Living with Paraplegia

Living with Paraplegia

MICHAEL A. ROGERS

with a Foreword by the Rt Hon Norman Tebbit MP

faber and faber

LONDON · BOSTON

Originally published as
Paraplegia: A Handbook of Practical Care and Advice, 1978
First published under this title 1986
by Faber and Faber Limited
3 Queen Square London WC1N 3AU

Photoset and printed in Great Britain by
Redwood Burn Limited Trowbridge Wiltshire
and bound by
Pegasus Bookbinding Melksham Wiltshire

Library of Congress Cataloging-in-Publication Data

Rogers, Michael A.
   Living with paraplegia.
Rev. ed. of: paraplegia. 1978.
1. Paraplegics—Rehabilitation. 2. Paraplegia—Great Britain—
Societies, etc.—Directories. 3. Paraplegia—Societies, etc.—
Directories. 4. Physically handicapped—Services for—
Great Britain—Directories. I. Rogers, Michael A.
Paraplegia. II. Title.
RC406.P3R62 1986   362.4'38'0941   85–29246
ISBN 0–571–13951–5 (pbk.)

British Library Cataloguing in Publication Data

Rogers, Michael A.
Living with paraplegia.
1. Paralytics—Care and treatment
I. Title
362.4'3   HV3011
ISBN 0–571–13951–5

FOR ELIZABETH

Contents

Foreword

Michael Rogers was born in 1937 and educated at Caldicott
School, Farnham Common, and Trent College, Nottingham. At
18 he joined the Army, serving in the Royal Electrical and Mechanical Engineers. On leaving the Army, in 1958, having spent two
years of his service with the Horse Guards in Cyprus, he returned
home to establish a plant machinery business. Only two years later
in 1960 an unknown virus infection of the spine left him almost
completely paralysed. Since then he has been a tetraplegic (quadraplegic), having all four limbs and most of his body paralysed.

In the early 1960s prospects of survival for tetraplegics were far
from good. During a year and half in a London teaching hospital
he experienced most of the complications likely to develop in paraplegia, and was in a serious condition when he was moved to Stoke
Mandeville Hospital. It then took three and a half years for
Michael to fight his way back to sufficient strength to be discharged in 1965, and to marry Elizabeth, the nurse who had seen
him through his worst hours and days. She is still a nursing officer
of Stoke Mandeville.

Michael Rogers' book tells a great deal about living with paraplegia, but his life tells a lot more. If not the longest surviving
tetraplegic, he is certainly among the longest surviving. That emphasises that no more than 40 or 50 years ago serious spinal injuries
were almost always fatal of themselves or by the complications
which developed. Even 25 years ago the prospects of survival for
those with high lesions (the tetra- or quadra-plegics) were poor
indeed.

That has changed and from now on, until research provides a
treatment to repair a damaged spinal cord and to restore its lost
function, there will be a growing number of survivors of spinal

injuries left with serious disabilities. Many paraplegics will live near normal lives, despite the inability to walk; other more severely disabled tetraplegics like Michael Rogers will find their own ways to extend their remaining abilities to accomplish far more than the able-bodied would believe possible.

This book is mostly about what the paraplegic needs to know, first to survive, and then to improve the quality of his life. It is also essential reading for the families and friends of paraplegics. Medicine and technology will do much to help those with spinal injuries. Implants to restore bladder control, artificial walking systems, better beds and improved wheelchairs (please!), together with word processors and computer systems able to enhance communication, perform household functions or simply to entertain, will play their parts.

But useful as all these are, none can replace the courage and determination of the paraplegic, nor the support and affection of his or her family and friends. Michael Rogers has all those in plenty. Hence his very survival, his ability to maintain so much independence (he shaves himself each morning) and to write a book, despite paralysis from the neck downwards. He and his wife Elizabeth did much to support my wife and me through many dark hours. I am sure this book will help many others through difficult times. Perhaps one day it will be followed by a sequel – 'Living with a Paraplegic' – to help those having that role both to think ourselves into the position of those who cannot even brush an unwelcome fly from their noses and to understand our own feelings.

Norman Tebbit

Preface

Almost a quarter of a century – literally half my life – has elapsed since the terrifying day in 1960 when I was admitted to St Mary's Hospital, Paddington, having contracted a viral infection to the spinal cord that ultimately left me totally paralysed below the shoulders. I spent 18 months in St Mary's where, despite conscientious and devoted care, I developed many of the now known to be avoidable complications associated with paralysis. Although my stay there was, on occasions, quite horrific, as my life frequently hung in the balance, in an ironical way it could be loosely construed as an extension to my education; for seldom a day passed when I wasn't visited by medical students who came to examine me and discuss my condition. By listening to the various doctors who lectured to them, I inevitably absorbed considerable knowledge. I became so interested in my own condition that I asked to be allowed to read medical books, regardless of the depressive effect the knowledge may sometimes have produced.

One painful way of learning about the complications of paralysis is through personal experience. On admission to the National Spinal Injuries Centre at Stoke Mandeville Hospital, where I was to spend the next three and a half years, I found myself under the care of its Founder Director, the late Sir Ludwig Guttmann, together with other members of his pioneer team. Sir Ludwig was a master in the art of teaching the subject closest to his heart – paraplegia. His ward rounds regularly lasted for hours, patients were stripped of their bedclothes – naked for all to see – and their conditions openly discussed. His knowledge flowed like water from a mountain stream and again it was impossible not to gulp some of it down – especially when it concerned myself. After I married in

1965, I was able to expand my knowledge even further with help from my wife, Elizabeth, formerly my ward sister.

When I left Stoke Mandeville Hospital my wife and I ran a nursing home until 1971, when Elizabeth was again offered employment at Stoke Mandeville. Shortly after, I undertook a part-time research job at the hospital, looking into the problems of employment for tetraplegics. As a result of this project, during which I heard many pleas for information concerning self-care, and on the basis of my own experiences together with knowledge I had acquired over the years (but without any medical qualifications) I wrote *Paraplegia: A Handbook of Practical Care and Advice*.

Since that book first appeared there have been changes and advances in many areas of care. In addition, I have been privileged to visit other spinal units at home and abroad; to attend meetings, lectures and discussions about the problems of disability; and to be invited to give lectures and write articles. I have also been afforded facilities to study several other aspects of spinal cord injury in greater depth. But above all, I've learned so much more from fellow paraplegics and tetraplegics in both this country and overseas. This present book is, therefore, the logical outcome of this wider knowledge.

Once again I have received help and guidance on technical matters from a spinal injuries specialist, a neurosurgeon, and a gynaecologist as well as from my wife, now Senior Nurse at the National Spinal Injuries Centre, Stoke Mandeville Hospital.

Because of the growing number of spinal cord injuries and the shortage of hospital beds, I have been explicit, blunt and frank, particularly regarding the complications associated with paraplegia, my sole object being to help individuals to keep healthy and *out of hospital*.

The chapter on sexuality has been written jointly with the help of my wife, who has devoted special attention to some of the problems faced by the female paraplegic and tetraplegic.

Due to sophisticated methods of treatment, combined with a shortage of National Health Service (NHS) funds, patients now tend to spend less time in hospital and, consequently, when discharged, are not always mentally or physically adjusted to the many problems that will remain with them for the rest of their lives. As a result of this, the newly discharged patient too often

The author using his Apple computer with a mouth stick to type this book

suffers early unnecessary complications requiring further hospital treatment.

Sir Ludwig Guttmann was dogmatic in his teachings to patients regarding the basic principles of individual and personal care. Only by strict adherence to his dogmas have I been able to stay so healthy. Patients treated today by modern methods in specialised centres and later discharged can look forward to a normal lifespan providing correct medical supervision continues. But, one fact cannot be overlooked: in most cases of traumatic injury, the paralysis, although varying in degree according to the extent and site of actual injury, is permanent. Patients will have to learn a new way of living if they are to survive and enjoy a worthwhile existence.

During the early months after discharge and return to the community, many things may appear to be utterly hopeless to the patient. The reality of leaving the protected environment of hospital and returning home often creates a feeling of despondency and apprehension. Jobs are not easy to find despite the fact that disabled people are sometimes found to be more highly motivated towards work than they were before their injury, and indeed more than many able-bodied persons.

Relatives and friends can play an important role at this time, by helping patients rediscover life and themselves and by displaying patience, love and understanding. The major prerequisite for success, however, is that a patient fully understands his new situation and this should include a sound, comprehensive knowledge of the medical condition, with all its ramifications and demands.

From the outset, it cannot be over-emphasised to patients that they must be prepared to maintain a high degree of vigilance throughout their lives to ensure that they adhere strictly to their new standards of living. Methods laid down by medical and nursing staff will need to be correctly maintained at all times.

Acknowledgements

In the writing of this book I have been indebted to many people – not least to numerous fellow paraplegics who have offered much encouragement.

First, I am immensely grateful to the Right Honourable Norman Tebbit MP for the splendid Foreword, written in the full knowledge of how the relatives, as well as the patient, have to restructure their lives when paraplegia suddenly strikes. I know that many readers will immediately relate to his words.

I would particularly like to thank Jack Hill, former South Coast correspondent of the *Daily Express*, for his endless help and support at all times.

To Mr I. M. Nuseibeh FRCS, Consultant Surgeon in Spinal Injuries, National Spinal Injuries Centre, Stoke Mandeville Hospital, my grateful thanks not only for vetting the medical details but also for his constant support.

To Mr P. J. Teddy BSC, BM, BCh, FRCS, Consultant Surgeon to the Department of Neurological Surgery, The Radcliffe Infirmary, Oxford, my grateful thanks not only for checking some of the medical details but also for his advice and support.

To Dr Marjorie J. Duckworth MD, DObstRCOG, my most grateful thanks not only for her help with the chapter on sexuality, in particular the female section, but also for her help, support and advice.

To Sister Dianne Cooper SRN, Fam.Plan.Cert., who contributed the section on contraception, I offer my most sincere thanks.

To Mrs Diana Gulland ALA, medical librarian, and Mrs Karen Evans, nursing librarian, Stoke Mandeville Hospital, I offer my most sincere thanks for their enthusiasm and continual support.

To the many other members of staff within Stoke Mandeville

Hospital who are far too numerous to mention individually, but have offered their personal help and advice, I give my most sincere thanks.

The female section of the chapter on sexuality is based on the findings of a research project involving numerous paraplegic and tetraplegic women throughout the United Kingdom (UK). To everyone who completed the questionnaire and shared so many intimate details of their lives with me, I am eternally grateful. I also express my gratitude to the consultants in charge of other spinal injury centres who also co-operated with me over this research.

Illustrations do much to allow a book to come alive, and I am grateful to Eva Janousek for taking the photographs, and Mrs Audrey Besterman for the line drawings. More particularly am I appreciative of the ready co-operation of patients and their families in allowing themselves to be photographed for use in this book. By this kindly action they give further support to the aim of this book which is to stress the ability of living with paraplegia.

Figures 6/1 and 6/3 and Table 6/2 are taken from *Pregnancy After Thirty* by Mary Anderson, and are reproduced by permission of the author and publishers, Faber and Faber.

Glossary

agoraphobia   A fear of open spaces

amenorrhoea   An absence of menstruation (the monthly period)

anaemia   A deficiency of red blood cells

automatic bladder   A bladder which will empty as the result of stimulation of its reflex action, for example by tapping

autonomic dysreflexia   The excessive rise in the blood pressure, resulting in a thumping headache, due to stimulation of the bladder, bowel or uterus. It is of a reflex nature, experienced mostly by patients with cervical or high thoracic region lesions

autonomous bladder   A bladder with no reflex action but which can be emptied by suprapubic manual pressure at regular intervals. It is usually found in patients with low thoracic or cauda equina lesions

catheter   A rubber or plastic hollow tube for introduction through a narrow canal to allow the passage of fluid as, for example, from the bladder of urine

cauda equina   Meaning a 'horse's tail'. The bundle of lumbar and sacral nerves at the base of the spinal column

claustrophobia   A fear of closed-in spaces

contracture   The permanent shortening of tendon or muscle fibres due, usually, to wrong positioning. It can be prevented by putting the affected joints through a full range of movements daily

ectopic pregnancy   The fertilisation of the ovum (female egg cell) in the Fallopian tube (oviduct)

electrotherapy   Treatment by electrical currents, e.g. faradism, galvanism, short wave diathermy, ultrasound, interferential

Guttmann's sign   The blockage of nasal air passages following injury to the cervical spinal cord. It is caused through interruption of the sympathetic nervous system. The blockage will impede respiration

hydrotherapy   Treatment by water, particularly exercises in a heated pool

hypertonic bladder   A spastic, often small and infected, bladder. It usually empties very frequently

intravenous urography (*formerly* intravenous pyelography)   A radiological (x-ray) examination using radio-opaque substances to show up the function of the kidneys, ureters and bladder

laminectomy   The operation to open the vertebral column by removal of the lamina(e) of the vertebra(e) to expose the spinal cord

osteomyelitis   Inflammation of the bone marrow

osteoporosis   Thinning of the bones due to reabsorption of calcium. It occurs frequently where there is disuse of limbs

paramedical   A term used to describe members of the professions supplementary to medicine other than doctors and nurses. The term includes physiotherapists, occupational therapists, speech therapists, radiographers, chiropodists, dietitians and others

rehabilitation   The process of restoration of a person after injury or illness to as near normal a condition as possible

spasms   Involuntary movements of muscles (sudden contractions). They may be due to certain stimuli, such as pain, to the lower motor neurones

spasticity   A state of increased muscular tone with exaggeration of the tendon reflexes

symphysis pubis   The bony prominence at the lower part of the pelvis where the two pubic bones join

trauma   Injury or damage caused by external violence to the body

traumatic   Relating to, or due to, a wound or injury

NOTE

Throughout this book, reference made to a paraplegic will include the tetraplegic unless otherwise stated.

Paraplegic   A person with paralysis which involves the lower limbs. Part or all of the trunk may also be affected

Tetraplegic (Quadraplegic)   A person with paralysis involving the four limbs. The trunk may also be affected

Historical Note

Injury to the spinal cord was recorded by an Egyptian physician over 5000 years ago. At that time, the condition was described as 'an ailment not to be treated'. This attitude persisted with members of the medical profession for thousands of years. Indeed, at the time of my birth – 1937 – 80 per cent of all spinal injuries failed to survive longer than three years (Thomson-Walker, 1937), and those that did often spent their lives in depressingly neglected states, either under institutional care or virtual prisoners in their own homes frequently shut away from society.

During the Second World War, several spinal units were established by the Ministry of Pensions on the recommendation of Dr George Riddoch, Neurological Consultant to the British Army, to provide care for war casualties, but those early units soon proved unsatisfactory. Not until the National Spinal Injuries Centre at Stoke Mandeville Hospital was founded in 1944 by Dr (later Sir) Ludwig Guttmann to cater for anticipated injuries following the Second Front invasion of Europe, could this dreadful situation be rectified. Prior to the opening of the National Spinal Injuries Centre medical treatment together with nursing and physiotherapy care had not been fully understood.

Within a comparatively short period of time, most of the earlier units closed and their patients transferred to Stoke Mandeville, where Guttman and his team were evolving techniques to care for the spinally injured. By 1951, when the Health Service took the Centre over, it had expanded from its original one small ward into a vast complex, ultimately totalling over 200 beds with a hostel for those unable to live at home.

Since those early days the situation has improved vastly. A comprehensive network of specialised spinal injury centres is now established throughout the UK and worldwide. New techniques have evolved, research has progressed and knowledge gained has completely transformed the outlook for paraplegics. In 1983, following a successful appeal headed by Jimmy Savile, the TV personality, the new spinal injuries centre at Stoke Mandeville Hospital was opened by His Royal Highness the Prince of Wales. Today patients are cared for in luxurious surroundings when compared with the original primitive and often inadequate wooden huts.

In spite of advancements in care during the past 40 years, management of the spinally injured still remains not always fully understood; indeed it has been described as the Cinderella of medicine. The finer points of the condition are not taught routinely in medical and nursing schools with the result that many doctors and nurses still have limited knowledge. Appreciation and consideration of this fact should encourage patients and relatives to take an active interest in furthering their own knowledge concerning all aspects of paraplegia. This can be achieved by supporting the various spinal injury centres and through joining the Spinal Injuries Association (see p. 162).

REFERENCE

Thomson-Walker, J. (1937). *Proceedings of the Royal Society of Medicine*, **30**, 1233.

1. Some Psychological Aspects of Paralysis

Following the admission to hospital of a spinal injury patient, close relatives will find themselves in a state of mental turmoil when they are told that their loved one is paralysed. The initial reaction is one of shock in a world of strange words, new faces, frightening hospital equipment and seeing disabled people in varying stages of treatment. Later, a patient or next-of-kin will want to know how and why paralysis has been caused.

Why does a person become paralysed when his spine is broken? A very good question, for some people do break their spines without becoming paralysed. This is because in their cases the spinal cord, made up of thousands of nerve fibres linking the brain with various parts of the body, has not been damaged despite a fractured or dislocated vertebra of the spinal column. Paralysis occurs only when nerve fibres have been damaged or broken during the spinal accident, as explained in detail in the next chapter.

The next question to be asked is: Will the patient recover? This is a difficult one for doctors to answer immediately. For, although they might be able to make a calculated diagnosis following neurological examination and after studying the x-rays, a period of time, known as the period of 'spinal shock' must elapse to allow the spinal cord to recover from the shock of injury. This period can take six or more weeks. For the patient, family and friends it is a time of tension, anxiety and heartache. To help people over this period, it is important to have an understanding of some of the psychological aspects of paralysis.

According to the *Oxford Dictionary*, psychology is the study of the human soul or mind. Therefore the psychological effect of paralysis is just another way of saying what goes on in the minds of patients and their families and friends. During the very early stages after becoming paralysed, whether the cause was traumatic, such as a motor car or diving accident, or non-traumatic, such as an illness, I think it is fair to say that the average patient is too frightened, as well as too ill, to think clearly about what has happened to him. He will ascribe little importance to the fact that he may be unable to move or feel certain parts of his body.

On admission to hospital, a patient puts his complete trust instinctively in the hands of the medical and nursing staff and subconsciously feels that all will be well. After a few days, most patients begin to feel a little better. Mental confusion subsides and the mind starts to recover its original pattern of thinking. But a sense of panic is often experienced at this stage and desperate questions fill the head. 'What has happened to me?' 'Why can't I feel or move?' 'Why can't I feel my bladder or bowels?' Also the embarrassment of being physically exposed every few hours for turns and medical procedures can be devastating.

Patients will begin to take notice of their surroundings, observe other patients in wheelchairs and listen to endless conversations between patients and staff about paraplegia, its problems and their day-to-day progress. At this stage many patients experience intense psychological disturbances and will, for varying periods of time, require all the love, care and understanding that can possibly be given.

Similarly, close relatives will be suffering the same feelings, possibly more so, for they will already have been told how serious is the situation. Unfortunately there is no quick and simple answer to the heartaches that must inevitably follow. There are no miracle drugs to put everything right. The process of psychological adjustment is slow and only time can heal the hurt mind successfully. As part of this process patients and relatives will have to live through a period of grief similar to that which may be experienced following the death of a close relative or friend. For, in reality, one is grieving for what constitutes a 'functional' death within a person's body. To help relatives through this desperate and emotive period, it is important that they begin to understand the various stages of paraplegia. It is even more important that relatives appreciate and understand the patient's feelings and reactions to this strange new world.

In the broadest possible terms, a similar and recognisable pattern of reaction exists among all paralysed patients whatever the level of injury.

The natural reaction of many is to wonder: 'Why me?' 'What have I done to deserve this?' Several try to dispel their emotions by crying or swearing at everybody and everything in sight. Some will pray endlessly, seeking an answer and trying to rid their minds of the reality of their condition. Close relatives, wives, husbands, mothers, fathers, brothers and sisters, boy or girl friends are those most likely to receive the brunt of this abuse, for it is human nature to hurt those you love most. The next to suffer will be the ward staff – the nurses in particular – orderlies, physiotherapists, and even the doctors. For nothing that anybody does can seemingly be right at this stage and equally it appears there is nothing that anybody can do to put matters right.

This can be a most distressing time for relatives. No matter what they say or do they are quite unable to alter the situation. There are, however, many things relatives *can* do to help at the hospital bedside; things that make the patient feel better at this most distressing and emotionally exhausting period. I list a few for guidance.

Try hard to maintain your natural normal everyday self. Do not suddenly adopt a different personality for this will only disturb and worry the patient. Spend as much time at the bedside as possible, doing the non-medical things the patient may ask you to do. Avoid being over-protective or too possessive. Do not be over-anxious to help, as this only emphasises the limitations of the patient. Above all don't be tempted to test for the presence or absence of movement.

In high lesions, especially those requiring artificial respiration, sensory loss is a particularly frightening experience. For several months following my initial hospitalisation, I was totally paralysed below the second cervical cord segment level. This involved complete sensory loss, with the exception of my face and the top of my head. Being also unable to breathe I was attached to a respirator – a frightening enough experience on its own. However, without sensation I could not feel the rib-cage expanding neither could I appreciate the passage of air entering and leaving my lungs. As a result I became convinced the machine wasn't breathing for me and that I was about to die. The only way *I* could eventually main-

tain tangible contact with life was through the stimulus of a re-
assuring touch to my face provided by a nurse, relative or friend.
Such physical contact is something relatives can easily provide,
especially for tetraplegics with considerable sensory loss; it can do
much to console and relieve the claustrophobic experience that
paralysis can bring at this stage (Fig. 1/1). (However, some people
do not like physical contact such as this, and, for them, this dislike
must be respected.) It is useful for relatives to involve themselves

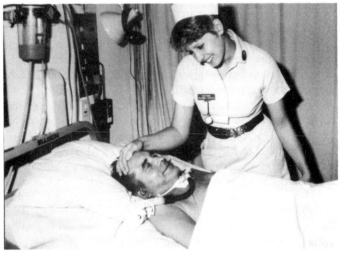

Fig. 1/1   Sympathetic support for a tetraplegic patient receiving
artificial ventilation

with the medical procedures taking place, by asking questions of
doctors, nurses, physiotherapists and other members of staff. This
helps the patient to appreciate that his family is interested in learning about his condition.

Medical experts in the field of spinal injury and its attendant
psychology, recognise the established fact that many patients suddenly become unusually aggressive at this stage. It can be most
disturbing and relatives need to understand that aggression during
this period is far better than mere apathy. It is known as 'reaction-
ary aggression' and is an expected sign. Aggressive patients,
although sometimes abrasive and abusive, have 'got fight'. The

mentally apathetic succumb far too easily and will have greater difficulty in rehabilitating to their new lifestyle.

During this initial period and for some time to follow, patients will be faced with soul-destroying and distressing situations. If a maximum effort is not made by all concerned to lessen these unusual and embarrassing situations, further psychological disturbances may follow. This is often more apparent in females, who may have led more sheltered physical lives than men.

It is usually necessary for patients to spend periods of time completely naked. Bedclothes will be removed for washing, bowel management, catheter drill, dressings, turns, physiotherapy, treatment and other regular examinations. During these procedures screens should be drawn around the beds. Staff sometimes forget this, or fail to close curtains tightly together, leaving patients to suffer unnecessary embarrassment through exposure. This can only retard mental adjustment. Relatives and patients can help each other by insisting on a high standard of privacy.

One would think that the psychological effect on a person of losing the use of all four limbs is greater than on a person losing his legs alone. Yet this is not always the case. It is relative to the individual and it is wrong to compare degrees of reaction.

Patients who have lost the use of their legs will lie in bed thinking of obvious things they can no longer do such as dancing, climbing, walking, football and other sports, and getting about the house and garden. At first they will give no thought to the many things that they *can* do. Patients with the loss of all four limbs will think about these aspects, but will be more concerned with scratching their noses, combing their hair, washing, brushing their teeth and feeding themselves or even holding the hands of close friends or relatives.

Paraplegics, as well as tetraplegics, with families and business interests frequently show more outward concern for their families and the continued smooth running of their business interests than they do about their immediate physical situation. Then there are the unusual complexes – such as I myself experienced for a few days. I was utterly convinced that the battery of my car – which I was positive was parked outside – would become flat and that I would be unable to start the car to go home when ready for discharge.

The forced confinement in bed coupled with restricted movement can also bring about reactive phobias, especially among the younger age group. Fear of fire and the inability to escape is genuinely experienced, as is agoraphobia when beds are wheeled outside as part of fire-drill, but, above all, claustrophobia of a physical as well as a psychological and social nature is the phobia most frequently felt. Constant reassurance, encouraging conversation, love and understanding, are the best supports relatives can offer.

Paraplegics will wonder about their sexual function, or the loss of it. But at this very early stage they will ask nothing, for they will not know what to ask. (This subject is fully discussed in Chapter 6.)

During the following weeks, the days will be filled with a tiresome but vital combination of routine treatments. There will be doctors' rounds, catheterisations to empty the bladder and turns three- to four-hourly day *and* night to prevent pressure sores developing, daily physiotherapy in the form of passive and, where possible, active movements of limbs to keep joints mobile and non-paralysed muscles active, and occupational therapy to maintain and strengthen existing movements, as well as keeping the mind alert. Throughout this routine treatment basic principles of future care become increasingly apparent. So when at last the initial stage of spinal shock has passed the dreaded question has finally to be asked – 'Doctor, am I going to recover any more?' This is a problem for doctors. Clinical judgement seems to vary considerably over exactly when and how they should answer this question. Some doctors are of the opinion that patients should be told immediately whereas others choose to put it off until directly asked. Obviously the patient's general condition, and his psychological state, have to be considered. But whenever the decision is made I would plead with doctors who read this book that they should be as certain as possible before answering the question. Please tell the truth – but with great tact, and with comforting words and reassurance regarding the future.

Although most patients will subconsciously know the answer before asking, the final shattering condemnation to a wheelchair is quite catastrophic.

Let nobody underestimate the psychological and physical effects of being told that you will never walk again; or the even worse effect of being told that you will never use your hands again. It can only be likened to a judge passing a life sentence.

No matter how distressing this might be, however, the truth is better than telling a patient he will be 'fine tomorrow'. For tomorrow never comes and the long-term depressive effect will be greater if the truth is withheld. The circumstances were slightly different in my own case. I had contracted a viral infection of the spinal cord and it was more difficult for the medical staff to estimate if I would recover. It was approximately 12 months after admission when I was told they were doubtful if I should ever walk again, but that they were convinced I would ultimately regain the use of my hands and arms. Six months later when I had been transferred to the National Spinal Injuries Centre, the complete truth was made abundantly clear – I would never regain the use of my limbs. Although subconsciously I was probably aware of this fact, true realisation of my physical state after 18 months of hoping and praying for even partial recovery reduced me to a profound state of depression.

Many patients choose to avoid asking if and when they will recover. This is either in the hope that they will, or from a fear of what they might learn. In these circumstances I believe it is the doctor's duty to make the situation perfectly clear and to reiterate the truth more than once. For some patients will say many months later that they were never told.

And no matter how tactfully patients are told that they will never walk or use their limbs again, initially many will wish they were dead and out of it. There seems so little left in life. This, too, is a perfectly normal and understandable reaction and one that is usually followed by prolonged bouts of depression mixed with aggressive outbursts. The most satisfactory method of dealing with this depression is by diversional therapy. This means anything that will keep the mind occupied – and such therapy should be applied by all members of staff as well as by friends and relatives during visits.

Nursing staff should talk about outside interests while carrying out routine nursing procedures. I always found it particularly stimulating and diverting to listen to nurses discussing the previous night's parties and dances which they had attended. Doctors can help by continued daily visits, even if there is nothing medically necessary for them to do. Physiotherapists should explain the aims of the treatment they are providing, in order to gain the patient's interest and co-operation. The occupational therapist can provide practical work, not only in the form of diversional therapy, but also to help strengthen and maintain existing movements. This is not always easy with tetraplegics, who may have limited movements. Friends and relatives can best help by visiting as often as possible and talking of day-to-day matters. Relatives should also seek advice from experienced hospital staff about the patient's domestic future, so that blunt questions can be answered truthfully. This will all help to ease a patient's mind gently back into normal routine thinking.

No matter how hard medical, nursing, and paramedical staff work to relieve depression they will not succeed unless the patient himself fights tremendously to overcome this despair.

Paraplegics can do a great deal to help themselves but tetraplegics will find it harder. Both paraplegics and tetraplegics should start by making an extra effort to talk, smile and be cheerful to staff and relatives. Staff themselves have extremely emotional and demanding pressures thrust upon them, particularly through seeing so many young lives shattered following injury. Patients and their relatives can help by trying to remember this and not underestimate the staff's feelings. This is not as easy as it sounds. It will require maximum willpower, but once a start has been made, co-operation, cheerfulness and optimism will come more naturally.

Reading is an excellent method of keeping the mind occupied. Bookrests are available in hospital, together with a large selection of books. Where difficulty is experienced in turning pages or holding a book, there are electrically operated page turners, and there is a 'talking book' service. This service, originally designed for the blind, provides books recorded on tape and all one has to do is wear a set of headphones and listen. This is easy, for it requires no physical effort and is a wonderful method of occupying the mind. A number of books recorded on cassette tapes for the modern individual compact and portable stereophonic radio/tape players are also commercially available, and are so easy to listen to. Television and radio provide relaxation and most hospital beds are fitted with headphones that can be switched to any station or channel required. With the advent of the micro-computer some spinal centres are able to offer patients the use of computers for word-processing, education, diversional games and even programming at a very early stage in their rehabilitation. Despite the different levels of injury the computer can be operated by a variety of methods using conventional keyboards. They can be controlled with normal finger movements or with mouth-sticks for high lesions. They can also be converted to pneumatic and optical control for patients with restricted head movements (Fig. 1/2).

It is so easy to lie in bed just counting spots on the ceiling and allowing the mind to wander and sleep. I know. That's exactly what I did for months; but in my case as I lay, being turned from side to side, it was the colourful parrots printed on the material covering the screens. I counted them so many times they eventually started flying. Beware. The longer this is done, the longer it will take to recover psychologically.

The majority of patients have domestic problems of one kind or another: hire purchase on a car or motorbike, mortgage repayments, rent and rates outstanding, employment problems, schooling of children and marital problems – just to mention a few. These problems are typical of the many things that patients turn over in their minds as they lie in bed. Coupled with the added worries of paralysis, both immediate and still to come, these domestic difficulties are often amplified or even invented.

I realise it is terribly easy to say 'don't worry', particularly where there may indeed be real problems. But worry really is the key to the whole situation. Try *not* to worry in advance. Take each day as it comes and close the mind to all future problems for the time being. By doing this, the mind is left clear to concentrate on a maximum effort towards rehabilitation. Finally, the problems often turn out to be not half as bad as anticipated. To help surmount this crucial period, patients and relatives should ask to see the hospital's social worker whose job it is to take over such domestic worries, and provide practical assistance.

Between 8 and 10 weeks from the time of the injury is the usual time taken for fractured bones to heal and for the spinal cord to recover from the state of spinal shock. Then the majority of patients will be ready to get up in a wheelchair. For myself, after initially spending nearly four years in bed during which time I desperately

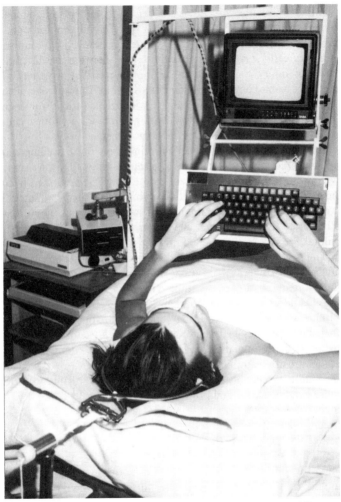

Fig. 1/2 A tetraplegic patient learning to use a computer while on cervical traction, within weeks of injury

looked forward to getting up, the first few days proved to be simply devastating. Only then does the true realisation of the disability hit you squarely between the eyes. The dishevelled appearance; the weakness of muscles; the tendency to faint as the blood rushes to one's feet; the wasted limbs and the terrible tiredness all have to be overcome. However, as each day passes patients will slowly but surely regain their strength, and at this stage it is essential that those who have not been fortunate enough to recover from paralysis must start to learn more about their physical condition, their limitations and how their body is affected. A simple explanation of their condition and how to cope with it is all that is required.

It does, however, need to be clearly understood and accepted philosophically that as a paraplegic and particularly as a tetraplegic the way of life will be different and a new pattern of living has to be evolved.

FURTHER READING

Treieschmann, R. B. (1980). *Spinal Cord Injuries: Psychological, Social and Vocational Adjustment*. Pergamon Press, Oxford.

2. Know Your Paralysis

ANATOMICAL UNDERSTANDING

The first thing patients need to learn is exactly what has happened to them. It is useless thinking because the neck or back has been broken and paralysis has resulted that there is no further need to be concerned about the injury or its cause and effects. To survive successfully, patients must understand why there is paralysis and how the body reacts to it. The parts of the body stricken without feeling or movement are by no means dead and need to be looked after very carefully.

If the brain is thought of as a central power house or information centre, then it becomes easier for a patient to understand why it is that he becomes paralysed when his spine is broken. Messages are generated in the brain, in the form of electrical impulses, whenever a physical action is required. The impulses from the brain reach the muscles via the spinal cord. If this line of communication is broken, then there can be no response.

The spinal cord is made up of thousands of tiny nerve fibres, like fine wires; the cord itself is about the diameter of a man's little finger and is situated in the centre of the tough, bony vertebral column for protection. The vertebral column is the spine. And inside the spine the cord is surrounded by a pad of fat for protection, as well as special coverings (the meninges). These coverings are separated from each other by fluid for extra protection. In effect it is nature's own form of armour plating (Fig. 2/1).

The vetebral column is constructed of 33 segments or vertebrae. Each segment is separated by discs of gristle which form pads and shock absorbers thus permitting smooth bending of the spine. When the spine is broken or dislocated the cord may be damaged.

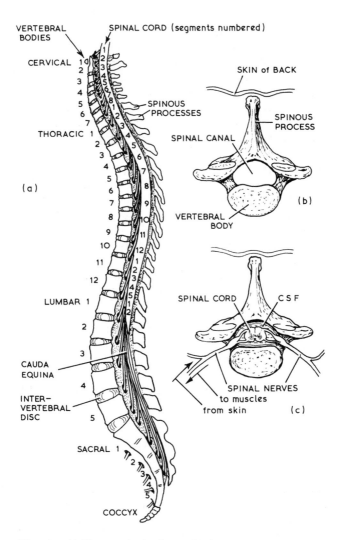

Fig. 2/1 (a) The vertebral column. (b) A vertebra. (c) Showing the spinal cord within the vertebra, with a pair of spinal nerves emerging

When this happens, messages from the brain to parts of the body lying below the site of injury cannot get through. Some injuries are termed 'complete lesions' while others are 'incomplete lesions'. This is simply a way of defining whether the cord has been wholly or partly damaged. When partly damaged there may be partial sensation or movement below the site of injury (Fig. 2/2).

Quite often a newly injured person will initially appear to have a complete lesion. After varying periods of time, as the spinal cord recovers from shock, swelling and bruising, so degrees of sensation and movement begin to return and some patients will make a total recovery. As yet, spinal nerves cannot be repaired or replaced. For reasons not yet fully understood, nerves of the spinal cord will not grow together once they are broken.

To estimate how much of the body is affected by a spinal cord injury detailed neurological examination is necessary. The severity of paralysis is dependent on which sections of the vertebral column and spinal cord were damaged during the accident or illness.

The vertebral column is divided into groups of vertebrae:

cervical vertebrae – 7 (the neck)
thoracic or dorsal vertebrae – 12 (the chest)
lumbar vertebrae – 5 (the waist)
sacral vertebrae – 5 (the pelvis)
coccygeal vertebrae – 4
    (sacral and coccygeal vertebrae are fused together and form
    the base of the spinal column).

The spinal cord runs down through the vertebral column, and usually finishes opposite the second lumbar vertebra (L2). Nerves leaving the cord below this point form what is called the cauda equina (the horse's tail) (Fig. 2/2).

There are nerves between the vertebrae which emerge on either side of the vertebral column and are known as the peripheral nerves. They carry messages to and from the brain, via the spinal cord, to various parts of the body such as the skin and the muscles.

Most spinal cord injuries affect the bladder, bowels and sexual organs. This is because the nerves which supply these functions stem from the lower end of the spinal cord. Damage to the cord in the cervical region will usually involve hands, arms, trunk and legs. Where the cord is damaged in the mid-thoracic region, the

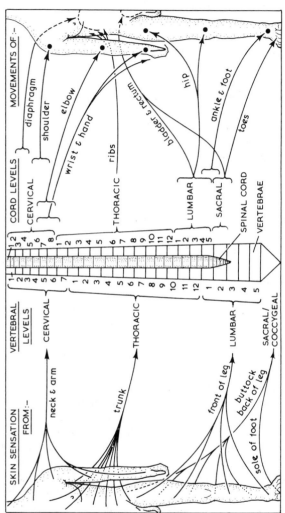

Fig. 2/2 Diagrammatic representation of levels of sensation and movement of the body. If you place a ruler at the level of your cord lesion you will see the possible extent of loss of sensation and movement. *Note* that cord levels are *not* the same as vertebral levels

lower limbs and part of the trunk will be involved, but the hands and arms will remain unaffected.

IMPLICATIONS OF PARALYSIS

The implications of a spinal cord injury are many and varied. While some complex physical changes take place that are unnecessary for a patient to study, other changes are more obvious and easily understood. These can be divided into: loss of movement, loss of sensation or feeling, loss of normal bladder and bowel function, and involvement of sexual functions.

LOSS OF MOVEMENT

Loss of movement is the most obvious implication, hence the need for wheelchairs. As a result of this, within a short time of injury, wastage of bone and muscle bulk can occur and the limbs begin to look thin. Daily supervised physiotherapy, in the form of passive movements, must be given to all paralysed limbs otherwise the joints will become stiff and tendons and muscles will contract. In the early stages of hospital treatment physiotherapy is most important to prevent stiffness and contractures, for any recovery of muscle power will be hampered by shortened tendons and stiff joints. Electrotherapy is sometimes given in the hope of maintaining specific muscle bulk, usually where recovery is evident. Its application to the whole of a paralysed body is impracticable.

Limbs not used for a number of years will obviously change in character. As well as muscle wastage, tendons will shorten and bones will decalcify and become brittle. This is known as osteoporosis, and is due to lack of weight-bearing and muscle pull. Regular standing under the instruction of a physiotherapist will reduce bone wastage, as will the taking of as much active exercise as possible (see p. 139). It is vital for children to stand as often and for as long as possible under the instruction of their doctor because, without weight-bearing, limbs will fail to grow normally.

Many patients develop spasms in their limbs. These are involuntary, jerky contractions of muscles, caused by over-active reflex movements resulting from damage of the spinal cord. Other patients may develop spasticity in their limbs – this is due to increased muscle tone resulting from the damage to the spinal cord. Sometimes spasms and spasticity have their advantages, including the maintenance of muscle tone, blood circulation and blood pressure. Because I have a very low blood pressure, over the years I have discovered that sudden jerky movements of my electrically operated wheelchair trigger the spasms in my legs thus pumping my blood pressure back to normal. This trick has often prevented me from fainting altogether. But remember: spasms can cause violent, involuntary movements of limbs throwing a person off balance (see p. 142). The first signs of spasticity occur at varying periods after injury and must not be interpreted as a sign of recovery. Physiotherapy and hydrotherapy, and good nursing care, will normally minimise spasms. Drug therapy may also be effective (see p. 142). In difficult cases, however, surgical treatment is sometimes required, and a procedure known as an 'alcohol block' may be necessary when spasms are extremely violent (see p. 143).

LOSS OF SENSATION

Sensation loss is probably the main factor in the many complications associated with paralysis. Without feeling or sensation there is no normal warning when the bladder or the bowels are full. Sexual functions also depend largely on sensation. I deal with these aspects in Chapters 4, 5 and 6.

Consider what other problems can arise during the course of a normal day, when there is loss of sensation. There is a danger in summer that paralysed parts of the body may become burnt by the sun (Fig. 2/3). This is best avoided by not sitting in direct sunlight on very hot days, by wearing a suitable hat and covering those parts without feeling.

In winter the need for extra heat often results in severe burns, which can be caused by sitting too close to open fires, against radiators or hot pipes. For a person's own benefit a hot water bottle or an electric blanket should *never* be used. Not only can bottles burst or leak, they can burn within a matter of minutes. Electric blankets, both the over and under types, can cause burns especially in circumstances when they might short-circuit due to accidental wetting. Scalding from hot baths, hot drinks and from cooking

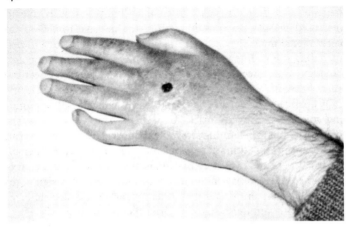

Fig. 2/3   The author's hand burned by sunlight while on holiday in France

accidents are other obvious dangers; avoid putting a cup of tea on the lap.

A combination of cold weather, loss of feeling and reduced circulation can result in frostbite on cold days. *Always* cover exposed limbs if you are going out when temperatures are low. If you are feeling cold, put on extra clothes or wrap up snugly in a blanket. It is far safer than sitting on top of a fire.

Sensation loss conceals normal pain which is a warning of possible complications. This makes a doctor's job of diagnosing internal problems more difficult. Patients must maintain constant and vigilant interest in themselves. This will include remembering what has been eaten, or drunk, as well as any drugs which may have been taken, also the appearance of stools and urine. Where there is any alteration from the normal motions, tell your doctor without delay.

HEAT REGULATION

In all cases of paraplegia there will be involvement of the body temperature mechanism, but patients with cervical and high thoracic lesions are more affected by the loss of the body temperature regulation mechanism. On very hot days the blood temperature can easily increase. The opposite occurs in extreme cold. Most patients will have heard how elderly people suffer from hypothermia (excess cold), and hyperthermia (excess heat). The same applies to the paralysed, but through a different cause.

The body temperature mechanism is very complex. It can be more easily understood by thinking of the many things within the human body that happen involuntarily. A good example is 'goose flesh' which is the erection of little hairs on the skin's surface, often triggered by a sudden flow of cold air. Another example is the digestion of food we have eaten. The regulation of the body temperature is similarly outside our control. The exertion of energy by physical movement or just sitting in hot sunshine causes skin and blood to increase in temperature. Several things occur to compensate for this. Sweat glands produce moisture on the skin's surface, and this evaporates and takes away body heat. Circulation is increased forcing more blood to the skin's surface where it is cooled and thereby reduces blood temperature. In an able-bodied person these two reactions to heat occur automatically. The situation is different for the paraplegic.

The heat-regulating centre is situated in the brain and, with the aid of the autonomic nervous system, controls hot and cold. The autonomic system is connected to the brain via the spinal cord, and consequently the autonomic nervous system is affected when the spinal cord is damaged.

On very hot days the increase in body temperature can be proved by taking the rectal temperature, and a rise of one or two degrees is quite usual. If the temperature is taken under the tongue in these circumstances it does not always register any increase. The effect of the increase on patients is most unpleasant, similar to having a temperature caused by infection. Other effects will include: constant thirst, dry mouth, loss of appetite, sleepless nights, claustrophobia, swelling of hands and feet, a severe feeling of being hot and bothered, and possibly blackouts due to reduced blood pressure. The combination of these effects may result in a feeling of complete physical and mental exhaustion.

There is a natural tendency to reduce body temperature by drinking excessive cold fluid. This can lead to further complications. There are other more satisfactory methods of cooling down. Spray or sponge cold water over the face and body and sit or lie in front of an electric fan – this simulates normal sweating. Wear light, loose cotton clothes. Do not drink anything hot and eat only cold light foods such as fruit and salad. Take a little extra salt. Drink cold fluids regularly but try to avoid drinking vast quantities.

During excessively hot periods patients with high lesions in particular should avoid direct sunlight altogether. If it is necessary to go out, a straw hat or similar head covering should be worn for protection, and a thermos flask of cold water and a battery fan taken along for emergencies. In very hot climates most people need air conditioning, and it may be essential for patients with high lesions. This should be remembered if holidays abroad are planned.

I advise all tetraplegics to purchase a good quality electric fan in anticipation of excessively hot periods and, if circumstances allow, the following will certainly help one to keep cool: when choosing a motor car, select a light colour which will reflect sunlight; if living in a hot climate all the year round, it might be worth considering air conditioning in the car as well as the house. A reasonably priced portable air conditioning plant that can be wheeled from room to room is now available (see p. 229).

The effect of cold is the complete reverse. Normally someone feeling cold will shiver, which is nature's way of making muscles work to produce heat. The flow of blood is redirected away from the skin's surface. Blood vessels close down to a minimum thereby conserving heat to protect vital organs and this leaves limbs 'blue with cold'. To overcome this, able-bodied people will rub their hands together and flap their arms to increase circulation.

In a paralysed person the blood still flows at the same rate on a cold day. Consequently it is quickly cooled by the cold skin and therefore there is rapid heat loss which leaves internal organs unprotected. If the body temperature is allowed to drop too much, the function of internal organs will be affected and patients will become seriously ill. This condition, known as hypothermia, results in death for many elderly people during unusually cold spells. Should this condition affect paraplegics, going to bed in a warm room is the most satisfactory method of regaining body heat. A special blanket, known as a 'space-blanket', which is made of heat-insulating material similar to tin-foil has proved very effective in raising body temperature (once the body temperature has become normal again, the blanket should be removed). Remember: *no* hot water bottles or electric blankets.

Other effects of extreme cold include the risk of frostbite, stiffness of joints and limbs, and possible low urine output. Poor concentration, lack of co-ordination, and a general feeling of being unwell may also result.

People who do not understand the needs of a paraplegic are often heard to say, 'Oh you will be all right on a hot or cold day because you can't feel.' This is true to a point. You will not feel hot or cold on the paralysed parts of the body. Neither will excessive heat or cold bother you too much for very short periods. But once you are exposed to either for prolonged periods the blood quickly takes up the surrounding temperature and you will feel the effects of extreme heat or cold. These effects are potentially harmful and certainly most unpleasant, so try and avoid them.

FURTHER READING

Fallon, B. (1984). *So You're Paralysed*. Spinal Injuries Association, London.

Walsh, J. J. (1973). *Understanding Paraplegia*. Reprinted by Dolphin Publishing, Aylesbury.

3. Pressure Sores

Unfortunately, there are still many people who refer to pressure sores as bed sores. This is misleading and does not help in the understanding of their true cause. While it is possible to get sores in bed it is not the bed that causes them (Figs. 3/1 and 3/2).

Pressure sores are caused by what their name implies – *pressure*. A simple way to demonstrate this is to apply pressure with the thumb of one hand on the back of the other hand. Continue pressing for 30 seconds and when the thumb is removed a white mark will remain. This is where blood has been forced away from the skin by pressure and, had this continued for several hours, the skin and underlying tissue would have died through being starved of its blood supply. This is the start of a pressure sore.

Exactly the same thing happens when one is sitting or lying in the same position for prolonged periods of time. Blood is forced away from the areas under pressure due to body-weight. Because of paralysis there is no advance warning of this pressure build-up by pain or discomfort which are nature's ways of telling us to move. There is a very good example of this advance warning system in the sleep of an able-bodied person. The moment he becomes uncomfortable, a message is sent to the brain from the nerves under pressure. A reflex action takes place and the person turns over during sleep; this removes pressure and permits blood to flow freely.

Blood is our lifeline; without it we should die. If the supply is cut off from areas of our body through pressure, then that area will die. A pressure sore is exactly that; an area of skin and underlying tissue which has died through pressure cutting off the blood supply.

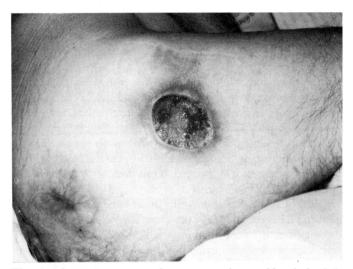

Fig. 3/1   A pressure sore over the greater trochanter. *Note* the healed
sore posteriorly

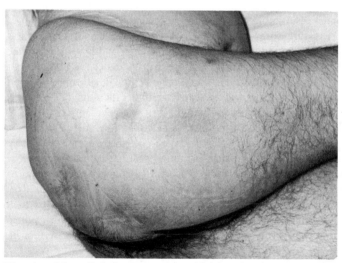

Fig. 3/2   After relief of pressure and careful dressing the same sore is
healed

HOW TO RECOGNISE THE START
OF A PRESSURE SORE

Pressure sores do not appear instantly or without logical reason. They occur more easily in newly injured and sick patients, due to shock and poor circulation. This is why these patients are turned more frequently.

The first sign of a pressure sore is redness over the area of skin that has been in contact with the mattress or cushion with the maximum weight on it (pressure). If this does not completely disappear after a few hours' relief by turning, and still more pressure is applied by further lying or sitting in the same position, the skin will turn bluish-red and may even break. Initially, this might only be a small area and the patient may think there is nothing to worry about. If, however, still further pressure is continued, the area will turn bluish-black and will enlarge. There will be more skin loss and possibly infection. If more pressure is applied, deeper layers of underlying tissue will die; infection will penetrate deeper and throughout a wider area and, if it is not treated, may enter the bone, resulting in osteomyelitis (infection of the bone marrow).

Pressure sores can start in other ways, such as knocks and scrapes when transferring from bed to chair and from chair to car. Knocks may bruise tissue and the damage under the skin will not be noticed. If pressure is then applied through sitting or lying on such an area, a sore will develop from under the skin. The reason is that such ruptured blood vessels (bruises) have not been able to heal and feed the surrounding tissue, which then dies.

Sores can start through septic spots, which are usually caused by a combination of pressure and skin bacteria that are always present. Pressure applied to a septic spot encourages the infection to spread, thus damaging a larger area. The pressure can be caused by creases in clothing, cushion covers, sheets or pillow cases. Creases in clothing can crack the skin, exposing it to bacteria. Moist skin is more easily bruised and broken, therefore it is vital not to sit or lie on wet clothing or sheets. Female paraplegics who wear pads for urinary incontinence are frequently plagued by cracks between their buttocks as a direct result of moist skin.

Too much talcum powder applied after bathing is another

danger. If the skin is not perfectly dry, the powder can become hard and lumpy, causing pressure, so it should be used sparingly.

Another type of sore caused through pressure is known as a bursa. This is a pocket of fluid that collects between tissue and bone. This can be caused through accidental bumps and knocks when transferring from bed to chair, or by prolonged sitting over a period of time. Not only does this add up to pressure of the normal kind, but also it does not give the pressure areas sufficient rest periods. Such pockets of fluid can be felt as jelly-like lumps over bony points. Sometimes the area will be red and swollen and the skin may also feel hot to touch.

PREVENTION OF PRESSURE SORES

Even after 40 years' proven treatment of the patient with a spinal cord injury, some members of the medical and nursing professions remain under the misapprehension that pressure sores are an integral and acceptable part of paralysis (Frankel, 1975). At one time this was assumed, but it is now known that it is not so. Once pressure sores and their causes are fully understood, prevention is relatively simple.

The answer to the problem lies in the name itself 'pressure sores', or sores caused by pressure. To prevent sores one has to mimic the able-bodied and constantly relieve pressure. This is not as difficult as it may sound – especially for those who are able to recall their lifestyles before injury occurred. Think. Think of the times it became essential to move to reduce the effects of pressure. Travelling from A to B in a car is a good example. After approximately 2 to 3 hours' travelling it becomes necessary to stop and stretch one's legs – thus relieving pressure. Become 'pressure minded' is a phrase often used to good effect. Awareness of pressure starts in the ward, where newly injured patients, regardless of the extent of injury, are turned day and night at regular intervals.

TURNING

The need for regular turning is constantly explained by nursing staff. Consequently, by the time patients are ready to sit in their wheelchairs, the need for regular lifts to prevent sores should be imprinted on their minds. Today there exists a variety of seat cushions and mattresses with which patients may be issued or which they may purchase themselves, but it should be clearly understood that all these items are only *aids* in the prevention of pressure sores. There is no substitute for turning when in bed and for lifting when in the wheelchair. This allows blood to flow freely again and feed the skin and underlying tissue. I repeat: *There is no substitute for turning in bed and lifting when in the wheelchair.*

Some patients find they can sit or lie in one position longer than others without causing damage. This is because no two people are alike. Some have more fat or padding over pressure areas than others; circulation varies from person to person and is also affected by the cord injury. Patients with limbs that are spastic often have better circulation because the involuntary contractions of muscles help to pump blood around the system. On the other hand, these involuntary movements themselves may cause continuous rubbing over prominent areas, producing sores.

Patients must learn how long they can sit or lie in one position without causing damage. This can be found only by trial and close examination of pressure areas after every turn and on return to bed. A good way of starting is by lying for 2 hours at a time when in bed and, after turning, the pressure areas should be closely examined with the aid of a mirror for signs of redness. The time between turns may be increased by 30 minutes until the maximum period is reached without any adverse effects to the skin. A maximum of 4 hours is the recommended period between turns. This period may well be extended by the use of pressure relief aids as further discussed. However, it is most important to establish one's maximum tolerance to pressure to cope in circumstances where aids may fail or not be available.

In the sitting position the situation is different. The aim is to stay up in the wheelchair for a regular day. To achieve this a more frequent pattern of lifting has to be adopted. Most patients will initially be issued with a 10cm (4in) thick latex foam sorbo-rubber cushion to establish their tolerance to pressure. With this basic aid, paraplegics should aim at lifting themselves every 15 minutes, supporting their weight for at least 20 seconds (Figs. 3/3 and 3/4).

Remember that circulation is not at its best, so the blood takes longer to return to the area under pressure.

Tetraplegics are not always able to lift themselves. Some learn to transfer their weight from side to side and this is quite satisfactory. Those unable to do this much, will require the help of an assistant to lift them (Fig. 3/5). Tetraplegics therefore have a more difficult job to find out how long they can sit without being lifted. This is best overcome by sitting for increasing periods and again closely examining the skin with a mirror on return to bed. Most tetraplegic patients, providing their skin is in good condition, should be able to sit on a new sorbo-rubber cushion for three-hourly periods without lifts. (Sorbo-rubber cushions should be replaced regularly, say 6-monthly.) Others will find one of the cushion aids can extend this period even further.

Many tetraplegics and some paraplegics find difficulty in examining their pressure areas because of limited movements and may require an assistant to hold a mirror. While this can prove awkward and impractical, they must not assume that an assistant will take responsibility for the state of the skin. It is a patient's personal responsibility to check his or her own pressure areas.

It is vital to examine pressure areas on return to bed. Any redness should be noted and relieved of all pressure. Should the redness persist next day, under *no* circumstances get up. Stay in bed relieving all pressure on the area until it is completely better. The same applies if there is loss of skin or bruising. A few days spent in bed to repair minor damage can save months in hospital later if the early danger signs are ignored.

This is not always as easy as it sounds. I know. I have ignored the golden rules on several occasions to fulfil pressing social engagements the results of which have confined me to bed for up to 4 weeks at a time. The paraplegic with strong arms and the ability to lift at more regular intervals may be fortunate and not sustain any further damage by sitting on dubious pressure areas. The paraplegic mother will have additional responsibilities preventing her from going to bed. Those in regular employment may find it difficult to take time off for what at first appears to be a trivial thing. Under these circumstances I can only advise keeping a very close watch on the area concerned. If it fails to improve there may be no alternative but to stay off it and to seek further medical advice.

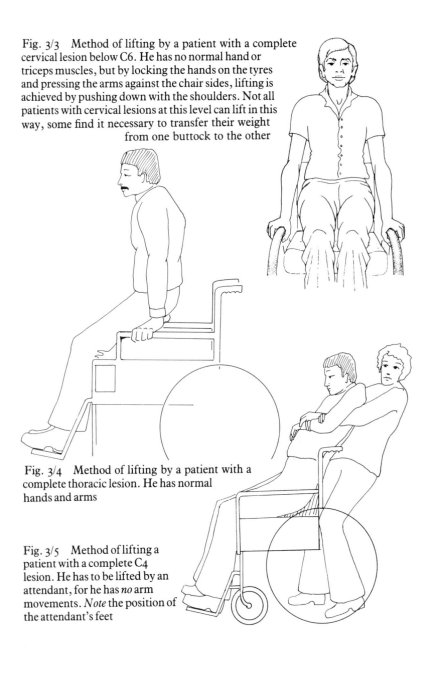

Fig. 3/3 Method of lifting by a patient with a complete cervical lesion below C6. He has no normal hand or triceps muscles, but by locking the hands on the tyres and pressing the arms against the chair sides, lifting is achieved by pushing down with the shoulders. Not all patients with cervical lesions at this level can lift in this way, some find it necessary to transfer their weight from one buttock to the other

Fig. 3/4 Method of lifting by a patient with a complete thoracic lesion. He has normal hands and arms

Fig. 3/5 Method of lifting a patient with a complete C4 lesion. He has to be lifted by an attendant, for he has *no* arm movements. *Note* the position of the attendant's feet

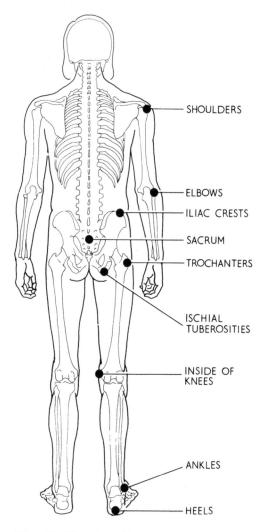

SHOULDERS

ELBOWS

ILIAC CRESTS

SACRUM

TROCHANTERS

ISCHIAL
TUBEROSITIES

INSIDE OF
KNEES

ANKLES

HEELS

Fig. 3/6   The vulnerable pressure areas of the
body

Every part of the body is prone to pressure sores, some areas being more vulnerable than others due to the shape of our skeleton. Where sharp and protruding bones are near the skin's surface and in direct contact with a mattress or seat cushion, these are the areas most vulnerable to pressure sores (Fig. 3/6).

SITTING

In the sitting position, the bony points on either side of the anus, called the ischial tuberosities (which form the base of the pelvis) are the points most prone to pressure (Fig. 3/7). These should be closely examined with a mirror on return to bed.

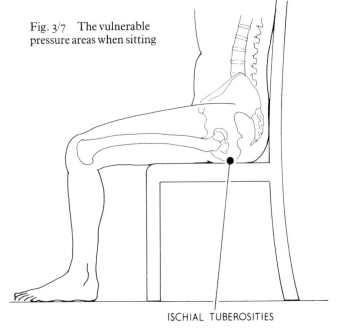

Fig. 3/7   The vulnerable
pressure areas when sitting

ISCHIAL TUBEROSITIES

The feet, particularly toes, backs of heels and ankles are areas most frequently damaged when sitting in a wheelchair. These areas are often damaged by pushing through swing-doors, the careless use of footrests, and allowing legs to drop on to the footrests without looking. Feet slipping over the edges of footrests can cause

the backs of heels to be scraped, while the backs of legs and surfaces of knees and elbows are examples of other areas subject to
pressure by knocks and scrapes when sitting in the wheelchair.
Never sit with bare feet.

Transferring from chair to bed, or in and out of cars, can result
in scraped or knocked hips. All these areas must be closely examined on return to bed and always before getting up the next day.
The constant examination of skin and pressure areas cannot be
over-emphasised – it *must* be a routine. The first time they are
ignored can be the moment when trouble starts.

LYING

When lying in bed, pressure areas can be protected in many ways.
A good quality mattress must always be used, and this should be
either spring-interior or sorbo-rubber. When lying on the back,
pillows should be placed between the knees and under the calves to
suspend heels. Pillows may be placed against the soles of the feet to
aid in the prevention of foot drop. When lying on the side, pillows
should be placed between knees and feet (Fig. 3/8). If difficulties
have been experienced with pressure over the hips, it will be
necessary to lie on double pillows with pressure points suspended
over the gaps. These may be either single, good quality sorbo-
rubber pillows, or double feather-filled pillows (two pillows in one
pillow or bolster case).

Patients with scars from old sores may have difficulty in finding
suitable positions in which to lie. Some may find it necessary to lie
prone, i.e. face down. If this position can be tolerated, it is most
satisfactory and one that permits much longer periods without
being turned. Care must be taken when lying prone. Ensure
breathing is not restricted, that there is no pressure from pyjama or
night-dress buttons, that urinals and drainage tubes are not
obstructed or causing pressure, and that toes, feet and knee caps
are positioned free of pressure.

CLOTHING

A very careful choice of clothing is all-important in preventing
pressure sores. Shoes should always be one or two sizes too large,

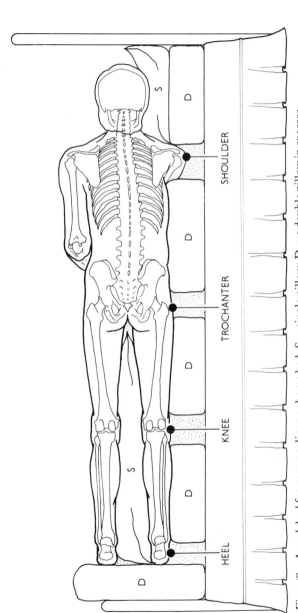

Fig. 3/8   A pack bed for use on a divan or home bed. S = single pillow; D = a double pillow in *one* case made of a soft material, and not tied tightly. This allows for swelling which often occurs through lack of movement especially during hot summer months. Paraplegics are usually advised to elevate the legs as much as possible during the day. If feet and legs continue to swell it may be necessary to wear knee-length elastic stockings; these are available on prescription and you should talk to your doctor about this problem. Trousers should have all the waist buttons and back pockets removed. In spite of tight trousers being in fashion, they must not be over-tight; men will require extra room for a urinal and the need to guard the testicles from damage, while over-tight trousers worn by females not only help to cause cracks between buttocks but have been known to cause vaginal and bladder infections. Trousers made of hard material and with thick seams should be avoided. If zips are inserted into trouser leg seams to allow the wearing of calipers, care should be taken to ensure that such zips do not cause pressure. Many patients choose to wear track suits during hospital rehabilitation. These are most suitable and easy to put on and take off. Some types of underpants are too tight or ride up in the sitting position causing creases which lead to pressure marks. Many of the older generation of patients discovered that pyjama trousers (not nylon) in place of underpants were most successful. These can be tucked into socks, which keep them pulled down and free of creases.

HARD OBJECTS

Hard objects normally kept in trouser pockets such as keys, coins and lighters, will cause pressure, even by their own weight, or they may be accidentally sat on. A bag attached to the side of the chair for carrying such daily requisites is suggested.

Prevention of pressure sores is a daily 24-hour job for 365 days a year. Once a routine has been established it becomes second nature. Until then, constant thought must be given to lifting or being lifted, turning in bed and regular examination of pressure areas. Both patients and their families must clearly understand the dangers to health through pressure sores. They are potential sources of infection that can lead to loss of blood and precious protein. Infection can affect all bodily systems. Indeed, extreme cases of pressure sores can account for the death of a patient.

AIDS TO PREVENTION

There are many aids now available to help in the prevention of pressure sores, some of these will be found listed on page 185. One particular product to which I should like to draw attention is the Spenco Dermal Pad. This is made of a synthetic fat-type material which feels much like normal tissue. It is self-adhesive and can be placed over pressure areas which may be lacking natural tissue padding, for example the sacrum, trochanters, ankles, heels. It is available from:

Spenco (UK) Limited, Tanyard Lane, Steyning, West Sussex BN4 3RJ.

SUMMARY

Sores are caused through prolonged pressure.
Ensure regular turns in bed.
Check skin for damage after every turn.
Check skin for damage before getting up.
Do not sit or lie on any damaged area.
If in doubt, stay in bed with weight off the suspect area.
Ensure regular lifts in the wheelchair.
Do not depend *totally* on mechanical aids to prevent pressure.
Do not wear over-tight clothing.
Avoid sitting or lying on a wet cushion or bed.
Keep well away from open fires or hot pipes.
Check your skin for damage on return to bed.

TREATMENT OF PRESSURE SORES

The treatment of pressure sores varies considerably according to the severity of the sore, clinical judgement and the availability of specialised equipment to relieve pressure.

Until recently patients undergoing treatment for sores in spinal injury centres were nursed on beds constructed of 'packs' or blocks or sorbo-rubber bound together with rubber sheets. These were then placed in wooden trays and positioned across the bed frame so that patients were able to lie with their pressure areas

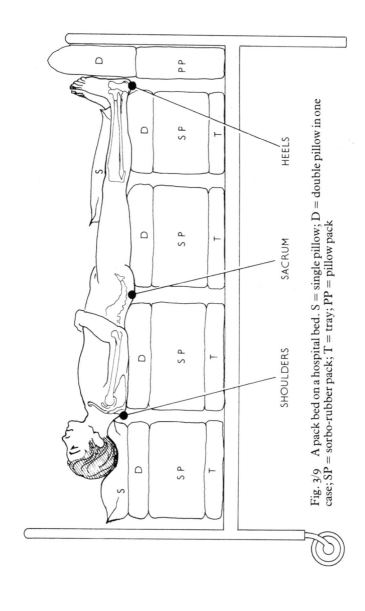

SHOULDERS   SACRUM   HEELS

Fig. 3/9   A pack bed on a hospital bed. S = single pillow; D = double pillow in one case; SP = sorbo-rubber pack; T = tray; PP = pillow pack suspended over the gaps (Fig. 3/9). Despite the effectiveness of these beds, today they are not so commonly used because of the sophisticated equipment which is now available to relieve pressure. In hospital and in the home pillows and pillow-packs are still widely used to relieve pressure and protect pressure areas in the treatment of less severe sores (see Fig. 3/8). These aids and others to prevent pressure are fully discussed later (see p. 185).

Regardless of the type of bed used, it is the relief of pressure which permits the free flow of blood that is the major factor in healing a sore. The treatment of very severe sores is best left to the specialist to determine. They may require surgery to remove dead tissue and possibly infected bone; they will certainly require prolonged hospital treatment – more than just the relief of pressure. Minor sores, knocks and scrapes that will certainly occur from time to time can be treated adequately at home with help from the family doctor and community nurse if necessary.

All paralysed people should keep handy a first aid kit containing all the equipment most of us need to have. Basic requirements of such a kit should include the following:

a good clean container
a sharp pair of scissors
a roll of Elastoplast
a roll of Micropore or Blenderm surgical tape
packets of sterile gauze swabs
a small roll of cotton wool
a bottle of sterile normal saline
a bottle of acriflavine
a bottle of Savlon or similar antiseptic
a bottle of ether meth (to remove plaster marks. Use sparingly, take care to prevent fire – highly inflammable)
a packet of Band-Aid dressings
a clinical thermometer

Individual paraplegics will obviously add other items as required. All these basic items can be obtained from a chemist and should always be available in the event of a knock or scrape, red mark and broken skin, or after a night out when the need for lifting was forgotten. Remember: do not sit or lie on the area; go to bed and stay there until it is completely better.

Method of dressing:

Clean the whole affected area with Savlon, saline or similar anti-septic; clean surrounding skin with ether meth and if the skin is broken, cover with a dressing of sterile swabs and acriflavine, secured with Elastoplast. It is important to use a reasonable pad-ding of swabs, thus ensuring that the dressing is not too tightly strapped down, for this will only add further pressure. Inspect the area after 24 hours and if necessary repeat the treatment until the sore is better. If the skin is not broken but just bruised, cover the area with wet saline swabs and again secure with Elastoplast, repeating the treatment every 12 hours until the bruise has totally gone. If a minor sore shows no sign of healing after 3 or 4 days, or if the dressings look dirty, then it is likely that the sore is infected and you should consult your family doctor or district nurse.

There are no hard and fast rules about which medications should or should not be used in these circumstances. Often medications used in hospital are not available from the local chemist but most paraplegics will soon discover something that suits them. I have found that Malatex cream used for a few days is excellent to clean a dirty sore, which will then heal naturally with almost any other preparation once pressure is removed. If bruises fail to disappear or if they look worse after a few days' rest, treatment in hospital might be required, so consult your doctor.

Septic spots, sometimes caused by skin bacteria and pressure, are a common problem. In certain cases they can be quite serious, requiring continuous rest in bed. Where they persist, try washing the area twice daily with Hibiscrub skin cleanser (available on prescription).

HEALING A PRESSURE SORE

Clean or infection-free sores will normally heal themselves pro-viding *all* pressure is removed. A high protein intake (unless other-wise instructed) will promote the growth of new tissue and healing. Open sores must be kept covered until totally healed to prevent the re-introduction of infection.

Table 3/1   Medications and drugs in common use in the treatment of pressure sores and minor injuries

CONDITION	MEDICATION
A. *Skin care*	
Persistent septic spots	Hibiscrub; surgical spirit; Betadine (povidone-iodine spray)
Itching; sunburn	calamine lotion, cream, ointment
Help in prevention of pressure sores	Ster-Zac dusting powder
Local skin inflammation	nystatin and calamine lotion
Bruised skin	normal saline packs (1 tsp of common salt to 1 pint *boiled* water) ice packs held over bruised area remove all pressure
B. *Cleansing sores*	
Cleaning infection-free sores	normal saline
Cleaning sores	hydrogen peroxide
Cleaning very dirty sores	eusol
Removal of sloughs	Malatex cream or lotion; Aserbine cream or lotion
C. *Healing infection-free sores*	normal saline; Aserbine cream; Flavazole in Carbowax; Jelonet (paraffin gauze); Bactigras
D. *Delayed healing*	
Infected sores	Fucidin H (gel or ointment)
Minor skin abrasions	Flavazole in Carbowax (this is a Stoke Mandeville Hospital preparation. Can be made up by a pharmacist – formula in *Martindale*)
E. *Burns*	
Minor	Bactrian cream, Cetavlex cream; Burneze spray; Aidex cream; Aciflex cream (all available without prescription)
F. *Boils and carbuncles*	magnesium sulphate paste antibiotics may be prescribed

The removal of black necrosed tissue from advanced and neglected pressure sores is normally a surgical procedure and best carried out in hospital. The removal of infected dirty slough from sores can be carried out safely at home under careful supervision. Eusol should be reserved for extremely filthy sores. It needs to be used with great care, because it can also remove healthy tissue.

Sores that show no signs of healing, or suddenly stop making progress, quite often when almost at the final stages, may continue to be infected. There are numerous antibiotic preparations available which might help; their usage should be restricted for fear of producing resistant infections.

BURNS

These may result from boiling water or hot drinks. The affected area should be doused immediately with cold water; if a hand is involved, hold it, or have it held, under the cold water tap for at least 10 minutes. If it is an area which is covered by clothing, don't waste time taking off the clothes. If the burn is severe, transfer to hospital immediately. Minor burns may be treated at home.

Table 3/1 summarises medications and drugs which are commonly used for treating pressure sores and minor injuries.

REFERENCES

Frankel, H. L. (1975). Traumatic paraplegia. *Nursing Mirror*, 6 November.

Martindale: The Extra Pharmacopoeia, 28th edition (1982). The Pharmaceutical Press, London. (This book is regularly updated.)

FURTHER READING

Barton, A. and Barton, M. (1981). *The Management and Prevention of Pressure Sores*. Faber and Faber, London.

4. Bowel Management

Management of the bowels is undoubtedly the most distressing aspect of paraplegia, especially to the newly injured. Because of limited alternatives, the methods of management have not changed significantly over the years. The aim is to regulate the bowels to open regularly at the same time, either daily, or on alternate days. This is most important in good rehabilitation for obvious social and domestic reasons. Although most paraplegics are incontinent, bowel action can be controlled successfully, and regulated with a combination of sensible eating and drinking, aperients, suppositories, automatic reflex bowel action or manual evacuation.

The secret of good bowel management lies, however, in regular, sensible eating habits. It is impossible to say exactly what people should or should not eat or drink, for no two persons are exactly the same. For example, if by eating curry the bowels are upset, or by eating eggs they become constipated, then these foods should obviously be avoided. The internal organs which comprise the bowels are particularly sensitive: they react to stress and abuse caused by worry, certain drugs, infection and foodstuffs that cause irritation or poisoning. When this happens, bouts of diarrhoea which may contain mucus, and/or blood, could result.

Most people prefer to attend to their bowels on alternate days, and this seems the most satisfactory routine. By taking an aperient the night before, faeces are moved into the lower bowel and rectum ready for emptying. The upper bowel will then be empty and the risk of accidents and constipation reduced.

There are numerous types of aperient available and some suit one person, but not others. There are no hard and fast rules governing the type to take. As long as a good result and a formed stool is obtained without accidents in between, then the individual choice is satisfactory. Difficulty may arise in measuring the exact dosage, too much can upset the bowels, while too little can produce a small result and possible constipation.

Senokot tablets are widely used in paraplegia and are very successful; the dosage can be easily measured to suit individual needs. Having taken an appropriate aperient the previous evening, suppositories are given before emptying the bowel. These are of two main types, bisacodyl (Dulcolax) and glycerine. Both are designed to aid the rectum to empty by stimulating it to contract automatically. Dulcolax suppositories promote a stronger action but take longer to act; up to one and a half hours compared with 30 minutes for the glycerine. Some patients may experience slight side-effects from the use of suppositories, such as stomach cramps and a temporary rise in blood pressure with a slight headache (autonomic dysreflexia). Such effects usually only last during the time the bowel is contracting to empty.

Those patients who have developed fully automatic bowel actions, usually with the aid of Dulcolax suppositories, will avoid the need for manual evacuation. This is always more satisfactory and certainly causes less inconvenience. Others usually require manual evacuation of the bowel with the aid of glycerine suppositories which are inserted into the rectum 30 minutes before the actual evacuation. Great care should be taken when doing this; a little petroleum jelly aids the insertion which should be upwards and towards the umbilicus – the natural position of the anal canal.

Manual evacuation, whether carried out by the patient or by the attendant, needs to be done gently: gloves are worn, and *one* finger only is inserted into the rectum. Nails should be kept short, to prevent damage to the lining of the rectum. If the evacuation is being carried out with the patient lying on the bed, he should be placed on the left side with the buttocks at 90° to the mattress. Availability of materials to assist in the procedure varies considerably and depends if the patient is in hospital or living at home (see Chapter 11). In hospital a plastic-backed incontinence sheet should be placed under the buttocks, ensuring that bedclothes are well protected. Holding the patient steady with the left hand, one well-lubricated gloved finger of the right hand should be eased gently into the rectum, rotated and withdrawn, bringing the faeces out with it. Between each insertion a few seconds should elapse, allowing the bowel to contract on its own, which then brings the faeces closer to the anus. This procedure should be continued until all traces of faeces have been removed. A clean incontinence sheet should then be placed under the buttocks and the patient left for a while to ensure that the motion has finished. Moist disposable wipes are used to clean the buttocks after evacuation, and both soiled materials and faeces are disposed of in plastic bags for incineration.

Manual evacuation can cause a sudden severe headache (autonomic dysreflexia) and increased spasms. If this reaction is severe and frequent it may be the sign of impending complications such as haemorrhoids (piles) or an anal fistula. If these are suspected, or if there is *any* bleeding, you should see your doctor.

In the home, and when on holiday, the disposal of soiled materials may prove to be more difficult. Although plastic-backed incontinence sheets are available through the community nursing services, I have found that an ordinary piece of plastic sheeting placed under the buttocks plus cellulose wadding (available on prescription) that has been halved in thickness, is perfectly adequate for bowel evacuation. The buttocks can be cleaned with standard soft toilet paper and everything, with the exception of the plastic sheeting, may be flushed down the toilet.

Obviously this procedure is not pleasant for the attendant, and is equally embarrassing for the patient. Attendants should wear protective clothing: a plastic apron, suitable plastic or rubber gloves and a paper face mask if required. A window should be opened and a fresh air spray used throughout the procedure.

Under normal circumstances the alternative method, that is giving enemas (the washing out of the bowels), is not recommended in paraplegia because the liquid cannot be retained and might also initiate severe autonomic dysreflexia. Because of sensation loss and possible weakness of the bowel wall, damage to the anus and rectum can also result. Nevertheless, there are a number of disposable enema sachets available which, under certain circumstances, have proved helpful both in relieving constipation and for bowel evacuation following surgery for the removal of haemorrhoids as well as other conditions. Their use is not recommended as a regular method of bowel management and should be used only after discussion with the family doctor or consultant.

Paraplegics and low level tetraplegics should be able to transfer on and off the lavatory where they can attend to their own bowels and, when this is possible, it is obviously the most satisfactory method. Under these circumstances aperients and suppositories will be required, but there is one advantage in this position and that is gravity. With the help of gravity, it may not always be necessary to perform a manual evacuation of the bowel. Quite often massaging the abdomen in conjunction with the use of suppositories has the desired effect. Excessive straining and sitting for prolonged periods should be avoided, for this can cause haemorrhoids and possible prolapse of the rectum. Both conditions are not uncommon in paraplegia; in the event of rectal bleeding consult your doctor.

The various aids to bowel management can be obtained on prescription and through the local DHSS in the patient's home area.

For certain tetraplegics who have limited hand movements, there is a suppository applicator available from the Spinal Injuries Association.

Throughout the country and also in many spinal units, there are aid centres which have complete toilet layouts, including a combined toilet and bidet. Visits can be arranged to these centres by appointment so that the equipment may be assessed for individual suitability. It should be noted that if patients wish to use a bidet, great care must be taken to ensure that only warm water is used, thus preventing burns.

Where problems do arise in the disposal of soiled materials it is unwise to try and flush everything down the lavatory for fear of blockage. Most local authorities have a 'Green Bag' service, where soiled materials can be collected in the bag provided. The social services should be able to supply full details. As an alternative, many patients choose to purchase an incinerator and burn soiled materials; where possible, this is perhaps the best solution.

CONSTIPATION

Constipation is a common complaint among paraplegics. It may be the cause of headaches, sweating, a slight rise in temperature, an increase in spasms and abdominal distension (this can make breathing laboured for the tetraplegic); if persistent, constipation can lead to other complications such as bladder dysfunction, which in turn may result in a urinary infection.

Short bouts of constipation are usually caused by changes of diet, daily routine, poor fluid intake, or drugs such as certain analgesics (pain killers) and some antibiotics. Quick relief can be obtained by taking extra measures of the chosen aperient and having the bowels evacuated daily until a normal pattern is reestablished. Invariably the paraplegic with an automatic bowel will require manual evacuation should he become constipated. Many patients make the mistake after being discharged from hospital of allowing themselves to become constipated, thinking this will prevent possible accidents. On the contrary, constipation is often the cause of diarrhoea.

A high fibre or roughage diet in the form of fruit, vegetables, high-bran breads and cereals is essential in the prevention of constipation. Fibre is the indigestible part of these foods: after normal digestion it combines with water in the large intestine to form bulk which ensures softness of faeces. The quantity of fibre required varies from person to person, and where constipation persists it can be supplemented by taking natural bran. This is the unprocessed and crushed outer layer of wheat available from health-food shops. This should be added a teaspoonful at a time to the normal daily diet. Where constipation still persists, a faecal softener such as dioctyl, or a bulk former such as Normacol may be required. These are available on prescription, and the family doctor should be consulted.

There are other stimulant laxatives for which a prescription is not required. These include cascara and Syrup of Figs. All will cause abdominal cramps with prolonged use, and as it is usually necessary for the paraplegic to depend on the use of laxatives, then the minimum dosage on alternate days seems the most satisfactory solution. In cases where constipation persists, the use of bulk-forming drugs and faecal softeners will greatly assist.

Soft soap enemas are not recommended, especially in pregnancy. They are likely to inflame the lining of the intestines and may cause damage due to sensation loss.

All drugs and medications required for bowel management are available on prescription and their use will be decided by the family doctor or consultant.

Table 4/1   Drugs and medications in common use for constipation

SUBSTANCE	SIDE–EFFECTS
Laxatives	
senna: Sennoside B; Senokot – tablets, granules or syrup (elixir)	Abdominal cramps. Prolonged use should be avoided. Not recommended during pregnancy. May colour urine red
danthron: Dorbanex – capsules, liquid mixture or liquid forte	Abdominal cramps. Prolonged use should be avoided. Urine may be coloured red. Avoid contact with skin or irritation may occur
bisacodyl: Dulcolax – tablets	Abdominal cramps. May cause gastro-intestinal disturbances. Avoid prolonged use. May cause gastric upset
magnesium sulphate (Epsom salts)	Colic. Very strong – should be used only very occasionally for rapid bowel evacuation
Bulk-forming drugs	
methylcellulose tablets	Flatulence. Abdominal distension
ispaghula husk (can be taken by patients who cannot tolerate bran; maintain good fluid intake)	Flatulence. Abdominal distension
Isogel granules; Fybogel granules	Flatulence. Abdominal distension

SUBSTANCE	SIDE-EFFECTS

sterculia granules (Normacol)
    sterculia standard, special or
    antispasmodic
	Flatulence. Abdominal
	distension

Faecal softeners dioctyl	None
Suppositories glycerol	None
bisacodyl (Dulcolax)	May cause local irritation and abdominal cramps

5. Management of the Urinary System

The urinary system consists of two kidneys, left and right, connected to the bladder by tubes called ureters. The bladder empties through a third tube called the urethra, which, in the male, lies through the centre of the penis (Fig. 5/1). Urine is the waste fluid secreted by the kidneys, and passes down the ureters into the bladder, where it is stored until ready for excreting via the urethra (micturition). The production and secretion of urine by the kidneys is a process designed to filter impurities from the blood to maintain life. It is therefore necessary to drink adequate amounts of fluid to keep the blood free of impurities and the urinary system flushed – especially when paralysed.

The urinary system is a delicate, sensitive part of the body and in a paralysed person is prone to complications. Great care must be constantly taken to prevent these from occurring unnecessarily. Recognising symptoms of problems and knowing what action to take is essential to survival.

The bladder acts as a reservoir for urine. Its opening is controlled by two sphincters (circular muscles at the bladder neck), an internal and an external. As the bladder contracts to empty so the internal sphincter opens to allow the urine to flow; once the urine has been voided the external sphincter relaxes. Able-bodied people can feel the distension of the bladder before micturition: they also have control of the external sphincter to check the out-flow if necessary. For a paralysed person, there is no normal warning sensation and, therefore, no control of the external sphincter (other than in the case of some incomplete lesions), and a urine collection device has to be used.

Immediately following injury to the spinal cord, the bladder emptying mechanism in most patients is non-functional due to

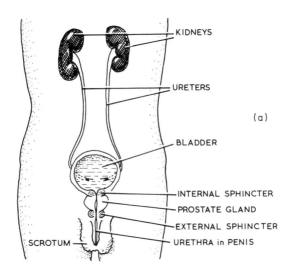

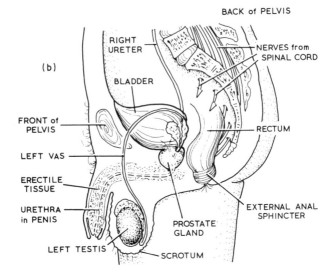

Fig. 5/1 The male urinary system. *Note* the spinal nerves which supply the pelvic organs (b)

spinal shock. To empty the bladder during this period, an indwelling catheter is frequently inserted before the patient is transferred to a spinal centre. The future management of the bladder from thereon varies according to medical opinion and the patient's overall condition. Whenever possible it is highly desirable ultimately to remove the catheter altogether, thus preventing infection. This is achieved by training the bladder to open regularly by the aid of tapping or expression. It may be necessary to carry out intermittent catheterisations, in conjunction with regulated drinking, until the bladder empties sufficiently well. Particular care is taken to do this under sterile conditions to prevent the introduction of infection.

In the majority of cases, as spinal shock subsides, the bladder either begins to empty automatically (like a baby's) or can be emptied by applying pressure over the lower abdomen above the symphysis pubis. The automatic bladder develops usually with cervical and high thoracic lesions that are spastic. An autonomous or flaccid bladder develops with flaccid paralysis, usually with low dorsal or lumbar lesions. Automatic or spastic bladders can be triggered into emptying by various methods. The most commonly adopted method is 'tapping' over the bladder area; stroking the insides of the thighs, or stimulating the anus with a gloved finger, are alternative methods. All methods are designed to stimulate the bladder to contract and allow micturition.

The autonomous or flaccid bladder has no muscle tone and will not react to this type of stimulation. These bladders are emptied by manual expression over the bladder area, or by abdominal straining, since abdominal muscles usually function in these lesions. (See page 94 for alternative methods of bladder management.)

The degree of efficiency will vary from person to person, but once a satisfactory method is found, patients are trained to empty their bladders every 2 to 3 hours. The objects are the establishment of a good system of emptying the bladder and the reduction of residual urine to below 100ml. The prevention of infection and other complications of a high residual urine, and the ability to prevent incontinence from interfering with rehabilitation and social activities are most important.

URINE COLLECTING DEVICES

The male paraplegic should regard himself as fortunate in having a penis on to which it is possible to attach a urinal. This is often taken for granted and the regular expression of the bladder forgotten. Over the years this can lead to a lazy and weak bladder that becomes difficult to manage. It is therefore important to stress that the bladder, whether of the automatic or autonomous type, should be expressed every 2 to 3 hours, or even hourly if the fluid intake is more than usual, regardless of whether a urinal is worn or not.

The majority of men will choose to wear the condom type urinal attached to either a GU suprapubic bag which is commonly called a 'kipper', or to one of several different types of disposable plastic urine collecting bag. There are other suitable urinals for the male paraplegic, such as the Stoke Mandeville type and the Thackray Male Urinal, but these are cumbersome, unsightly and seldom used by the modern generation of patients.

The condom type urinal is fixed to the penis by either a skin adhesive, or by an adhesive strip. These should be changed at least every 24 hours as instructed.

CONDOMS

Basically there are two different types of condom.

1 The contraceptive type which is attached to a length of rubber tubing by a plastic button.
2 The moulded one-piece construction type, where the tubing and condom are moulded together.

There are variations of both designed to suit different circumstances. They are available through either the DHSS at Blackpool (see p. 100), or on prescription from the family doctor.

The DHSS supply the following: (1) rubber tubing and plastic buttons; (2) Payne's condoms; (3) the Durex non-allergy condom. Of these, the Payne's condom is the most popular, leaving the non-allergy type for a minority of people who find they develop an allergy to other types of rubber sheaths after several years' use. Both condoms should be secured with a skin adhesive.

Included in the vast range of the 'moulded' types of condom available on prescription from the family doctor are:

1 The Posey Sheath. This has a foam rubber insert to protect the end of the penis from pressure, and should be secured with a skin adhesive.
2 Warne Secure. Attached with the aid of an adhesive foam strip.
3 Conveen Male Incontinence System. Attached with an adhesive strip and designed to be attached to their own urine collecting bags.
4 Down's Uromale condom. Again attached to the penis with an adhesive strip and designed to be attached to their own urine collecting bags.
5 Franklin Portasheath. Attached to the penis by a double-sided adhesive strip.
6 Bard Penile Sheath. Attached to the penis by skin adhesives.
7 Squibb Accuseal External Catheters. Attached to the penis by skin adhesive and specially designed for tetraplegics with poor hand movement to attach it to their own drainage bag.

SKIN ADHESIVES

These are available on prescription from the family doctor and include:

1 Saltair Ostomy Solution
2 Chiron skin adhesive.
3 Dow Corning Medical Adhesive B. Available in aerosol spray or brush-on liquid. The brush-on type is ideal for fitting condoms to the patient with a very small penis – such as a child.

There may be considerable confusion concerning the most satisfactory condom and adhesive to use. I would recommend patients to start with the Payne's condom, and to use either the Chiron or Saltair skin adhesives. The Dow Corning adhesive is extremely expensive and is specially produced as a non-allergic adhesive. The other types of condom are expensive, some costing about £1 each. I feel they should be reserved for patients who experience difficulties using the other types.

Prolonged erections can cause pressure sores from the rubber ring of the condom. To prevent this, after the condom has been fitted, cut the ring with a pair of scissors, or better still wear a condom that has no ring such as the Warne's Secure. When fitting a condom, always ensure that at least 2.5cm (1in) of free condom is left to prevent pressure on the end of the penis from the plastic button.

Both the tubing and the plastic buttons must be sterilised before fitting. At home this can be done either by boiling for five minutes, or by soaking overnight in a solution made with Milton sterilising tablets, or a weak solution of household bleach. Before sterilising, the tubes and buttons should be thoroughly cleaned in hot soapy water. Mineral deposits on plastic buttons can be removed by soaking in 5% hydrochloric acid. Condoms are disposable.

URINE COLLECTION BAGS

All urine collection bags are available on prescription from the family doctor. These include the disposable bed collection bags, disposable leg bags, and bags such as the GU 532 suprapubic bag – the 'kipper'. With the exception of the last bag, all the others are designed to be disposable and most are designed to go with a specific condom produced by the same company. To cut the cost, several of these bags can be adequately washed out and used more than once, especially at home where there is less likelihood of cross infection. Disposable urine collection bags include:

Bardic '500' Dispoz-A-Bag leg bag.
Bardic '500' Dispoz-A-Bag leg bag with extension tube.
Bardic '500' Dispoz-A-Bag leg bag/bedside bag with connection tube.

Other makes are available (see pp. 100–2).

Application of condom urinal

To apply a condom urinal the equipment required is: a new condom sheath, condom rubber tubing approximately 12.5cm (5in) long, a plastic condom connecting button, an orange stick or 'pricker', gauze swab or cotton wool, ether meth, skin adhesive and the urinal or 'kipper'.

Method: Gently remove the old condom taking care not to damage the skin; if it is difficult to remove, use ether meth to dissolve the adhesive. Thoroughly clean all traces of adhesive from the penis with a swab and ether meth, then wash the penis and scrotal area with warm soapy water. Dry carefully and examine the penis for skin damage. It is advisable to wait an hour after removal before putting on a fresh condom. Should there be skin damage, a fresh condom should *not* be affixed. The damaged area should be covered with a sterile dressing and you should stay in bed using a glass or disposable urine collecting bottle until the skin is completely healed.

The new condom and tubing should be assembled ready for application. This is achieved by placing the plastic button in the end of the condom, then pushing it into the rubber tubing. The rubber of the condom which then lies across the end of the plastic button is pricked out leaving the way clear for the free flow of urine. A moderate coat of adhesive should then be applied to the shaft of the penis, waiting a few seconds for it to become tacky before rolling the condom down the shaft of the penis. Use a little finger-pressure to aid adhesion. The best results are obtained if the condom is fitted to an erect penis.

In some spinal units patients are instructed to attach the condom to the base of the penis using Elastoplast rather than skin adhesive. The disadvantage of this is that the condom may be detached and the skin may be damaged when the Elastoplast is removed.

Instructions for the application of the other types of condom with either a single- or double-sided adhesive strip are given clearly with the products. Many patients, in particular those who have reflex erections, have found that these types of condom are easily pulled off and cause leakage. To overcome this problem, many patients use skin adhesive *plus* the adhesive strips.

On their discharge from hospital patients are given a certificate stating that they wear a condom urinal. This should be sent to the DHSS with the initial request for supplies.

A complete guide to the range of incontinence aids is available from: Thames Valley Medical, 119 Chatham Street, Reading, Berkshire RG1 7HT (0734 595835). Alternatively your local chemist can supply information on the aids available.

URINARY PROBLEMS FACING WOMEN

So far, no one has been able to invent a suitable urinal for the female paraplegic. Some have been produced, but all cause pressure and should be avoided. Consequently females have to work very hard indeed to develop a good automatic or autonomous bladder, together with very strict drinking and bladder emptying routines.

Women faced with this problem usually succeed better than men in organising their bladder routine, for obvious social and domestic reasons. Those physically able to use the lavatory, do so every 2 or 3 hours, expressing the bladder in the normal way. Others may use a female urine receiver sitting in the chair with a split cushion, or may lie on the bed. To prevent possible accidents in between, women can wear absorbent pads and plastic pants. These are available through the social services, and you should contact your social worker or community nurse for full details. More attractive pants can be bought from firms such as Basingstoke Hygiene Products, and some women may wish to consider buying these themselves.

For the younger strong-armed paraplegic who is able to transfer unaided, this routine is usually satisfactory, but for the tetraplegic dependent on others to lift him on and off either toilet or bed, such a routine can prove very demanding.

Problems can arise in social activities such as shopping, going to the theatre, eating in restaurants, in finding suitable places to express the bladder. Special consideration is necessary when travelling. At such times many females choose not to drink at all. While this may prevent them from getting wet, it often leads to infection of the bladder and further problems. It is better to decrease the amount of drinking before going out, then compensate for it later by drinking extra fluids on returning home. A little research and a few telephone calls should be made to find out if a particular place has accessible toilets, or a satisfactory room that can be used. Do not wait until you arrive only to find there is nothing suitable. This can lead to bad temper, frustration, getting wet and the risk of pressure sores.

The necessity to attend to bladder function in this way, combined with the endless struggle against getting wet, invariably dominates women's lifestyles. This may be so acute, that one of the alternative methods of bladder management could be considered (see p. 94).

BLADDER TRAINING

There are various approaches to bladder training depending on medical opinion and the state of the bladder. Basically, the object of training the bladder to empty automatically or by manual expression is in order to eliminate the need for an intermittent or indwelling catheter, and whenever possible to maintain the urinary tract free from infection as well as avoiding back pressure to the kidneys.

Because urinals are readily available for the male paraplegic, there is a natural tendency for him to instinctively depend on the urinal to collect urine expelled from the bladder, rather than regularly expressing the bladder in the toilet as is practised by women. It is possible for the male to avoid wearing a urinal and remain dry, in particular the low level spinally injured paraplegic with a flaccid bladder. It is also possible for many women to stay dry in between bladder expressions.

To achieve this the bladder *must* be free from infection and *must* be expressed at regular and frequent intervals. An infected bladder is sore and irritated, consequently it will be contracting and emptying more frequently. Fluid intake must be regular and not in excess of the bladder capacity. For example: if a bladder will only hold 500ml, then to drink 1000ml and not empty the bladder for 3 hours would make remaining dry very difficult.

No two people are exactly the same. Similarly, the capacity of the bladder will vary from person to person – as will the need to express the bladder. With a normal average fluid intake of no less than 2 litres daily the aim should be to try and express the bladder every 2 or 3 hours. More frequent expressions will, obviously, become necessary if the fluid intake is increased, during the summer months for example.

Precisely when the intake of fluid should occur following the emptying of the bladder will be up to each individual to discover by trial and error. However, I would suggest that to drink a large amount immediately following the expression of the bladder will shorten the period of time an individual can last before the bladder is again full and ready to be expressed.

SUPRAPUBIC BAG GU 532 ('THE KIPPER')

The kipper urinal cannot be sterilised; it can only be disinfected and therefore it is necessary to have two – one on and one off. The kipper can be used with the condom urinal, and by men and women who require an indwelling catheter.

After use, the screw top should be removed and the urinal drained and rinsed in warm water. The urinal should then be thoroughly washed in warm soapy water, rinsed and left to soak for 2 to 3 hours in a disinfecting solution. Milton sterilising tablets, available from most chemists' shops, are ideal for this purpose. Should these not be available, a 5% solution of household bleach can be used – in this case the urinal should not be soaked for more than 2 hours.

Careful attention should be paid to cleaning the screw top and the drain tap. Where mineral deposits are found, a fine brush may be required to clean the holes. When thoroughly clean, the screw top should also be soaked in the disinfecting solution. After soaking, urinals should be rinsed again in warm water and finally hung up to dry with the drainage tap open.

Urinals should not be exposed to direct heat or the rubber will perish. Normally they will last between 5 and 6 months with careful use. The rubber first starts to perish near the tap, or splits along the seams, so regular inspection is advised.

Patients are advised to carry a spare urinal *always* plus condom and any other incontinence devices they may use whenever they are away from their home, no matter how short the journey.

The suprapubic bag GU 532 is available on prescription and can be supplied in either black or white rubber. A waist support strap is also available, but must be specified on the prescription as must the colour.

THE INDWELLING CATHETER

For various reasons, such as chronic infection, defects in the urinary system, or where the bladder is unable to expel urine and all measures to make it function have failed, drainage may become necessary by employing an indwelling catheter. Various types of catheter can be used, but the one found to be most satisfactory is the Foley. Having been inserted, it is retained in the bladder by an inflatable balloon.

To minimise infection and reduce the formation of stones, a standard Teflon-coated Foley catheter is changed twice weekly and a daily bladder washout given. Regular catheter changes also relieve pressure to the urethra, thereby reducing the risk of pressure sores. The silastic Foley catheter, made of a softer material should be changed every 4 weeks and daily bladder washouts given.

Catheters often become blocked and difficulty may arise in obtaining a doctor or community nurse, especially at night or weekends. It is therefore *essential* for those living outside hospital or an institution to be taught, themselves, how to change their own catheters and do their own bladder washouts, or for their attendants to be taught (see bladder retention, p. 92).

Patients requiring indwelling catheters will be supplied with all equipment necessary for both changing the catheter and doing daily bladder washouts.

Inserting the indwelling catheter

Having talked with many patients who have experienced great difficulties in obtaining professional help at times of emergency when catheters have blocked, I feel justified in outlining the technique of catheterisation: *but* readers must obtain professional instruction before attempting the procedure unattended.

Before a new catheter can be inserted, the old one must be removed gently. First a syringe should be inserted in the catheter's valve and the fluid withdrawn. The capacity of the balloon is clearly marked, thus ensuring that the appropriate quantity of fluid has been obtained in the syringe. Once the balloon has been fully deflated the catheter can then be withdrawn gently. Should difficulty be experienced in deflating the balloon, then leave the syringe in the valve for several minutes *without* applying suction, this will usually have the desired effect. Should this fail, and providing the catheter is not blocked, then inject 10ml of liquid paraffin into the balloon. This should then cause the balloon to perish during the next 12 to 24 hours, allowing the catheter to be removed in the normal manner. Should the catheter be blocked, and if it cannot be removed, patients should seek medical assistance from the nearest hospital without delay. *Never*, under any circumstances, cut any part of a catheter for this will make the hospital's job of removing it very much more difficult.

Catheterisation

Catheterisations must be carried out under sterile conditions to prevent the introduction of infection. All equipment must be sterilised. In hospital this is usually done by a central sterilising department which prepares all equipment needed in a pack; the user has only to open the pack and find everything ready. At home, similar pre-sterilised packs are available and supplied through the community nursing service or on prescription from the family doctor. In certain circumstances, such as holiday periods, or when pre-sterilised packs are not available, patients may have to resort to the old-fashioned but effective method of boiling some equipment for 5 minutes.

Foley catheters. These are available on prescription and are supplied in many sizes. Under normal circumstances a size 14 or 16 for males, and a size 16 or 18 for females should be selected. If the size of the catheter is increased, the danger of pressure within the urethra and stone formation on its balloon is more likely. Many patients who have a chronic bladder infection, which almost always accompanies the long-term use of indwelling catheters, may find the smaller catheter easily blocks with sediment produced by the infection. Medical advice should be sought before inserting a larger size, as it may be possible for the infection to be treated to reduce the degree of sediment.

Method of catheterisation: Thoroughly scrub hands and carefully open the catheter pack without touching the contents. Place on a clean surface, such as a table or trolley previously swabbed with Savlon or similar antiseptic. Break the external catheter packet covering and shake the internal packet on to a sterile paper sheet. Scrub the hands again and put on sterile disposable gloves.

1 Place the sterile paper sheet over the abdomen with the penis protruding through the cut-out hole. A similar paper sheet with larger cut-out hole is supplied for females.

2 Place a gauze swab around the penis, and for females between the labia.

3 Thoroughly swab the glans of the penis with 4 or 5 swabs soaked in Savlodil and held with forceps. For the woman, the swabbing should commence from the top and outside lips of the labia, working inwards towards the urethra.

4 Lignocaine gel, which is a combination of local anaesthetic and lubricant, should then be injected into the urethra from the tube, and the end of the penis held for 2 minutes to retain the lubricant. For a woman, the catheter is lubricated with gel before insertion.

5 With a clean pair of forceps, the catheter should then be threaded from the inside packet container into the urethra and bladder.

6 Ensure that the catheter is well into the bladder and that urine is flowing before inflating the retaining balloon with 5ml of sterile water.

7 Gently withdraw the catheter until resistance is felt.

8 Connect to drainage bag.

Bladder washouts

Bladder washouts can be carried out by most patients or their relatives. Understanding this technique can obviate long waits for community nurses. It may also be of value in relieving catheter blockages that often occur.

Bladder washouts must be carried out under sterile conditions to prevent the introduction of new infection. All equipment must be sterilised.

Daily washouts with sterile normal saline will keep the bladder clear of sediment as well as helping to prevent stone formation. Washouts are best carried out first thing in the morning. After a night's rest sediment will have collected in the bladder. I stress that this is a sterile procedure even if the bladder is already infected.

Equipment required may be supplied from hospital prior to

discharge, and may differ from supplies available from community nursing services. Hospital supplies will include: Stylex syringe and plastic measuring jug or tin-foil tray, receiver or plastic kidney dish, disposable gloves and sterile normal saline. Adequate sterilising can be obtained by soaking the equipment in a solution made with Milton sterilising tablets.

Method: All equipment necessary should be sterilised and placed on a clean surface, such as a table or trolley swabbed with Savlon. Scrub the hands thoroughly and put on sterile disposable gloves.

1 Lay catheter in receiver and swab the connection to drainage bag before parting the two.
2 Fill Stylex syringe with 60ml of warm normal saline. Expel air and inject fluid into bladder.
3 Immediately withdraw fluid to 45ml, then slowly for remaining 15ml and discard.
4 Repeat this procedure at least three times until a clear return of fluid is obtained.
5 Reconnect the catheter to the drainage bag.

If your doctor has prescribed a local antibiotic for the bladder this should be injected into the bladder through the catheter after the washout is complete, and then clipped off according to medical advice but usually for 10–15 minutes before reconnection to the drainage bag. Usually the amount of antibiotic will be determined by the doctor, but where no instructions are given 10–15ml is normal.

Due to the possibility of reflux, and because the bladder which has received continual drainage over a long period of time will have a small capacity, it is important that only 60ml is injected into the bladder at a time. Where there is a known reflux, 30–40ml of fluid should be injected slowly. It should then be withdrawn immediately and not simply left to trickle out of the catheter, thus ensuring that all sediment stirred up and suspended in the saline is removed. On occasions it might be impossible to withdraw the fluid immediately because the bladder goes into spasm – in that case, let the saline run out on its own.

A new technique for doing bladder washouts has been devised by CliniMed Ltd, and is being widely used in both hospitals and the community. This is with pre-sterilised disposable sachets of various solutions. The solution known as 'Suby G' has been found most effective in preventing blockage of catheters and bladder stone formation. The sachets are available on prescription.

DRINKING

Unless instructed otherwise, patients should aim at maintaining a high non-alcoholic fluid intake of 3 litres (5 pints) or more in every 24 hours. This is all-important for those paralysed as it prevents stagnation of urine, which leads to infection. A concentrated urine will deposit minerals in the system leading to the formation of stones which, together with bad emptying of the bladder, will encourage infection.

'Moderation at all times' is the best advice available concerning the consumption of alcohol. This advice is even more important to the paraplegic, for the following reasons. First, due to paralysis the circulation, although normal, is easily affected by circumstances, including circulation through the kidneys. Making the kidneys work harder by drinking excessive amounts of alcohol only adds to the strain they already suffer. Second, alcohol has bad effect on bladder function. Not so many years ago alcohol, in large quantities, was given before crude surgery was performed in place of an anaesthetic. Most people will have experienced the effect of too much alcohol. They become drunk, weak, lose balance and are unable to stand properly. This is because alcohol in large quantities is a depressant poison, thus the paraplegic will forget to attend to his bladder. It also depresses the action of the automatic bladder.

Those with an automatic bladder depend on good muscle tone for its emptying. Alcohol relaxes this muscle tone, and because these bladders work automatically, there is no normal warning sensation to indicate when it needs emptying. Consequently the bladder will not empty, it will overfill and becomes stretched out of shape; there will be stagnation of urine which will become infected and there will also be the possible risk of kidney damage due to a build up of back pressure.

Excessive alcohol also encourages forgetfulness, especially the need to lift in the chair and to empty urinals, which can burst. It can cause loss of balance leading to falls from the wheelchair, which may result in bone fractures. Even small quantities of alcohol can interact with various drugs that individuals might be taking – so always check with your doctor. Some paraplegics, those with high cervical lesions in particular, may find that alcohol reduces their already low blood pressure – I most certainly do.

Regular intake of excessive amounts of alcohol will lead to an increase in weight and eventual damage to the liver. So, I repeat – 'moderation' is the key word. A glass or two of beer or wine will do little harm. Spirits such as whisky, gin and brandy have a high alcohol content and should be taken with respect, or better still avoided altogether.

TAKING A URINE SPECIMEN

Under ideal circumstances a urine specimen should be taken by a nurse, doctor or trained orderly at a hospital in order that the specimen can be swiftly taken to the pathology laboratory for examination. This is not always possible at home and as it is often necessary for the paraplegic to have a urine test, I feel this aspect should be covered.

A urine specimen can be collected in two different ways: either by passing a catheter, or by collecting a mid-stream sample of urine. I will deal with the latter method first.

A mid-stream sample (MSU): This is taken while passing urine, not when starting, and ensures that any contaminant is washed away and not collected in the jar. Particular care must be taken in preventing the jar from coming in contact with skin or clothing, for this could lead to the sample's becoming contaminated and thus an inaccurate laboratory result.

The equipment required for taking an MSU includes a sterile urine collection jar, sterile gauze swabs, Savlon, and a kidney dish or receiver.

Approximately 45 minutes before taking the specimen, a good drink of water should be taken. The procedure should then be as follows. Thoroughly wash hands, soak swabs in Savlon, then thoroughly swab the end of the penis. This should be repeated at least three times, using a clean swab each time. The same procedure should be applied with females who should thoroughly swab the urethral area by holding the labia apart with a sterile swab. Swabbing should be from the outside and from the top in a downward direction only, working towards the urethra. Swabbing should be done at least five times, using a clean swab each time. Ensure the top of the specimen jar is not too tightly closed. Stimulate the bladder in the normal manner and, when urine is flowing freely, remove the top of the jar and insert into stream, collecting about 2.5–5cm (1–2in) of urine. Replace the lid on the jar quickly and take it to a hospital pathology laboratory as soon as possible.

Patients with indwelling catheters can obtain a specimen by clipping off the catheter for 10 to 15 minutes after a good drink of water. Thoroughly wash the end of the catheter in Savlon; remove the clip and again collect a mid-stream of urine, not the first flow from the catheter.

Catheters should not be left clipped off for more than 15 minutes at a time, thus preventing the possibility of infection travelling up the ureters to the kidneys.

If specimens cannot be taken directly to a hospital pathology laboratory, they should be kept in the bottom of a domestic refrigerator until transport is available.

COMPLICATIONS

It is important to acquire some knowledge and understanding of the more obvious complications which can occur in the urinary system, in order to recognise possible symptoms and to know what action to take. It is not necessary to learn every detail about possible complications. The majority of problems will be connected with infection in the following: the bladder (cystitis), the kidneys (nephritis), the pelvis of the kidneys with the ureters (pyelitis), and the urethra (urethritis). Other problems may include bladder retention, high residual urine, reflux of urine, and the formation of bladder and kidney stones.

BLADDER INFECTIONS (CYSTITIS)

Infection of the bladder is the most common problem, and if

untreated, infection of the whole urinary system can follow. Symptoms are easy to recognise: dirty, cloudy urine which may be foul smelling; possible bleeding from the bladder (haematuria); headache; sweating; and sickness. There may be a rise in body temperature; possible rise in pulse rate; and frequent passing of small amounts of urine with automatic bladders. Also possible is an increase in spasms; or, as I have discovered, a reduction of spasms accompanied by a severe reduction in the circulation to the lower limbs, which turn blue and are cold to touch; there may be a burning sensation in the bladder or lower abdomen (where there is sensation). There may also be shivering and rigors, although these occur more often with further infection of the urinary system.

At the first sign of infection a urine specimen (collected in a sterile manner) should be sent to a hospital pathology laboratory for examination. Arrangements for this should be made with the family doctor or community nurse. To prevent infection from spreading to the remainder of the system and possibly causing a 'flare-up' the family doctor may prescribe an antibiotic that can be changed, if necessary, when the laboratory result is known.

A 'flare-up' is the term used to describe a sudden rise in temperature, rigors and vomiting, due to infection of the urinary system. It is usually associated with pyelitis.

I cannot over-emphasise the importance of sending a urine specimen for examination when infection is suspected. Only too often, at the first signs of infection, patients put themselves on to an antibiotic that they have in their cupboards in the hope that it will provide a cure. I'm equally guilty, and so are many family doctors. The 'hit or miss' approach may sometimes work. But when it fails, then more resistant strains of the infection grow and be very difficult to clear up. When the appropriate antibiotic is confirmed, it is *essential* to complete the full course unless instructed otherwise. This is to ensure that the infection has been completely cleared. Again, if an insufficient course of an antibiotic is taken, new strains of bacteria grow.

The urine of a paraplegic tends to be alkaline in reaction, due to the presence of bacteria in the bladder. Consequently the doctor may follow a course of antibiotics with an acidifying and antiseptic drug, such as ascorbic acid, or G500 (a mixture of methionine 250mg and hexamine mandelate 250mg), in an attempt to make the urine acid to discourage infection and stone formation. The use of these acidifying drugs should be carefully monitored – if used for prolonged periods gastric upsets may occur.

INFECTION OF KIDNEYS AND URETERS (PYELITIS: NEPHRITIS)

One cause of infection in the kidneys and ureters is that of an infection of the bladder that has travelled up the ureters. Other less common virulent infections may find their way to the kidneys through the circulation. Additional symptoms to those of bladder infections are: a high rise in both body temperature and pulse rate; a possible rise in respiration rate; rigors, shivering and hot and cold spells; pain in the loins, back and shoulders; increased spasms; and a loss of appetite. A definite feeling of illness will be experienced, which requires staying in bed for at least 24 hours after the body temperature has returned to normal. As in the case of a bladder infection the family doctor must be called and a urine specimen taken.

If, as is often experienced, the temperature is very high, two aspirin tablets taken every 6 hours will help reduce it (soluble aspirin is more easily digested). Tetraplegics in particular will suffer, and an electric fan, sponging and cold drinks will all help to reduce body temperature. The added risk of pressure sores must be remembered at such times, hence the need for more frequent turns.

Kidney infections are dangerous and should not be ignored; if they are not treated immediately permanent damage to the kidneys will result, impairing function. Repeated infections of either the kidneys or the bladder will certainly require investigation, since causes can usually be treated if discovered in time. The need for regular check-ups to monitor kidney function is essential (see p. 153).

INFECTION OF URETHRA (URETHRITIS)

Infection of the urethra can occur without infection to the remainder of the urinary system, although it is usually associated with at least an infection of the bladder. Those requiring permanent indwelling catheters are most prone to this condition, because the infection is introduced during catheter changes.

Symptoms of infection in the urethra are usually a discharge of pus from the urethra, or from around the catheter. The condition is fairly common, especially in those having indwelling catheters. It should not be ignored because further complications can arise. In men, particularly, a fistula can form. This is a hole through the wall of the urethra caused by a combination of the infection and pressure from the catheter. The general practitioner should be consulted, and he may prescribe treatment or refer patients to a spinal specialist or urologist.

The risk of infection to the urethra, or the formation of a fistula, can be minimised for those with indwelling catheters by thoroughly washing the penis and catheter daily, and ensuring that any crusty deposits from around the catheter are removed. The penis and catheter should then be wrapped in a clean gauze swab and secured with a piece of adhesive tape.

KIDNEY AND BLADDER STONES

The formation of stones in either the bladder or the kidneys is not uncommon in paraplegia and is usually associated with infection, the use of indwelling catheters, or low fluid intake.

During the early months following injury there is a higher risk of stone formation. This is because calcium is given off from the bones due to lack of movement and weight-bearing. This is then excreted by the kidneys in the urine. With a combination of infection, low fluid intake and output, together with excess calcium there is a chance of deposits being formed in the urinary system, leading to the growth of stones. This can be reduced to a minimum by regular drinking, turning, and careful catheterisation to prevent infection. Milk is rich in calcium and should be restricted at all times, especially during the early months following injury.

The formation of stones can usually be seen on the x-ray when having an intravenous urogram (IVU). Should they be discovered, the spinal specialist will decide what course of action to take. More often than not, small stones in the bladder can be removed through the urethra. Those that form in the kidneys may require more extensive surgery for their removal.

It is less likely for stones to form in a sterile acid urine, which again emphasises the need for the system to be kept free of infection. For reasons not fully understood a number of patients do commence the growth of stones many years after injury.

People who require permanent indwelling catheters usually have a chronic bladder infection and become more prone to stone formations. This is because mineral crystals in the urine tend to collect on the balloon of the catheter. These then grow together, forming a stone. To reduce this risk, daily bladder washouts must be given and catheters changed regularly (see p. 83).

REFLUX OF URINE

Reflux of urine is simply the flowing back of urine from the bladder up the ureters, and is often associated with a high residual urine and possible infection. When this happens, and it is usually first suspected on the IVU, the pelvis and possibly the ureter of the kidney involved may become enlarged, and the patient is said to have hydronephrosis.

Confirmation of reflux can be obtained by a special x-ray examination (a cystogram). For this, the bladder is filled with a special dye, through a catheter, and the movement and flow of the dye observed under x-ray control. When reflux is confirmed, any treatment will be decided by the spinal specialist. Prevention of reflux can be helped by maintaining the urine in a sterile condition and ensuring that residual urine is low. Regular expression of the bladder will aid this.

RESIDUAL URINE

Residual urine refers to the amount of urine left in the bladder after it has been emptied in the normal manner. To measure it, either a catheter is inserted into the bladder immediately after micturition, the remaining urine then being drained and carefully measured, or the remaining urine can be estimated with the aid of ultrasound equipment. This latter technique has the advantage of preventing the possible risk of introducing infection by catheterisation.

Ideally, residual urine should be less than 100ml. If it is higher, there is a possibility of infection due to stagnation, and bladder and kidney damage. Causes of high residual urine vary, the most common being obstruction at the outlet of the bladder, which impedes emptying, weak muscle tone of the bladder, and failure on the part of patients to express their bladders at regular intervals, leading to overstretched and weak bladders.

After investigation of kidney and bladder function by IVU and cystogram or urodynamics, any treatment will be decided by the specialist. For men this might be cystoscopy (examination of bladder interior); a transurethral resection (TUR) – this is the removal of obstruction in the bladder neck, to widen the outlet; dilatation of the urethra; or division of the external sphincter.

Because of the female anatomy, removal of a section of the sphincter is not normally carried out due to technical difficulties. Where there is a high residual urine in women, the sphincters are usually dilated or stretched, thus allowing a free flow of urine. This procedure may need to be repeated at regular intervals to maintain the desired effect.

In certain circumstances bladder function can be helped with specific drugs, as well as with very frequent and regular expression.

BLADDER RETENTION

This is quite common in paraplegia, and means that for some reason the patient is unable to empty the bladder. The causes vary, but usually it is the symptom of impending infection. The symptoms will include a thumping headache, sweating, increase in spasms, or the complete reverse, a distended bladder, flushing of the face and possibly a slow pulse rate. Over and above these symptoms, I have observed a significant reduction in the circulation of the lower limbs, which turn blue and become cold to touch, as with infection to the bladder. If the bladder refuses to empty by stimulation or by expression normally carried out, usually a straightforward catheterisation is needed to empty the bladder.

In these circumstances, if the individual or his family are unable to carry out this procedure, a doctor or community nurse should be called, and if they are unable to provide immediate attention then the patient must be taken to a hospital without delay. *This is an emergency* and is particularly important in patients with high thoracic and cervical lesions where, due to the over-filled and distended bladder, there will be a reflex action on blood pressure which rises sharply and causes a thumping headache (autonomic dysreflexia).

Until the bladder can be emptied, do not eat or drink, remain sitting up, try to remain calm.

Bladder retention is more common with patients who normally require indwelling catheters. This is caused through blockage of the catheter by sediment which collects in the bladder.

SWEATING

Sweating, as opposed to normal sweating due to the increase in body temperature, can prove a confounded nuisance to many paraplegics. High thoracic and particularly cervical lesions are most prone to outbursts of sweating which may be either above or below the level of the lesion.

In the majority of incidences, these outbursts of sweating are associated with the bladder. Alternatively, they can be caused through constipation, pressure sores, certain drugs, pregnancy and pain. Many paraplegics start to sweat immediately their bladder is full; while this might be a useful indication to express the bladder, it can be socially distressing. However, the prime reason for sweating is the failure of the bladder to empty adequately.

Many paraplegics discover they can empty their bladder more easily when sitting or lying in one position rather than in another. More often than not, difficulty arises when sitting up in the wheelchair, which may indicate the need for treatment to the bladder. Infection is another cause of sweating. The infected and irritated bladder is constantly contracting, which causes autonomic dysreflexia and sweating. Paraplegics with indwelling catheters frequently experience problems of sweating. In their case it is due either to the bladder shrinking in size through continual drainage, which then causes the tip of the catheter to irritate the bladder wall, or the bladder has become over-active due to chronic infection (hypertonic bladder).

Treatment for excessive sweating will be decided by the spinal specialist, but will certainly require extensive investigations to establish the true cause.

ALTERNATIVE METHODS OF BLADDER MANAGEMENT

THE INDWELLING CATHETER

The indwelling catheter, as previously discussed, is generally the most widely accepted alternative method of managing the paralysed bladder. There is, however, considerable difference in opinion concerning its use. Many regard the use of indwelling catheters to be totally abhorrent, while others philosophically accept their use.

In an ideal world patients are undoubtedly better off without an indwelling catheter, for its continual presence will result in chronic bladder infection, the additional possibility of stone formation and a gradual shrinkage of the bladder's capacity. The presence of an indwelling catheter may also cause undue irritation to the bladder, causing sweating and autonomic dysreflexia. Catheters can be psychologically distressing, particularly to younger people who regard them as an appendage and infringement to their bodies. Catheters may also interfere in sexual relationships for both males and females (see Chapter 6).

Most, if not all, of these problems and difficulties can be surmounted, and sometimes the social and medical advantages of having a catheter outweigh the disadvantages. This must certainly be true for many female paraplegics and tetraplegics who otherwise would have to depend on others to transfer them on and off the toilet every 2 or 3 hours. And to be free of the hellish necessity to find an accessible toilet at such frequent intervals, plus preventing the embarrassment of getting wet, are all points in favour of the indwelling catheter.

Occasionally patients who have had good automatic bladders for a number of years, enter a period where they are plagued with repeated infections regardless of all treatment available. In these circumstances the introduction to the indwelling catheter most certainly improves the quality of life. For a well-managed catheter is more satisfactory than a badly-working bladder, and kidneys must be preserved at all costs.

SUPRAPUBIC DRAINAGE

Suprapubic drainage of the bladder is another form of catheter drainage, but in this case the catheter is introduced through the abdominal wall directly into the bladder, rather than through the urethra.

Suprapubic drainage with a small gauge catheter may be the method selected for particular patients with new lesions until their bladders commence to empty automatically. The long-term use of suprapubic drainage is usually associated with some defect in the urethra making it unsuitable for the catheter to be passed in the normal way.

URINARY DIVERSION

A urinary diversion (urinary conduit: ileal conduit) is the diversion of urine from the bladder by transplanting the ureters into an isolated loop of small intestine which is then brought out through the abdominal wall. A urine collecting bag is then worn strapped to the abdomen.

This method of bladder management is sometimes selected for particular patients, but is normally reserved for both male and female paraplegics who have developed complications involving the bladder. The procedure involves major surgery and the main disadvantage is that future examination of the kidneys is made more difficult.

INTERMITTENT SELF-CATHETERISATION

Intermittent self-catheterisation is principally carried out by female paraplegics as a method of controlling incontinence. To a lesser extent men carry out the same procedure as a method of emptying the bladder in preference to having an indwelling catheter.

The technique involves passing a specially produced catheter at regular intervals throughout the day to drain the bladder completely, following which the catheter is withdrawn. This procedure is similar to the intermittent catheterisation carried out when newly injured. The disadvantages must be the ever-present risk of introducing infection, and the continual trauma applied to the urethra.

Catheters for this procedure are available on prescription, and are semi-disposable. Paraplegics must be fully instructed before adopting this method of bladder management. Full details can be obtained from the various spinal units (see p. 236).

DRUGS AND MEDICATIONS IN COMMON USE

There is a vast range of drugs and medications used to treat the disorders of the urinary tract found in paraplegics. Most drugs have known side-effects which range from the very minimal to the more pronounced. Patients should always discuss any possible side-effects with their doctor before commencing treatment so that they may be able to recognise and understand any unusual feelings should they occur. As the majority of problems are associated with infection, antibiotics will probably be the most commonly used drug. The correct selection of antibiotic to treat a particular infection can only be made after the urine has been tested.

Through experience it has been established that infections in the paralysed patient respond better to large doses of the chosen antibiotic given over longer than usual periods of time. Many antibiotics have side-effects, ranging from gastro-intestinal upsets to optical disturbances and as it is essential to *complete* a full course of an antibiotic, your doctor will consider possible side-effects against advantages before prescribing a course.

An irritated and spastic bladder caused by infection may give rise to autonomic dysreflexia – a rise in blood pressure and a thumping headache.

Table 5/1 gives a selection of drugs which are used for urinary disorders. There is an enormous list of drugs available and this Table indicates only a very limited range. No drug or medication should be used to treat bladder and urinary complaints without consultation with a doctor.

Table 5/1   Drugs used for bladder disorders

DRUG	SIDE-EFFECTS
Autonomic dysreflexia	
diazepam	Dry mouth, drowsiness, dizziness, headache (see also p. 000)
propantheline bromide (Pro-Banthine)	Dry mouth; constipation; cardiac disturbance
To increase urine acidity	
ascorbic acid (vitamin C)	Gastro-intestinal upsets after prolonged use
G 500 (hexamine mandelate 250 mg and methionine 250mg)	Gastro-intestinal upsets after prolonged use
Bladder washouts	
sterile sodium chloride solution (normal saline)	
chlorhexidine (Hibitane) 0.01% 'Suby G'	Stronger solutions should not be used as they irritate the bladder

RADIO-LINKED BLADDER CONTROL

Radio-linked bladder control is a new technique developed to empty the bladder of both male and female paraplegics and tetraplegics by electrical stimulation.

The technique involves the surgical implant of a small radio receiver subcutaneously over the lower ribs and connected by cable tunnelled under the skin to the sacral nerves within the spinal column. The procedure is normally carried out in two stages. Stage one involves a delicate, lengthy and complex operation to attach electrodes to one or more of the sacral nerves, S2, S3 and S4, which control bladder function. The second, much shorter, operation carried out about a week later involves the implant of the radio receiver.

To empty the bladder, a compact radio transmitter held in the hand is placed over the implanted receiver and the current switched on (Figs. 5/2 and 5/3). The bladder is thus stimulated and completely emptied in a matter of seconds. After the bladder is emptied in this manner, the residual urine is almost non-existent,

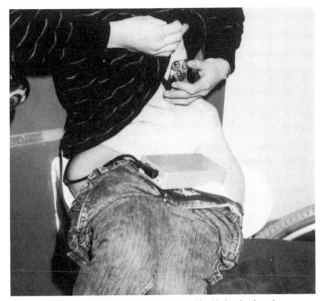

Fig. 5/2 Female paraplegic using a radio-linked stimulator to empty her bladder

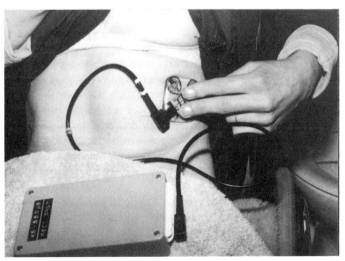

Fig. 5/3 Close-up of the radio-linked stimulator

which considerably reduces the probability of infection and many other complications of the urinary system. In most cases the need for catheters to be passed is eliminated. Women can stop wearing pads and waterproof pants while men can stop wearing urinary devices because the bladder can be emptied as and when required, and if emptied just before going to bed should last until morning.

The implant stimulator has also been found to produce substantially long-lasting penile erections in a number of male recipients (Brindley, 1982).

The physical and psychological benefits of this method of bladder control are immeasurable. At present, the selection of suitable patients initially depends whether the nerves running from the isolated spinal cord to the bladder are intact; they also have to undergo extensive urinary tract investigations – intravenous urography (IVU) and urodynamic studies – to ensure that the outflow from the bladder is not constricted.

Patients who have complete lesions and those who have *not* undergone bladder neck resections or sphincterotomy may possibly be selected as the more suitable subjects, although those who have undergone such surgery are by no means eliminated. There are many in these categories who have successfully received radio-linked implants.

The decision to undergo implant surgery must be balanced between possible benefits and possible hazards. In the first instance, the initial stage is a big operation involving a laminectomy (the removal of bone of the vertebral column to expose the spinal cord) between the third lumbar vertebra and the second sacral vertebra. Should the stimulator malfunction or not work, the whole operation would have to be repeated to remove or replace the implant. The same might apply should it become infected. Other hazards can include the loss of reflex erections in males should the device fail to give implant stimulated ones. Changes in bowel function, and the likelihood of an increase in autonomic dysreflexia exists in certain patients when the stimulator is switched on.

Tetraplegics with poor dexterity will have difficulty at present in holding and in operating the radio transmitter, consequently they may not be considered suitable subjects, but it could be operated by an attendant until such time as it could be modified for their use. Paraplegics and tetraplegics wishing to be considered for implant surgery should initially contact their general practitioner or spinal specialist for referral to either a specialised neurosurgical unit, or to a spinal unit offering this treatment.

REFERENCE

Brindley, G. S., Polkey, C. E. and Rushton, D. N. (1982). Sacral anterior root stimulators for bladder control in paraplegia. *Paraplegia*, **20**, 365–81.

FURTHER READING

Accounts about successful implants by persons with them may be read in the following issues of the Newsletter published by the Spinal Injuries Association.

Issue 23 – Judy Jackson – a paraplegic with a T7/8 lesion.

Issue 30 – Susan Abbott – a paraplegic with a T10 lesion.

Issue 32 – Margaret Maughan – a paraplegic with a T11 lesion.

USEFUL ADDRESSES

The following is a list of suppliers of incontinence aids, most of which have been mentioned in the text.

Argyle-Sherwood Medical
London Road, County Oak
Crawley, West Sussex RH10 2TL
0293 34501
   Producers of catheters, including those for self-catheterisation and other urinary incontinence aids

Bard Limited
Pennywell Industrial Estate
Sunderland SR4 9EW
0783 343131
   Produce a variety of incontinence aids – drainage bags, catheters (including short ones for women). Also the Bard penile sheath

Basingstoke Hygiene Products Limited
Brevitt Hospital Products
PO Box 98, Cocklebury Road
Chippenham, Wiltshire SN15 3QA
0249 56438/9
Suppliers of 'Brevitt' waterproof knickers

CliniMed Limited
Pilot Trading Estate
West Wycombe Road
High Wycombe, Buckinghamshire HP12 3AB
0494 444027
Produce Uro-Trainer bladder washout solutions, e.g. 'Suby G'

Coloplast Limited
Bridge House, Orchard Lane
Huntingdon, Cambridge PE18 6QT
0480 55451
Manufacturers of incontinence equipment, condoms, drainage systems

DHSS, Room 111 Government Buildings
Warbreck Hill Road
Blackpool, Lancashire FY2 0UZ
0253 52311
Supply Payne's, Durex non-allergy condoms. Plastic buttons, connector buttons, and rubber tubing

Down's Personal Products
Church Path
Mitcham, Surrey CR4 3UE
01–648 6291
Produce a vast range of incontinence aids – urine drainage systems, condoms, catheters, bed and leg bags

Peaudouce UK Limited
Rye Park Industrial Estate
Rye Road, Hoddesdon EN11 0EL
0992 445522
Suppliers of the very effective Slipad incontinence padding system

Raymed (a division of Chas. F. Thackray Limited)
47 Great George Street
Leeds LS1 3BB
0532 430028
> *Produce 'Aquadry' Freedom self-adhesive condom sheath. Also urine drainage bags*

Simpla Plastics Limited
Phoenix Estate, Caerphilly Road
Cardiff CF4 4XG
0222 621000
> *Produce Simpla bed and leg drainage bags. Plus a vast range of urine incontinence aids*

6. Sexuality

'The sexual problems of disabled people have received much attention of late. In fact, it could be argued that sexual aspects of disabled people's lives have received too much attention and that they should be returned to where they belong – to people's lives' (Oliver, 1983).

In principle I agree with Oliver's sentiments. Nevertheless, interruption of normal sexual function in both male and female paraplegics, and especially in tetraplegics, although recognised as a serious aspect of rehabilitation, has, in my opinion, been grossly underestimated and inadequately catered for. In writing this chapter my sole aim is to provide paraplegics with as much factual information as I have been able to collate in order that people may re-arrange their own sexual lives, if they so wish.

When I first became paralysed the thought of sex was the last aspect of my predicament to enter my mind. This, in spite of being newly married and surrounded by numerous attractive members of the opposite sex, is a fairly typical reaction following the onset of sudden paralysis, especially when complications are present. It must have been between two and three years afterwards, when I had been restored to good health and the prospect of a second marriage had presented itself, that my mind recalled the joys and happiness that close sexual relationships can bring. Today, 25 years later, when I've almost forgotten how useful it is to have hands and arms that function normally – the legs being incidental – and only someone with a C4 lesion will understand that – strangely, the desire to participate in the sex act and to have normal sexual responses remains as strong as it did before paralysis. In other words, from my own experience, time does not appear to heal this aspect of injury quite so well.

It is often said that: 'To be a stranger in a large city is the most lonely experience in the world.' I would qualify this statement by saying: 'To be disabled and a stranger in a large city is the most lonely experience in the world.' Life's greatest tragedy is not to be loved, and at some stage in life everybody wants to be needed. When one is confined by physical limitations and the rigours of daily care, it becomes increasingly more difficult to form relationships. This is even more apparent for the young tetraplegic living at home, unable to go out unaided, and dependent on the family for basic bodily care. A similar situation exists for those living in institutional surroundings. The opportunity and freedom to meet partners are limited and controlled by the rules and regulations governing the smooth running of the establishment. Although it must be said that many such homes are extremely liberal in their outlook.

In the majority of spinal cord injured people, the ability to experience orgasm is lost. Often a new approach to the whole subject is required, for sexual relations (either in or out of marriage) are based on much more than simply the physical enjoyment of orgasm, although this experience is undoubtedly the fulfilment and climax of the sexual act. When this sensation has been removed an alternative outlet has to be found. An understanding of normal sexual function, which is something many patients are not clear about, and how it is affected by injury to the spinal cord are the bases for finding an outlet and in maintaining, as far as is possible, a happy and contented sexual relationship.

MALE SEXUAL FUNCTION

The external and visible parts of the male reproductive organs comprise the penis and scrotum (see Fig. 5/1, p. 72). The penis provides a dual purpose: through its centre lies the urethra, whereby urine from the bladder is passed; the urethra also provides a passageway for the ejaculation of semen. The penis is formed largely of erectile tissue which is normally flaccid, but, when stimulated, either by physical contact or by erotic thoughts, the blood vessels that supply the penis open up, thus permitting extra blood to flow into the penis under pressure. This then causes the penis to become erect in preparation for sexual intercourse. These two forms of erection are known as reflex and psychogenic.

The scrotum contains the two testicles (testes) – oval-shaped firm masses that hang side by side (see Fig. 5/1b). The purpose of the testicles is to produce sperm, the male seed, and testosterone, the male sex hormone. Testosterone is responsible for the changes from boyhood to manhood, the breaking of the voice, growth of the beard and pubic hair, and the development of muscle and bone growth. Its secretion into the blood is controlled by the release of an additional hormone produced by the pituitary gland situated in the brain. Each testicle contains around 250 lobes within which are coiled tubes (the tubules) from which are produced the sperm cells.

From the tubules, the sperm travels to the epididymis where they gain motility. At the time of sexual arousal, and immediately before ejaculation takes place, sperm travels from the epididymis along the vas deferens, where it mixes with fluid secreted from two seminal vesicles which lie behind the bladder, and also from the prostate gland. These secretions provide the sperm with nutrition. Following sexual intercourse sperm swims through the cervix and into the uterus where it may enter an ovum (the female egg) and allow fertilisation to take place (Fig. 6/1).

At the time of ejaculation, either during masturbation or sexual intercourse, the internal bladder sphincter closes tightly and the external sphincter opens to permit the sperm to be ejaculated through the urethra, and not backwards into the bladder. The control of this function is partly reflex in nature and partly controlled from higher centres within the brain via the spinal cord.

SEXUAL FUNCTION AFTER SPINAL CORD INJURY

Following injury to the spinal cord the male paraplegic is faced with three main problems: (1) the inability to produce either a psychogenic or reflex erection; (2) the inability to maintain a reflex erection; (3) the inability to ejaculate semen containing sperms. As the neurology of sexual function is complex, it is impossible to group all male paraplegics together and describe just one situation.

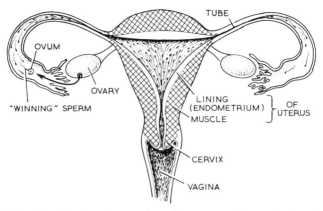

Fig. 6/1   Fertilisation: the meeting of the sperm and ovum in the tube

The level at which the spinal cord has been damaged and to what extent, will determine the sexual potential.

The nerves that supply sexual functions stem from the lower segments of the spinal cord and therefore most patients with cord injuries will have their sexual functions affected (see Fig. 5/1b). Patients with damage to the upper segments of the cord, in particular cervical injuries, are often able to have good and lasting erections, but may not be able to ejaculate in the normal manner. Those with lower levels of injury may not be able to maintain an erection or produce sperm in the normal way. Only patients with incomplete lesions will stand a chance of experiencing orgasm.

There is no known treatment to restore lost orgasm. Some patients claim to reach orgasm through stimulation of the nipple area or other erogenous parts of the body above the level of injury. Others have experienced a type of para-orgasm, or 'phantom' orgasm. Such claims are open to conjecture. I think this may be a psychological response – with the mind playing tricks, recalling previous experiences. I have never heard such claims from males who became paralysed before the age of puberty and had not previously experienced orgasm.

There are numbers of things that can be done to help males father children and sustain erections of sufficient duration to partake in sexual intercourse, thereby giving sexual satisfaction to their partners. And to be able to see orgasm in one's partner can be compensation for not experiencing it oneself.

The production of sperm continues after injury to the spinal cord, although production diminishes and deteriorates after several months. The problem lies in finding an artificial way to stimulate the ejaculation of sperm so that they can be collected for artificial insemination, or kept in deep-freeze storage until children are wanted. Ejaculation normally happens only during the climax of the sex act. Several years ago it was the practice to inject a substance, prostigmine, into the spinal canal which stimulated the nerves responsible for ejaculation. This method although quite successful had its drawbacks, mainly that of autonomic dysreflexia – a rapid rise in blood pressure. In recent years it has been possible to stimulate the prostate gland and seminal vesicles to produce semen by using a finger-shaped electronic probe placed in the rectum. The semen produced is then collected and if found to be suitable it can be stored or used for artificial insemination, as with the previous method. The advantage of electro-stimulation is that, should there be a rise in blood pressure during the procedure, the apparatus can be switched off until the pressure returns to normal.

It may also be possible to produce semen with the aid of a powerful vibrator placed on the glans of the penis.

Yet another method of possible value in producing an ejaculation is the radio-linked implant for bladder control (see p. 97). Brindley et al. (1982) found that in 9 men who had implants, stimulation of the second and third sacral nerves (S2, S3) produced erections in 5 of them which lasted for at least 10 minutes.

A weak erection can sometimes be helped by the simple application of a moderately tight rubber ring around the base of the penis. By constricting blood flow this often maintains the erection long enough for intercourse. It *must* be removed directly intercourse is finished, to prevent skin damage. Erections may sometimes be improved by drug therapy and by treating infection in the bladder. Hormonal therapy and vitamin E have been found to improve fertility (Guttmann, 1976).

It is also helpful to know that the majority of paraplegics who are able to have erections do so because of a reflex action depending on touch not controlled by sexual desire or will. Lack of this understanding may lead to embarrassment when paraplegics are being washed, catheterised or dressed. A reflex erection may more easily occur when the bladder is full. This might be useful to know, but it is unwise to attempt intercourse with a full bladder. At such times there is a danger of urine retention in the bladder and it might be necessary for a catheter to be passed. To avoid this, always ensure that the bladder is empty before intercourse and do not drink for an hour or two beforehand.

Males requiring indwelling catheters are advised to remove the catheter before intercourse, though some patients claim the catheter helps to maintain an erection, and this might well be true. To leave a catheter in could be dangerous, for movement may pull the balloon through the sphincter of the bladder thereby causing serious damage. If, however, it is preferred not to remove the catheter, it is advisable to fold it back along the shaft of the penis applying a liberal coat of KY jelly and then applying a condom for protection.

For paraplegics unable to obtain an erection there are several surgical procedures designed to implant various devices into the penis either manually to initiate an erection or to leave the penis permanently semi-rigid. So far, reports about these are not altogether favourable, and they are considered dangerous on medical grounds. Males would be better advised to develop the technique of 'stuffing' the limp penis into the female vagina and rhythmically rubbing against the female clitoris to satisfy their partners. Another alternative is to use one of the sexual aids available (see p. 132).

Surgery to the bladder, designed to relieve the problems of high residual urine, can have adverse effects on sexual function. When the internal sphincter is made wider following a TUR (see p. 92) it becomes more likely that the ejaculation of semen, produced when stimulating the vesicles and prostate gland artificially, will enter the bladder rather than flow out through the urethra.

Division of either the internal and/or external sphincters may sometimes affect the ability to produce an erection – though this may only be temporary. Patients should discuss this aspect with their spinal specialist before undergoing such surgery.

In the future it is hoped that sperm will be routinely collected from patients soon after injury and kept in deep-freeze storage for future artificial insemination. The technique is available, although it should be made perfectly clear it does not necessarily work for every patient. Storage facilities are available, although this is not always made known. Patients should ask for details of these procedures as a routine aspect of rehabilitation (see p. 135 for addresses).

Table 6/1   Drugs used in connection with sexual function

DRUG	EFFECT/USE
Hormones – testosterone and gonadotrophin	May increase fertility. Must only be given under medical supervision
Vitamin E	May increase fertility with hormones or by itself
Potensan	May improve weak erections
Antibiotics	For treatment of bladder infections

A doctor must alway be consulted before starting any drug therapy aimed at improving sexual function.

FEMALE SEXUAL FUNCTION

Figure 6/2 illustrates the female reproductive system. It is not proposed to go further into detail and the interested reader is referred to the book list on page 134. Certain aspects will be mentioned in as much they relate to specific actions.

The ovaries which lie on either side of the womb (uterus) are the organs that produce the female eggs (ova). They are, therefore, similar to the male testicles. The ovaries are responsible for producing the female hormones, oestrogen and progesterone. Unlike the male testicles which are connected to the sperm ducts, the

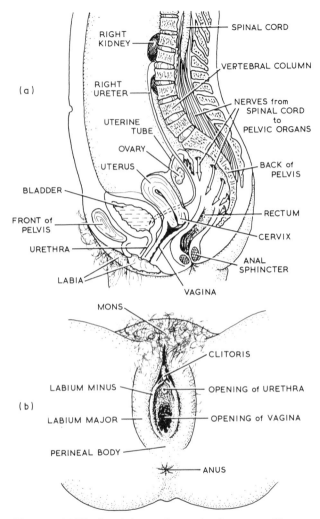

Fig. 6/2 (a) The female internal reproductive organs. *Note* the spinal nerves which supply the pelvic organs. (b) The female external genitalia

ovaries are not actually joined to the Fallopian tubes (oviducts).

The Fallopian tubes end in finger-like suckers rather like a sea anemone. These waving fingers attract and direct the ovum from the ovary into the tube. Once inside, the ovum moves towards the uterus, perhaps meeting a sperm on the way (see Fig. 6/1).

The vagina provides access for the male penis during intercourse and it is here that sperm are deposited during ejaculation. They then make their way through the cervix into the womb and so to the Fallopian tubes. It is while travelling along the tubes that an ovum may be met and fertilisation may take place.

Whereas the male depends on one hormone, testosterone, the female depends on two, oestrogen and progesterone. These control the menstrual cycle whose mechanism is shown in Figure 6/3 and Table 6/2.

Table 6/2   A summary of events leading to menstruation

NO. OF DAYS

1 After menstruation a follicle ripens: oestrogen is produced: the endometrium proliferates	10
2 Ovulation	
3 The corpus luteum appears: progesterone is produced: small amounts of oestrogen persist: the endometrium becomes secretory	14
4 The corpus luteum degenerates: oestrogen and progesterone levels fall: menstruation	4
Total	28

If during the proliferative phase synthetic oestrogen is given, the production of the follicle stimulating hormone from the pituitary is inhibited, which in turn prevents stimulation of the ovaries – consequently no egg cell is produced. This basically is how oral contraceptives work, for example 'the pill' (see p. 117).

Ovulation generally occurs between the 12th and 18th day of the cycle in women who have a regular 28-day cycle (see Fig. 6/3).

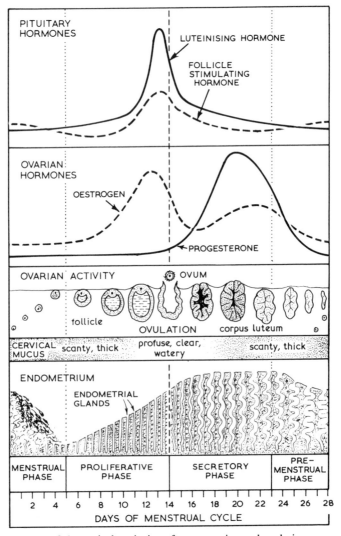

Fig. 6/3 Schematic description of menstruation and ovulation

SEXUAL FUNCTION AFTER SPINAL CORD INJURY

Following injury to the spinal cord the female reproductive system is less dramatically affected than in the male. True, there is usually a temporary cessation of the menstrual cycle and, with complete lesions, orgasm is abolished. Many women, in particular those with lesions below T5, do claim they are able to experience an orgasm through stimulation of other areas of the body, such as their breasts, neck and ears. These areas, known as the erogenous zones, also include the mouth, lips, nipples, the genital areas, inside of thighs and in particular the skin above the sensory level of the spinal lesion. In all these areas or zones, there is a concentration of nerve fibres, making them more sensitive. As a percentage of women do make this claim, while others do not, it would seem that perhaps this form of tactile stimulation is an art and needs considerable practice to attain.

Following the return of the regular menstrual cycle, usually within a matter of weeks following injury unless there are additional complications, women with either complete or incomplete lesions are able to become pregnant. There are certain dangers and difficulties, similar to those experienced by able-bodied women, but these difficulties are more pronounced, particularly for women with cervical lesions. Therefore medical advice should be sought regarding contraception, and must certainly be sought if children are wanted.

MENSTRUATION

The 'monthly period' for the paraplegic, and even more so for the tetraplegic who is unable to care for herself, combined with incontinence of both bladder and bowel, exaggerated by the non-existence of a suitable urine-collecting device, must surely present a hellish picture for many women.

For women without sensation there may be no warning signs of the onset of their period. Providing the menstrual cycle is regular a careful calendar check may suffice; if not, then it is wise to apply protection in advance. A high proportion of women report an increase in their spasms and swelling of their breasts prior to and during their period. Regardless of lesion level, many still feel pain from slight to normal degrees. Mild pain killers of individual choice – and most are available without prescription – can relieve both the pain and the increased spasms.

Management of the menstrual flow can lead to accidents and embarrassment to many women, in particular for those unable to apply or change pads/tampons themselves. It is usually best controlled with a combination of tampons as well as with pads of various types, especially if the flow is heavy. Whatever is used, they should be changed at more frequent intervals than normally practised, combined with careful washing. By doing this the likelihood of accidents and of introducing infection to both bladder and vagina is kept to a minimum. Women who possess the Closomat type toilet will certainly find it a great advantage for washing at this particular time.

Most women will have discovered which type of tampon or sanitary pad suits them best. Many still prefer to make their own from cellulose wadding and cotton wool. Others keep to the standard incontinence rolls as supplied through the community nursing service. The commercially-available pads that stick on without the need to use pins and straps are easier to change and they also cause less pressure. Problems may sometimes arise in inserting and removing tampons. For those unable to do this for themselves, the Tampax type with applicator may be more satisfactory. If the Lilet type is preferred, a little KY jelly applied to the tip will make insertion easier.

Some writers recommend the simultaneous use of two tampons for people unable to change them at frequent intervals. This practice may possibly present problems of pressure, interfere with bladder function or cause the by-passing of urine around indwelling catheters. But above all, should the innermost tampon be overlooked, then infection to the vagina and uterus could result.

Paraplegic women who suffer from severe, prolonged, irregular or excessive bleeding during their periods should ask their family doctor to refer them to a gynaecologist for investigation. Don't suffer unduly month after month. It is quite possible that a simple dilatation of the cervix and curettage (scraping) of the uterus, (a D and C), or treatment by hormone therapy will dramatically improve the situation.

PREMENSTRUAL TENSION (PMT)

This may be observed in some women between 2 and 12 days prior to the commencement of menstruation. The exact cause is unknown, but is thought to be due to an imbalance of hormones, particularly progesterone. As the hormone level drops, a number of women feel increasingly 'on edge', irritable, frustrated, bad-tempered, agitated, hysterical, depressed and sometimes suicidal. Women who have previously suffered from PMT may, following injury to the spinal cord, feel those symptoms to be even more exaggerated due to the additional frustrations of paralysis.

Treatment to help overcome the anguish of PMT is available and women should not have to feel they must simply put up with the situation. A doctor experienced in treating PMT and with knowledge of paraplegia should be consulted before diuretics are taken. A number of women find that vitamins taken at various stages throughout the monthly cycle are most effective in reducing the disturbing symptoms. Clinical opinion varies about the effectiveness of vitamin treatments, but since many women derive relief from their use, I feel justified in including the most recommended vitamin, B_6 (pyridoxine). But again I emphasise that medical advice must be sought before commencing treatment. Women who become unusually agitated and aggressive may derive benefit from mild tranquillisers. A low-salt, high-protein diet may also be helpful as may be taking a hot bath and trying hard to relax. But, above all, understanding the condition, tolerance, patience and reassurance from family and friends are possibly the most useful.

Table 6/3   Drugs used in the treatment of premenstrual tension

DRUG	DOSE
Vitamin B_6	50mg twice daily for 10 days prior to the onset of the monthly period
Mild tranquillisers	To be decided by your doctor; diazepam is commonly used
Hormones, e.g. Duphaston	As prescribed by your doctor

CERVICAL SMEARS AND BREAST EXAMINATION

As with able-bodied women, paraplegic women should ask their family doctor to carry out regular cervical smear tests. Paraplegia does not eliminate the risk of cervical cancer, neither does it reduce the risk of breast cancer. Where possible, self-examination of the breasts for any abnormalities should be carried out routinely every month. Immediately following a period is a suitable time, or perhaps on the first day of every month if the menopause has been reached.

CONTRACEPTION

For the fertile spinally injured woman obtaining sound advice on suitable methods of contraception is an important part of the rehabilitation programme. A reliable method of contraception must be used if unwanted pregnancies are to be avoided, and the method selected should be compatible with the patient's physical as well as mental capability, medical condition and lifestyle. Before a decision concerning a suitable method of contraception can be taken, newly injured women normally require advice and guidance from staff familiar with the medical and physical aspects of the spinal injury.

All methods of contraception have advantages and disadvantages. These may become more apparent for women with spinal cord injuries. In the first instance the woman's personal preference must be considered. This may be influenced by previous use, recommendation or cultural beliefs. Women should be able to obtain contraceptive advice from their spinal centre. Others may prefer to continue with advice from their family doctor or from a family planning clinic. Should either of the latter sources of help be selected, it should be remembered that members of staff within these clinics may have little understanding of the special needs of paraplegia, but the staff in most clinics are helpful and willing to help with transfers.

METHODS OF CONTRACEPTION

ORAL CONTRACEPTION (THE PILL)

There are two different types of oral contraceptives available: the combined pill and the progestogen-only pill (mini-pill).

The combined pill

This contains oestrogen and progestogen and prevents the ovaries from producing an egg cell. These pills are normally taken for 21 days, then stopped for 7 days and started again. Some brands include a further seven tablets which do not contain oestrogen or progestogen – designed to help women who have difficulty in remembering to restart the pills after a 7-day break. Other brands of the pill are designed to have changing levels of oestrogen and progestogen during the course (triphasic or biphasic pills). All pills are packaged clearly, displaying the name of each day for each pill and a clear arrow indicating the next day.

During the 7 days of the cycle when no pill containing oestrogen and progestogen is taken, a bleed will occur, caused by the withdrawl of the hormones.

Advantages: They offer the most effective method of contraception, providing they are taken correctly. They are easy to use, one tablet being swallowed daily for either 21 or 28 days of the menstrual cycle. Their use reduces the monthly bleed in volume and duration. This may be of great advantage to a disabled woman who may have difficulty in managing her personal hygiene. Abdominal cramps associated with the periods can be reduced by taking oral contraceptives. Finally, the woman can be in complete control of her contraception without involving her male partner.
Disadvantages: Some women have minor side-effects like nausea, breast discomfort and headaches initially, but these usually disappear, but it is known that the oestrogen content of the combined pill predisposes to the risk of thrombosis (blood clotting). This is a serious complication but occurs in very few women and usually only when there are predisposing factors like obesity, raised blood pressure, smoking, diabetes and a family history of thrombosis. Medical opinion varies concerning the additional risk of

thrombosis in women with spinal cord injury who take the pill. Generally speaking doctors prefer to wait 12 months following injury before prescribing oral contraceptives. Women with spastic lower limbs are less likely to develop thrombosis and may be considered suitable for oral contraceptives at an earlier stage. The loss of normal sensation in the legs means that the early signs of thrombosis, i.e. pain and heaviness, may be missed. The effectiveness of the pill is reduced when certain other drugs are being taken – for example antibiotics. It is advisable that additional precautions, such as the sheath or spermicidal pessaries, should be used during the time when a woman is taking antibiotics and for 14 days following the completed course. The combined pill is not normally prescribed to heavy smokers (more than 15 a day), women over 30 years of age, nor to women who are over-weight, have a raised blood pressure, a previous history of cardiovascular (heart) disease, deep vein thrombosis, or pulmonary embolism. If none of these contra-indications is present women can stay on the combined pill until they are aged between 40 and 45. The packaging of the pill may present problems for tetraplegic women to take it privately unless a sympathetic chemist is willing to place the pills in a more suitable container.

Progestogen-only pill (the 'mini-pill')

This contains progestogen only and has the advantage of reducing the risk of thrombosis, yet still possesses a fairly high degree of effectiveness. The progestogen works in three ways. It thickens the mucus in the cervix which forms a plug preventing sperm from entering the uterus; it causes changes to the lining of the uterus and it reduces movement in the tubes, which delays the egg cell's passage to the uterus. The progestogen-only pill is taken by mouth every day, preferably at the same time. Efficiency is impaired if the pill is delayed by more than 3 hours.

Advantages: It is an effective method of contraception, with less risk of thrombosis than the combined pill. It is easy to use – one tablet daily – and it is safe to be used by older women, as well as by mothers who are breast feeding.
Disadvantages: There is a possible risk of ectopic pregnancy (the attachment of the fertilised egg cell to the wall of the Fallopian

tube) due to the reduced movement of the fertilised egg cell along the tube. Bleeding can be irregular as can the quantity; the unpredictable cycle may make coping with hygiene difficult.

Injectable progestogen

An injection of a long-acting progestogen is given usually between every 2 to 3 months. It is an efficient contraceptive which suppresses ovulation.

Advantages: One injection can cover 3 months' contraceptive needs. Therefore it can be very convenient. Temporary amenorrhoea (the absence of the monthly period) may occur after a couple of injections, thus alleviating the problems of coping with bleeding. It is also a very effective method of contraception.
Disadvantages: These are few and provided they are explained to the patient they are usually acceptable. However, many women do not like the absence of their periods, and there can be irregular bleeding. The point which must be stressed is that it becomes less efficient towards the time for renewal. The woman must be aware of this, and possibly additional protection should be used by her partner. Fertility may take several months to return following discontinuation of the drug. The action of the drug cannot be reversed during the duration of its activity, and there is also a risk of ectopic pregnancy.

INTRA-UTERINE DEVICES

Intra-uterine devices are produced in a variety of shapes and are made of plastic or of plastic and metal. They are inserted in the uterus by a doctor and when in position only the two fine threads of the device remain in the vagina. The device works by a complex mechanism not fully understood.

Advantages: Once inserted the device can remain in position for several years before it requires changing. It also avoids the need to take drugs or the fitting of an appliance (cap or sheath) immediately prior to sexual intercourse.
Disadvantages: The device may be difficult to insert if the woman has abdominal spasms, and it may be expelled by excessive

spasms. Fitting of the device may cause abdominal pain or spasm, although this normally settles within a few days. The device often causes an increase in the menstrual flow, thus making personal hygiene more difficult. There is a slight increase in the incidence of inflammatory disease of the pelvic organs, and in paraplegics loss of normal sensation may hide the early warning signs of pain and discomfort which are suggestive of infection. The threads of the device should be checked following the monthly period to ensure that it remains in the correct position, but many disabled women may find this difficult to do. Some paraplegic women may be more prone to bladder infection when an intra-uterine device is used. This is thought to be caused by the threads which may favour the 'tracking' of infection.

BARRIER METHODS

Caps, including diaphragms

These are rubber domes inserted into the vagina to cover the cervix prior to intercourse. They prevent sperm from entering the uterus and should not be removed for washing for at least 6 or more hours after intercourse. They can in fact be left in position for up to 24 hours. Initially a cap should be fitted by an experienced doctor, and should always be used in conjunction with a spermicide. The cap can be inserted several hours prior to intercourse, providing the spermicide is topped up.

Advantages: This method does not involve any drug taking, so that metabolism is unaffected. It does not affect the menstrual cycle as does an intra-uterine device.
Disadvantages: Insertion can be difficult for many women, if not impossible for the tetraplegic. Weak pelvic and vaginal muscles may allow the device to slip out of position. The regular tapping and expressing of the bladder may dislodge the diaphragm, as may muscle spasm.

Sheaths

Sheaths are made of disposable latex rubber and they are applied to the erect penis prior to any form of penile vaginal contact. They work by retaining sperm in the sheath following ejaculation. They should be used in conjunction with a spermicide, and several types of sheath are coated with spermicide.

Advantages: They can be obtained easily either over the counter or by mail order. The method eliminates the need for drugs or vaginal insertions. A sheath also helps to protect against sexually transmitted diseases. It allows the male partner to assume some of the responsibility for contraception.

Disadvantages: A sheath may split during, or come off after, intercourse (see post-coital, p. 122). If the woman uses a permanent indwelling catheter, this should be taped across her abdomen, otherwise the sheath could possibly tear due to friction against the catheter. Friction against the catheter causing a tear may still be experienced through the wall of the vagina. The sheath may reduce the degree of sensation for one or both partners.

SPERMICIDES

Spermicides are chemicals produced in the form of either pessary, cream, foam or jelly. They are inserted into the vagina prior to intercourse and are designed to destroy sperm.

Advantages: Spermicides are available in shops as well as being obtainable on prescription.

Disadvantages: Spermicides are not effective on their own. They should only be used in conjunction with the cap or the sheath. Insertion of the pessary and other spermicides may prove difficult for some disabled women.

CONTRACEPTIVE SPONGE

The contraceptive sponge is a relatively new method of contraception. It is a polyurethane sponge impregnated with a spermicide. It is inserted in the vagina and positioned to cover the cervix. It works by absorbing and killing the ejaculated sperm.

Advantages: The sponge is available in the chemist's shop. It is soft and flexible making it less likely to slip out of position.

Disadvantages: It may be difficult to insert for some women. It does not provide a very high safety factor, and although obtainable free of charge at family planning clinics, it is in short supply and is very expensive.

RHYTHM METHOD

The rhythm method of contraception is designed to avoid intercourse around the time of ovulation, thus reducing the likelihood of fertilisation. Intercourse therefore should not take place for several days before and after ovulation.

Advantages: The rhythm method may be the only method of contraception permissible to some religious or cultural groups. It also avoids the risks associated with the taking of drugs and the use of internal devices.

Disadvantages: The rhythm method has a high failure rate due to changing patterns of ovulation in many women. Figure 6/3 shows how the cervical mucus changes in consistency during the menstrual cycle; noting these changes in the feel of the mucus will enable the woman to more accurately chart the 'danger days' when conception is more likely to occur. An accurate record of the menstrual cycle must be kept (see the Further Reading on page 134 for helpful titles).

THE WITHDRAWAL METHOD (COITUS INTERRUPTUS)

The withdrawal method is the responsibility of the male partner, for he must withdraw the penis from the vagina prior to ejaculation. This method requires no contraception preparation, drugs or devices. The disadvantage is that the woman has to trust her partner, who has to exercise considerable self-control. This method has a high failure rate.

POST-COITAL 'MORNING AFTER'

Post-coital contraception is an emergency measure only, for example following rape or a split sheath. It should not be used regularly and has to be applied under medical advice. There are two methods available – the insertion of an intra-uterine device up to 5 days after unprotected intercourse has taken place, or a high dose of oral contraceptive given under medical supervision up to 3 days after unprotected intercourse. Both are available at family planning clinics.

STERILISATION

Sterilisation is a surgical procedure which can be carried out on either the man or the woman. Although the procedure has been reversed in some cases, it cannot be guaranteed and sterilisation should be regarded as a final method of contraception. Consequently, before the procedure is carried out, extensive counselling of the individuals concerned should be undertaken.

In the female the tubes are either cut and tied, or a ring is placed over the tube obliterating its cavity, thereby obstructing the pathway of the egg cell. It is an ideal solution, providing the woman is positive that she no longer wishes to have children. The procedure requires hospitalisation and a general anaesthetic, although modern techniques using a laparoscope have made it simpler to perform.

In the male the vasa deferens from the testes are cut and tied, thus obstructing the pathways of sperm to the urethra. This procedure can be carried out under local anaesthetic and does not require hospitalisation. The procedure is not *instantly* effective. Subsequent examination of the semen (male ejaculate) should be made to ensure that all stored sperm have been ejaculated. Until 3 specimens are clear of sperm, protection *must* be used.

There is no easy solution to the choice of contraception. Any method is better than none at all if unwanted pregnancies are to be avoided. Whichever method is adopted, it will be successful only if used correctly and consistently. The degree of the woman's disability will probably dictate the most suitable method, and to this end a woman's sexual partner should be encouraged actively to assist the woman if necessary over the application and checking of the contraceptive. After discussion with a knowledgeable doctor or nurse, careful consideration of the advantages and disadvantages of all methods of contraception should be made by both partners before making a final choice. If a woman is not totally happy with the method selected, it is likely she will fail to use it correctly, thus rendering it ineffective.

The method of contraception chosen may vary at different stages in a couple's life, depending on various factors such as age, health, desire for any or further children.

With the increased training of doctors in contraceptive work and the improved knowledge of methods, techniques, drugs, devices and appliances, there should be fewer problems in finding an acceptable method of birth control. Anyone unable to obtain satisfaction should seek advice at a Family Planning Clinic, where suitable methods will be correctly taught.

Family Planning Clinics produce excellent leaflets describing the individual methods of contraception, and in some areas clinics offer a domiciliary service.

SEXUAL INTERCOURSE

Sexual intercourse for the female paraplegic is slightly less difficult than for the male. The most commonly adopted posture is the conventional missionary position, i.e. lying on the back. This by no means excludes other positions, for many women choose to lie on their sides, others prefer to lie on their stomach enjoying entry from the rear, while a number kneel astride their male partner. Obviously the choice of position will largely depend on physical ability. But should the woman be tetraplegic, then lying on the back is probably the most satisfactory position, and under such circumstances the able-bodied partner should take care not to restrict the woman's breathing by supporting part if not all his weight on his elbows.

As with males, women should empty their bladders before intercourse; the risk of retention is less, but it exists. The prime concern is to prevent the embarrassment of becoming wet. For obvious reasons it would be unwise to attempt intercourse on the night a laxative has been taken. A woman with an indwelling catheter need not remove it before intercourse, but should spigot it and tape it securely to the abdomen, thus preventing it from being pulled out.

Depending on the level of injury to the spinal cord and whether it is a complete lesion or not, will determine whether the Bartholin glands are still able to lubricate the vagina in readiness for penile penetration. Should they not function, then an additional lubricant such as KY jelly may be necessary. A lubricant such as petroleum jelly, which is not soluble in water, should be avoided for it can harbour bacteria.

Where over-spastic legs prevent satisfactory sexual intercourse it might be necessary to secure them with suitable soft ties. Care should be taken not to tie too tightly, for this can result in skin damage and also the fracture of bones. Where drugs are being used to control spasms, as well as pain, then regulation of their intake prior to intercourse may well improve the situation. A careful choice of surface on which to have intercourse is all important, because skin damage and bruising can easily occur.

If problems persist that prevent good sexual relations, such as over-spastic legs, there is often a simple answer or some treatment available that will help the situation. Do not withdraw altogether from sexual relations if you do not really want to, but discuss the problem with your family doctor, community nurse or spinal specialist.

PREGNANCY

Let me first allay the fear that a paraplegic or tetraplegic woman will give birth to an equally paralysed or disabled baby. This is simply not the case. A baby born to a paralysed woman does *not* acquire its mother's paralysis. Occasionally a baby may be born to a paralysed mother with other congenital abnormalities but these are no more likely to occur than with able-bodied mothers.

In an ideal world children should be planned and careful thought given to the many implications of bringing up a family. In cases of paraplegia, and more so tetraplegia, the planned decision to start a family is more desirable on health and social grounds. The first question a paraplegic woman should ask herself is: Can I adequately look after a newly-born baby from my wheelchair? Most paraplegic mothers have unquestionably proved they can, with or without varying degrees of help (Fig. 6/4). Not many tetraplegic women have had children following injury because of their associated medical and inevitable social difficulties. Of those that have, considerable domestic help has most certainly been necessary.

After the social aspects have been thoroughly explored and a positive decision to have a baby has been taken, the next stage is a thorough medical check-up including an IVU. This is very important since the kidneys are subjected to considerable strain during pregnancy. This initial examination is probably best carried out by the spinal specialist who will then refer the woman to a gynaecologist. Thereafter the spinal specialist together with the family practitioner and gynaecologist will be able to monitor the pregnancy.

If there are no difficulties regarding conception, then for the first 4 months of the pregnancy there is little difference from that experienced by able-bodied women. Many paraplegics and tetraplegics suffer from morning sickness of unpredictable duration, but only a minority of women have reported the need to take drugs to combat this. It is during the last 5 months as the baby grows larger that problems and difficulties begin to emerge. These include general fatigue as the daily routine becomes harder when carrying additional weight. Transferring from wheelchair to toilet, bed and car becomes an art. Fluid retention which causes swelling of the legs and arms can become a problem and extra rest may be required to control this. Indigestion and heartburn, probably intensified by the sitting position can cause considerable discomfort. A good supply of indigestion tablets should be obtained. Car drivers are perhaps advised to discontinue driving after 7 months, purely on safety grounds. There may not be a lot of room between your enlarging abdomen and the steering wheel! But a number of women continue driving almost to term.

More serious problems include repeated infections to the bladder, caused by the baby pressing on it and making it more difficult to express. In many circumstances it may be necessary to insert an indwelling catheter, especially during the final weeks of pregnancy. The prevention of pressure sores can be another additional problem. Due to fatigue many women are unable to lift and turn themselves as much as they should. To combat this, the use of additional pressure prevention aids for the bed and wheelchair are

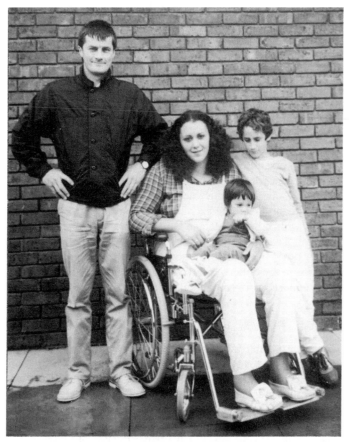

Fig. 6/4   Paraplegic mother with her husband and 2 sons both conceived and born *after* her injury

recommended (see p. 185). Paraplegic women are more prone to anaemia during pregnancy and this is a major factor in the cause of pressure sores. To overcome this problem iron tablets may be prescribed. Iron has a tendency to cause constipation which can be most distressing for the paraplegic. Normally additional dosages of the chosen aperient are taken (see Chapter 4) to relieve constipation. Senokot is not recommended during pregnancy, neither are soap enemas. Prevention of constipation will be helped by increasing the amount of fibre in the diet, and anaemia can be reduced by eating foods with high iron content, such as spinach.

As the pregnancy advances there is a likelihood of increased spasticity or the complete reverse; sweating, back pain (often around the site of the original spinal fracture), carpal tunnel syndrome (pain, numbness and tingling in the hands) may also be present. But above all, an increase in blood pressure is the most serious complication which might occur. Regular check-ups with the family practitioner, spinal specialist and gynaecologist are essential. For a paraplegic mother attendance at ante-natal clinics may not always be practicable. But if this can be arranged then relaxation and breathing exercises are of great benefit as is social contact with other expectant mothers. Advice from the family doctor or community nurse should be sought. A last word of advice: heavy alcohol consumption during pregnancy carries a high risk to the unborn child. Smoking can cause stunted growth to the unborn baby – try and give them up.

LABOUR

Whenever possible it is advisable for the paraplegic mother to be admitted to hospital 4 or more weeks before the baby is due, not only to monitor general health and thereby prevent complications, but because premature labour in paraplegics can be anticipated. The commencement of labour in complete lesions above T10 may prove difficult to diagnose owing to lack of sensation. Patients with lesions below this level may have reduced levels of sensation and can quite easily be unaware they are in labour. I recall a conversation with a paraplegic mother with a mid-thoracic lesion, who explained to me how she almost gave birth while sitting on the toilet and was unaware of anything unusual. Another paraplegic mother explained how she did not want to hurt the baby and therefore slept with her legs wide apart in case she gave birth while asleep. Women with incomplete lesions will obviously have varying degrees of sensation according to the incompleteness of their lesion. Consequently they should receive some indicative messages when contractions commence. These might be very similar to sensations experienced during bowel contractions – sweating, goose-flesh, headaches and flushing.

The nature of delivery will be decided by the gynaecologist. There is no reason to assume it will be anything but normal. However, women with lesions above T5 frequently experience an increase in blood pressure – autonomic dysreflexia. To overcome this and to avoid unnecessary trauma to the mother, delivery may be assisted. This is a particularly dangerous time for mothers with high thoracic lesions and even more so for tetraplegics. Unless expertly controlled, the blood pressure can rise to such a level as to cause cerebral haemorrhage. It is this aspect that may encourage doctors to advise tetraplegic women against having children.

The duration of labour varies enormously and probably is no different from that of non-paralysed women. The hospital stay may, however, be slightly longer in order to retrain the bladder and the bowels. A number of women claim that these never work quite so well again. Additional bed-rest may also be necessary to reduce the swelling of limbs, to rest pressure areas and to allow episiotomy incisions to heal.

CHILD CARE

It is possible only to generalise on the difficulties that paraplegic mothers may experience on return home with their babies. The health visitor, midwife, district nurse and general practitioner will all be able to help and advise over the immediate care of the child and welfare of the mother. In most areas the social services should be able to provide additional support from the home-help service, and maternity grants will provide additional financial help.

Whenever practicable breast feeding is more beneficial for the baby, and many paraplegic mothers have no difficulty providing this. A carry-cot on wheels that can be pushed around and parked alongside the bed is useful, especially for night feeding. Some mothers combine night feeding with their own routine toilet visits which prevent them losing valuable and much needed sleep during the first few, often quite exhausting months.

A baby-sling worn around the mother's neck which supports the child's head is an ideal method of carrying the baby while in the wheelchair. Hands and arms are thus left free to push and carry on with domestic chores. Carrying the baby on one's lap alone can be dangerous but a pillow tied to the wheelchair's handles provides an ideal platform for this purpose. Bathing the baby from a wheelchair can sometimes be tricky, as can changing nappies. But what better place than the already converted kitchen sink and draining board? Make sure it is cleaned before and after use.

There are many organisations and publications available to provide help and advice over domestic difficulties. Perhaps the best source of information would be from a similarly paralysed person. I am sure your spinal centre or the Spinal Injuries Association would put you in touch with another 'Mum'.

THE MENOPAUSE

There is no reason to assume that spinally injured women do not experience menopausal symptoms. Possibly such symptoms may be less obvious than in non-paralysed women and overshadowed by the more urgent complications of paralysis, or simply misdiagnosed altogether.

Symptoms of the menopause occur in women between the ages of 40–55 and mark the commencement of cessation of menstruation. Symptoms may include hot flushes, sweats, depression, irritability, fatigue, difficulty in sleeping, aches and pains in joints, light-headedness, nervousness, palpitations and shortness of breath. It should be remembered that many women pass through this phase of life without any difficulty but, as with premenstrual tension, treatment is available to relieve the more unpleasant symptoms, and women should not feel they have to 'put up' with their lot. Women should feel able to ask their own doctor for advice or to refer them to a menopause clinic.

RELATIONSHIPS

Spontaneous intercourse for either the male or female paraplegic is not always possible. Tetraplegics may require help from their partners over transferring from wheelchair, undressing, emptying their bladders, removal of urinals and in selecting the most satisfactory positions. It therefore becomes quite understandable that many people regard such additional difficulties as complete obstacles and withdraw altogether from attempting any form of sexual activity. Couples married before injury may, initially, feel like this, for the new style of relationship is so totally foreign.

To help overcome this feeling of isolation, I would strongly advise couples to refrain from attempting intercourse for several nights following discharge from hospital. Instead, gradually get to know each other again and slowly discover each other's capabilities. Frank and open communication is essential to explore individual likes and dislikes, until amicable agreement over the nature and style of future physical contact is understood. The situation is similar but somewhat different for couples who, like myself, entered into a marriage after becoming disabled. Although such a decision should not be taken lightly, the advantage is that the marriage starts with the physical limitations clearly understood, and providing these have been closely analysed and openly discussed, then most difficulties can be overcome.

Considerable patience, trial and experiment are required before satisfactory relationships can be reached when one partner is paralysed. It must be remembered that when two people are in love, any physical contact that is agreeable between each other is acceptable. One partner may want to try a certain position for intercourse but the other partner may at first feel awkward and not wish to participate. This is understandable but wrong. Try everything, more than once, until a satisfactory relationship is reached. Many disabled people gain great satisfaction from oral sex; many able-bodied practise oral sex too. There is nothing wrong with oral sex; it is a healthy contact between two people to be enjoyed. Again there is a positive need to take great care and not forget the probable loss of normal sensation which could result in damage to skin and tissue from over-indulgence.

The involvement, and its enjoyment, of sexual activity by paralysed people of both sexes can be a leading factor in psychological rehabilitation. Because there may be loss of normal sexual outlet through orgasm, this is no reason to assume that sexual drive or desire is also lost. On the contrary, sexual drive and desire do remain strong and it is this fact that always makes me shudder when the paraplegic or tetraplegic individual is referred to as impotent. Here I include spinally injured homosexual men and women. Loneliness is the worst thing in the world and if love and companionship can be obtained with a member of the same sex then it should not be condemned. There are organisations that exist especially to cater for the needs of disabled lesbians and male homosexuals (see p. 136).

Young people injured before experiencing intercourse and orgasm, may spend the rest of their lives wondering what they have missed, while those fortunate enough to have experienced intercourse before injury will have their memories. I believe it is this problem that often leads many newly disabled to drink more alcohol than is good for them in an attempt to numb their minds to reality. Again there is no quick and simple answer and periods of frustration will be experienced. In marriage, as in other close re-lationships, much of the sexual frustration experienced is more easily expelled by seeing sexual satisfaction and happiness in the able-bodied partner.

PROSTHETIC DEVICES

It is possible to obtain prosthetic devices, or marital aids, which in certain circumstances can be of great help and benefit to disabled people. Some aids can be regarded as nothing more than sex toys. Others have been designed under medical supervision to cater especially for disabilities of all kinds. Should people wish to try using any of these aids, then an open mind must be adopted and continuing trials made.

Such aids include an artificial penis that can be strapped to the male partner when it has been impossible to obtain an erection. Another type of artificial penis is of hollow construction into which the penis can be inserted and held by an inflatable balloon device. This is useful when only a partial erection can be sustained. There is also a hand-held penis, a 'Dildo', which can be used in the hand by either partner. Should patients wish to try an artificial penis, a lubricant such as KY jelly or Johnson's baby oil should be used.

There are also various types of vibrator designed to stimulate males and females. These are easily fitted with suitable straps to enable the tetraplegic to handle them. All these items can be studied by contacting or visiting one of the many sex shops, or by writing directly to the suppliers for catalogues (see p. 136).

ARTIFICIAL INSEMINATION

There are many couples who desperately want to have a family but for various reasons are unable to conceive in the normal manner. It might be that artificial insemination by donor or by husband could resolve the problem. This service is now available on the National Health Service. People wishing to take advantage of this facility should speak with their family doctor in the first instance, or write to The Medical Director, The Margaret Pyke Centre, 27–35 Mortimer Street, London W1A 4QW. This centre is one of several in the country that can provide basic information on request. There might however be a centre nearer your home, so speak with your family doctor first.

Women wishing to undergo artificial insemination, either by donor (AID) or by their husband (AIH), should have gynaecological investigations in advance to eliminate any abnormalities and to ensure that there is a maximum chance of becoming pregnant.

Waiting lists for appointments and investigations for artificial insemination, in particular by donor, are in most instances extremely long. The same facilities are available privately. These are equally suitable and for a reasonable fee will eliminate much of the frustration brought about through waiting. General practitioners or fertility clinics will be able to supply names and addresses of private clinics offering this service.

ADOPTION

Couples unable to have children of their own, may wish to consider adoption: in the United Kingdom adoption is not easy and is subject to rules, regulations and waiting lists. The chance of a couple being offered a child for adoption when one partner is paraplegic is not impossible but is certainly less favourable and will take considerable time to negotiate.

Couples seeking further advice and information concerning the

possibility of adoption, should contact an adoption agency (see p.
135). An alternative of fostering children may be possible. Local
social services departments will be able to advise.

REFERENCES

Brindley, G. S., Polkey, C. E. and Rushton, D. N. (1982). Sacral
anterior root stimulators for bladder control in paraplegia.
Paraplegia, **20**, 365–81.

Guttmann, L. (1976). *Spinal Cord Injuries. Comprehensive
Management and Research*. Blackwell Scientific Publications
Limited, Oxford.

Oliver, M. (1983). *Social Work with Disabled People*. Macmillan
Press, London.

FURTHER READING

Anderson, M. (1983). *The Menopause*. Faber and Faber, London.

Campling, J. (ed.) (1981). *Images of Ourselves*. Routledge and
Kegan Paul Limited, London.

Comfort, A. (1972). *The Joy of Sex*. Mitchell Beazley, London.

Cornwell, M. (1975). *Early Years*. Disabled Living Foundation,
London.

Delvin, D. (1974). *Book of Love*. New English Library, London.

Disabled Mother
Available from Equipment for the Disabled, 2 Foredown Drive,
Portslade, Sussex BN4 2BB.

Greengross, W. (1976). *Entitled to Love: Sexual and Emotional
Needs of the Handicapped*. National Marriage Guidance Council,
Rugby.

Heslinga, K. (1978). *Not Made of Stone. Sexual Problems of Handicapped People*. Woodhead-Faulkner, Cambridge.

Kitzinger, S. (1983). *Woman's Experience of Sex*. Dorling Kinders-
ley Limited, London.

Llewellyn-Jones, D. (1986). *Everywoman. A Gynaecological Guide
for Life*, 4th edition. Faber and Faber, London.

McCarthy, B. (1981). *Disabled Eve. Guide to Coping with Problems
of Menstruation*. Disabled Living Foundation, London.

Marshall, J. (1979). *Planning for a Family: An Atlas of Mucothermic Charts*, 2nd edition. Faber and Faber, London.

Mooney, T. O. et al. (1975). *Sexual Options for Paraplegics and Quadraplegics*. Little Brown, Boston. Available from Quest Publishing, 145a Croydon Road, Beckenham, Kent.

Stewart, W. F. R. (1975). *Sex and the Physically Handicapped. The Report of a Research Project*. National Fund for Research into Crippling Diseases.

Stewart, W. F. R. (1979). *The Sexual Side of Handicap. A Guide for the Caring Professions*. Woodhead-Faulkner, Cambridge.

USEFUL ORGANISATIONS

ADOPTION

British Adoption & Fostering Agencies
11 Southwark Street, London SE1 1RQ   01–407 8800

Independent Adoption Society
121–123 Camberwell Road, London SE5 0HB   01–703 1088

ARTIFICIAL INSEMINATION/SPERM BANKS

British Pregnancy Advisory Service
Austy Manor, Wootton Wawen, Solihull
West Midlands B95 6BX   0564 23225
The British Pregnancy Advisory Service operates a number of clinics throughout the country that are equipped to deep freeze sperm which can then be used for artificial insemination at a later date. They also possess sperm banks for artificial insemination by donor. The British Pregnancy Advisory Service will also offer free tests and advice over such matters as abortion.

The Margaret Pyke Centre
27–35 Mortimer Street, London W1A 4QW

COUNSELLING

Marriage Guidance Council
Herbert Gray College, Little Church Street
Rugby CV21 3AP   0788 73241

Sexual and Personal Relationships of the Disabled (SPOD)
286 Camden Road, London N7 0BJ   01–607 8851

The Outsiders' Club
Box 4ZB, London W1A 4ZB   01–741 3332

FAMILY PLANNING

Family Planning Association
27–35 Mortimer Street, London W1N 7RJ   01–636 7866

HOMOSEXUAL ADVICE

Gaydaid
c/o 36 Pembroke Street, Bedford MK40 3RH   0234 58879

Gemma
Box 5700, London WC1N 3XX

Lesbian Line
Box 1514, London WC1N 3XX   01–251 6911

PROSTHETIC DEVICES

Blako Limited
Medical Division, 229 Putney Bridge Road
London SW15 2PY   01–870 4251

House of Pan (Dept MOH)
Unit 18, Roman Way, Coleshill Industrial Estate
Coleshill, Birmingham B46 1RL

WELL-WOMAN CLINICS

Women's National Cancer Control Campaign
1 South Audley Street, London W1Y 5DQ   01–499 7532

Family Planning Association
27–35 Mortimer Street, London W1N 7RJ   01–636 7866

7. Physiotherapy and Related Topics

Physiotherapy plays a major role throughout the whole treatment of the paraplegic and is aimed at strengthening and keeping the body in the best possible condition to provide maximum independence and confidence. Early treatment consists of daily passive movements to the paralysed limbs, thus ensuring the maintenance of a full range of movement at all the joints, as well as muscle length, thereby preventing contractures and stiffness. Active, or assisted active, exercises will be encouraged for all unaffected muscle groups. Electrotherapy is sometimes given to stimulate weak muscles and keep open nerve pathways; ultrasound and other forms of heat treatment may be given to painful muscles and joints. Breathing exercises and chest physiotherapy are often required to treat or prevent chest complications, particularly in patients who have cervical or high thoracic lesions.

Once the stage of active rehabilitation is reached, patients are taught to strengthen the unaffected muscle groups through exercises, weight lifting, and springs and pulleys. They are taught balance control sitting on a plinth in front of a mirror, by using the muscles of the trunk and neck to compensate for the loss of leg and other movement. This is part of the training to enable them to sit in the wheelchair without losing balance, and leaving their hands and arms free.

Training will also include learning to transfer from wheelchair to bed, to car, on and off the lavatory and from the ground to chair. In addition paraplegics will be helped to stand wearing leg plasters or while strapped to a tilt-table, using a standing frame (Fig. 7/1) or with orthoses (calipers). Where possible they will be taught to walk with the aid of crutches or sticks. All these skills are part of the normal routine of rehabilitation. While I do not intend to go

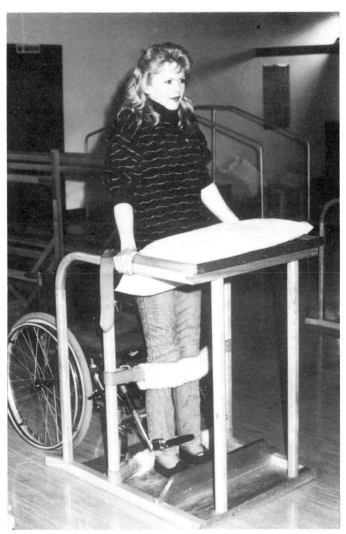

Fig. 7/1   A paraplegic using a standing frame

into details, I should like to emphasise some points stressing the value of continuing treatment after discharge.

PASSIVE MOVEMENTS

These should be continued to all paralysed limbs at regular and frequent intervals, especially for those limbs that are spastic. Not only do they help to preserve a full range of movement, they also help to maintain a good circulation, which is so important in preventing pressure sores. From a cosmetic angle they help in the prevention of deformed and contracted hands and arms, which are often seen in old patients with cervical lesions and can be unsightly and difficult to manage.

STANDING

This is a most beneficial part of treatment and should be practised as often as possible. Many patients become lazy about standing, and forget the benefits which include better drainage of the urinary system, thus aiding prevention of infection and formation of stones, and the weight-bearing which helps to prevent bones becoming brittle (osteoporosis). Standing helps the ankle joints and in particular the prevention of foot drop due to the contraction of the tendo calcaneus (Achilles tendon) which prevents the foot lying flat on the floor. Standing reduces spasms, improves circulation and prevents sores, as well as helping in the general effect of well-being; morale is boosted by being able to talk to others at the same standing level. Tetraplegics, like myself, who make regular 'standing-transfers' as a routine method of daily management, will benefit from weight-bearing in this way.

PREVENTION OF CHEST COMPLICATIONS

The prevention of chest infection is all important. This is more difficult for patients with high lesions who are unable to expand their lungs as normal. Regular daily deep breathing exercises will help maintain the elasticity of lung tissue. Regular changes of position, turns in bed, standing and leaning forward in the wheelchair all assist the lungs to drain naturally. During the summer months, as much time as possible spent in the fresh air will be beneficial to the lungs. During the winter months, try and avoid going out unnecessarily, stay in the warm and avoid mixing with people known to have a cough or cold.

Where a chest infection is suspected, a doctor must be consulted immediately, particularly by those persons who have a cervical lesion. Sore throats and head colds should not be ignored and often a day or two spent in bed with a cold will prevent the infection travelling to the chest. Some patients may find difficulty in breathing through their noses. The cause is sometimes attributable to the spinal cord injury and the disturbance of the nervous system. This condition, Horner's syndrome, has a number of effects, one being blockage of the nasal passages known as Guttmann's sign. Should this persist, consult your doctor who may prescribe decongestant drops or spray.

CHEST CARE

Good understanding of chest care is important, particularly for patients with cervical and high thoracic lesions. Such people will have paralysis of their abdominal and chest muscles resulting in an inability to cough normally. Because of this, a chest infection or the inhaling of food, drink and of vomit can prove fatal. The lungs are made in such a way that it is normal for the lining tissue of the tubes (bronchi) to produce mucus. This keeps the tubes moist and clean; in addition, this lining has tiny hairs (cilia) that are constantly on the move carrying mucus through the lungs until it reaches the throat. An automatic reflex is then triggered and we cough to clear the throat.

With high lesions this reflex is still present, but due to the paralysis of the chest and abdominal muscles it is not possible to cough up mucus in the normal manner. Any irritation tends to cause the person to inhale sharply thus drawing mucus back into the lungs which is followed by an attack of choking. When this happens, assistance is usually required to cough and keep the throat and lungs clear.

Assisted coughing

Assisted coughing is a method of helping the patient to react as he would if his chest and abdominal muscles were working normally. Coughing is simply the forcing of air out of the lungs under pressure. As the air is expelled, it takes any foreign matter with it. Nature's way of doing this is for the abdominal muscles to force the diaphragm upwards. At the same time the intercostal (chest) muscles contract the rib cage thus forcing air out of the lungs under pressure. When these muscles are paralysed it is necessary to mimic nature by applying external pressure over the rib cage. This is done by an assistant placing her hands on either side of the chest and squeezing the chest as the paralysed person exhales. Care has to be taken not to squeeze too hard for fear of damaging the ribs.

An alternative method is to place the hands over the abdominal muscles and, as the paralysed person exhales, push inwards and upwards. The diaphragm is thus pushed upwards forcing air out of the lungs. Both methods of assisted coughing require practice; when necessary they will be taught to the relatives by a physiotherapist.

With experience patients soon learn how to keep their throats clear by trick coughing techniques, combining a weak cough, exhalation of air and contractions of the throat. By coughing *before* mucus can start an irritation and choking attack, normal lung excretions can usually be cleared effectively without assistance. When irritation is caused by infection or smoking, assistance will certainly be required to keep the airways clear.

SMOKING

Smoking is the classic example of an unnecessary irritation causing the formation of excess mucus. Not only does the smoke cause the lungs to produce more mucus, but the nicotine in the tobacco stops the movement of the cilia that carry the mucus along the tubes in the lung.

Smoking can, therefore, cause two problems: the formation of an excess of mucus, and the prevention of nature's own method of cleaning and lubricating the lungs. This then results in a blockage of the bronchioles which may become infected leading to a reduction of oxygen, with consequent breathlessness and, ultimately, chronic bronchitis. An able-bodied person with his normal coughing mechanism can overcome the excess mucus caused through smoking, but the paralysed person who continues to smoke will be bothered by chest problems leading to lung conditions. Put simply, nobody *should* smoke, and patients with high lesions should *never* smoke.

SPASMS

Many spinally injured people are bothered by spasms – the involuntary muscular contractions that flex and extend limbs outside their control. Severe spasms that can throw patients out of their wheelchairs or from their beds will obviously require treatment. In circumstances when extensive physiotherapy and hydrotherapy have not reduced spasms significantly, drug therapy may be necessary. There are various drugs currently in use, all of which have side-effects which may influence a person's daily routine (Table 7/1).

Table 7/1   Anti-spasmodic drugs with possible side-effects

DRUG	SIDE-EFFECTS
diazepam	Drowsiness, dizziness, dry mouth, headache. May affect ability to drive. May increase the effects of alcohol. Prolonged use and abrupt withdrawal should be avoided. May become addictive
dantrolene sodium (Dantrium)	Weakness, fatigue, drowsiness, diarrhoea. Treatment may take several weeks to take effect; until stabilised, patients are advised not to drive
baclofen (Lioresal)	Nausea, vomiting, drowsiness, fatigue, confusion and low blood pressure. Abrupt withdrawal should be avoided

As a number of patients may be prescribed a combination of these drugs, it is clear that driving under their influence could prove hazardous.

Where drug therapy has proved ineffective, surgical procedures to lengthen tendons, divide muscles or, possibly, interfere with the nervous system may be considered. For the minority with intolerable painful, violent and uncontrollable spasms to their legs, a procedure known as an alcohol block which prevents muscle activity in the lower limbs may be suggested by the consultant.

COMPUTERISED MUSCLE STIMULATION

In recent years much publicity has been given to computerised muscle stimulation as an artificial method of walking. This technique, whereby paralysed muscles, externally stimulated, are linked to a computer to simulate normal walking, was developed in the USA by Dr Jerrold Petrofsky at Wright State University, Ohio.

A similar system, developed in the UK by Dr Hugh Grenfell at Swansea, is presently undergoing clinical trials. It should be clearly understood that computerised systems *do not* provide a *cure* for paralysis. Much research and development is necessary before nerves from the spinal cord can be re-joined and thus restore movement and sensation.

PAIN

One of the most difficult complications of spinal cord injury to diagnose and treat is pain. It can vary from very mild, being no more than burning sensations, to intense and severe degrees of pain occurring in an assortment of places throughout the body.

The most commonly experienced pain is that of a less intense nature, being a burning or tingling in those extremities that, in theory, should have no sensation if the lesion is complete. Such pains could be linked with the 'phantom limb' syndrome, where people who have had limbs amputated still feel pain. Patients with low lesions in particular may sometimes suffer regular bouts of acute pain that are probably initiated at the site of their cord injury. Tetraplegics sometimes suffer pain to the neck, shoulders and arms. Hypersensitivity in certain areas of the body can be unpleasant if not painful; sometimes the pain is persistent along a well identified area of the body which is supplied by a spinal nerve originating, usually, near the site of the damaged spinal cord – this is known as *root pain*.

A vast range of treatments have been tried to relieve pain, including drugs, physiotherapy, hydrotherapy, heat and ultrasound, surgery and local anaesthetics. Trying to discover under what circumstances the pain is triggered may provide a clue to some degree of relief. For example: I suffer quite intense degrees of pain to my limbs when cold and overtired. This takes 14 hours in bed to rectify. One of the latest techniques being used to treat the more difficult forms of pain is by electrical stimulation of nerve pathways both within and outside the spinal cord. Some patients have reported varying degrees of relief using these techniques. Patients suffering acute pain should consult their spinal specialist who may refer them to a pain clinic for investigation (see p. 146). Probably the most effective antidote in overcoming the less acute forms of pain is by diversional activities which occupy the mind.

POSTURAL HYPOTENSION

Postural hypotension describes the lowering of blood pressure when changing from the lying position to sitting up in bed or in the wheelchair. This condition, literally caused by the pooling of blood to the lower limbs and abdominal organs is experienced by many patients, in particular those with lesions above T_5 and, more so, those with cervical lesions. The cause is due to vasomotor paralysis (the mechanism which regulates the tone of the walls of the blood vessels) which is abolished by injury to the spinal cord.

In most circumstances the repeated changes of position from the supine to the erect gradually overcome the effects of hypotension. These effects include fainting, preceded by a blurring of vision; ringing in ears; and acute weakness in neck muscles and the inability to hold the head erect. Patients with cervical lesions, and in particular high cervical lesions, may be plagued with this problem every time they get up – I most certainly am. The wearing of elastic stockings and an abdominal binder may improve the situation. If not, it might be necessary to sit up in bed gradually and elevate the foot-rests when in the wheelchair. When all such methods have failed, the taking of a drug, such as ephedrine, to increase the blood pressure 30 minutes before getting up may be necessary. This must only be done after consultation with your doctor who will prescribe the dose.

Under certain circumstances postural hypotension may be made more acute. Eating before getting up should be avoided as it leads to natural pooling of blood to the stomach for aiding digestion. Alcohol dilates the blood vessels and lowers blood pressure. Hot climates also lead to a lowering of blood pressure, as does the taking of certain drugs which may have been prescribed for other complications. If this is the case do see your doctor.

SURGICAL RECONSTRUCTION OF THE TETRAPLEGIC HAND AND ARM

Over the past 50 years, a number of orthopaedic surgeons through-out the world have collaborated in evolving surgical techniques to improve upper limb dexterity in tetraplegic patients.

Surgical reconstruction procedures, particularly tendon trans-fers, can, in carefully selected cases, provide a grip between index finger and thumb and allow extension of the arm from the elbow when the triceps muscles are non-functional.

Not every tetraplegic will be considered suitable for such sur-gery. In the first instance those with incomplete lesions are advised to wait between 18 months and 2 years following injury for any latent signs of recovery (Guttmann, 1976). The procedures are lengthy, and the ultimate result will depend upon patience, deter-mination, co-operation and total confidence in the surgeon and his team.

The benefits of such surgery are difficult to estimate, but are probably best measured against the pre-operative physical con-dition. The few people to whom I have spoken who have undergone a deltoid to triceps transfer (affecting the ability to straighten the arm), as well as the reconstruction of the hand to provide a grip, have spoken of greater independence and improved quality of life, thus confirming that a little movement does mean a lot.

A tetraplegic wishing to be considered for a tendon transfer should ask his doctor to refer him to a spinal centre or orthopaedic hospital for assessment.

Reports by patients who have undergone tendon transfers can be read in the *Spinal Injuries Newsletter*, No. 35, May 1985.

FURTHER READING

Bromley, I. (1980). *Tetraplegia and Paraplegia. A Guide for Physio-therapists*, 2nd edition. Churchill Livingstone, Edinburgh.

Downie, P. A. (ed.) (1986). *Cash's Textbook of Neurology for Physiotherapists*, 4th edition, chapters 13 and 14. Faber and Faber, London.

Guttmann, L. (1976). *Spinal Cord Injuries. Comprehensive Management and Research*, chapter 33. Blackwell Scientific Publications Limited, Oxford.

PAIN CLINICS

Pain Relief Unit, Abingdon Hospital, Abingdon OX14 1AG
Pain Relief Unit, The Royal Sussex Hospital, Brighton BN2 5BE
Pain Relief Foundation, Walton General Hospital,
    Liverpool L9 1EA
Pain Relief Unit, The International College of Oriental Medicine,
    East Grinstead RH19 1TZ

8. Return to the Community

DISCHARGE FROM HOSPITAL

Besides the physical and mental turmoil that paraplegics often experience during their long periods of care and protection under hospital conditions, final discharge back into the community can be, and often is, as traumatic as when they were first admitted to hospital. Although most patients will have spent time with their families in hospital-provided accommodation, and progressively longer periods at home before discharge, it is not until they are finally at home on their own that the true impact of everything that has happened during the preceding months really registers with dramatic clarity.

In previous chapters I have outlined some of the psychological and physical difficulties associated with the immediate effect of a spinal cord injury. I have also supplied guidelines directed towards good physical care for the future. The importance and value of all the information provided may not register for a long time. Readers might well wonder how they can manage to prevent or avoid some of the complications mentioned. The most positive, effective, and probably the only way of doing this is to aim to remember the points I have stressed and try hard and conscientiously to live by the rules. I should be naive indeed if I were to say there are no inevitable complications to paralysis. There are: and everybody will, from time to time, experience problems, some minor and some more serious. One thing is certain; if paraplegics do not try and live their lives within the rules, then they will be inviting problems.

This is sometimes difficult to understand immediately for after discharge there is a natural tendency to try and resume life as it was before the onset of paralysis. A normal enough reaction; but whereas the mind might be anxious and willing to do this, the body is not always able to cope. I am not saying one cannot enjoy life. On the contrary, a vast majority of paraplegics and tetraplegics live very full, happy and contented lives and are fine examples to many able-bodied people. Nevertheless it takes time both to re-adjust to a new code of living and to develop a natural balance between mind and body.

Depending on domestic circumstances, discharge from hospital/ spinal centre, may be either to the person's own home, to institutional care, such as a Cheshire Home or a young disabled unit, or to a further rehabilitation unit or a job retraining centre. In some circumstances discharge might be to a hospital near a patient's own home. Regardless of where patients are discharged, fear and apprehension are often experienced. Tetraplegics who are totally unable to fend for themselves are frequently terrified that institutional staff or relatives will not be able to care for them in the manner to which they have become accustomed.

To enable patients to settle down after the initial discharge period, staff and relatives will need constantly to offer comfort and reassurance, remaining even-tempered for as long as necessary.

I believe that however long patients initially spend in hospital following injury, they will not psychologically adjust to their new circumstances for at least 12 months after discharge. This is equally true from the physical aspect; merely experiencing the effects of living outside hospital through all the changes of the seasons in a wheelchair is sufficient in itself.

Those who are able to be discharged back to their old home, or even a new one, will, it is hoped, have had any necessary basic entrance and doorway adaptations carried out before their return to give them reasonable access. This is not always the case because rehabilitation sometimes works faster than social integration! More detailed internal adaptations and conversions are best carried out when the individual concerned has settled in, and been able to assess more accurately what is required. It is impossible to describe how individuals of all ages and from all walks of life manage to rehabilitate after their discharge. The majority do settle into a new lifestyle after a reasonable period of time, particularly those who return to caring families, and employment.

There is, however, a minority of patients, often young, sometimes depressed, over-sensitive, self-conscious or unstable individuals who have great difficulty, mentally, adjusting to facing life from a wheelchair.

Somewhere in their lives or during their rehabilitation they seem to have lost all sense of responsibility. They waste their lives by sitting in front of television, backing horses, drinking too much alcohol, indulging in drugs or just looking out of the window. Why some people react in this way may be attributable to factors such as unemployment, educational and social backgrounds or even failure on behalf of the rehabilitation professionals – who knows? Here is excellent material for a behavioural psychologist to study.

Some paraplegics admit that massive compensation settlements and social security benefits take from them any incentive to work. Up to a point, this might well be right, for such financial security does provide people with a means to live without working. I am not necessarily suggesting that people should seek employment at this stage, but I do maintain that a 'temporary' occupation will stimulate their brains and prevent them from vegetating. If, at a later stage, they should wish to seek more lasting and satisfying employment, and circumstances permit, so much the better. By being occupied there is less opportunity to think about disability and gradually the mental anguish lessens.

Undoubtedly domestic circumstances have a large bearing on people's activities. In institutional surroundings it is not always easy to follow an occupation of one's own choice, for the whole home has to be considered. Happily, however, many of these establishments are understanding, and free and easy in their outlook. If a patient is in receipt of DHSS benefits, there are limitations to the amount that is allowed to be earned within the term 'therapeutic earnings'. But there can be no limitation on the amount of unpaid work or occupational therapy undertaken – the more the merrier.

I am often asked what motivated and inspired me back to life. Quite simply, it was my wife. But likewise I have asked many others the same question. The conclusion reached is that it is not just one person or just one thing in particular that may happen on a certain day, but a series of events and circumstances that accumulate over an unpredictable period.

The initial responsibility in hospital for motivation lies with the medical, nursing and paramedical staff. These are the experts who have to start the task of restoring a patient to the best possible physical and mental condition. As part of that treatment they should create the correct atmosphere for patients to relearn that life is still worth living despite the severity of the disability.

The medical consultant usually leads the team, and consequently directs and demonstrates the style of treatment. This is usually achieved through regular ward rounds, and case conferences when individual capabilities and achievements are discussed. Ward sisters who maintain a happy, efficient, progressive manner, do much to instil enthusiasm and if one vital word can describe what it is that motivates anybody to do anything, then it must be enthusiasm. The enthusiasm exhibited by all members of a medical, nursing and paramedical team working closely with patients, will create a little spark of motivation in the patients' hearts by the time they are ready for discharge.

This is only the start; motivation must also come from within and, as I have said, will depend largely on domestic circumstances. It is quite understandable for someone to become withdrawn, depressed and disinterested in everything life can offer if, for example, he has been rejected by family and friends and packed off to an institutional home full of strangers. Where an atmosphere of love and caring exists and the disabled person is made to feel wanted, he will then respond by wanting to give all he can in return, encouraged by a purpose for living and a reason to make something of life. The desire to be wanted is by no means exclusive to the disabled. It applies equally to people in all walks of life. A disabled person has to cope with the extra burdens and frustrations of fighting his disability, and so it is vitally important for him to receive support and encouragement in his endless struggle.

There are numerous organisations and charities well equipped and experienced to help disabled people rediscover themselves, by providing information and guidance (p. 162).

Besides the many charitable organisations willing to help the disabled, the DHSS can offer a wide range of practical help in the form of family doctor and hospital services, aids and equipment, financial benefits, and help from local authority social services. Most of the Department's help is obscure and patients do experience difficulty in obtaining facts: DHSS booklet HB1 *Help for*

Handicapped People explains how such services and help may be obtained. The booklet is available from post offices, public libraries and Citizens Advice Bureaux, or by post from the local DHSS office. It is a booklet which should be obtained by anyone who is disabled, as should leaflet FB2 *Which Benefit*.

Disabled people may like to purchase a copy of the Chronically Sick and Disabled Persons Act 1970. It is available from one of Her Majesty's Stationery Offices (see p, 163) or through any bookseller. It outlines a disabled person's legal entitlements. Broadly speaking, this Act is an extension of the 1948 National Assistance Act and when sections apply to local social services in particular, they tend to interpret the Act according to their circumstances. Consequently this leads to considerable variance in the help provided from area to area. In order to ensure that disabled people receive adequate help, a means test may be required before requests are considered.

THE CARERS

Although there are many professionals who are involved in providing care for the disabled, it is only the wife, husband, mother, father and other close relatives and friends who provide the 24-hours-a-day, 365-days-a-year total care for the more severely disabled and dependent person living at home.

This army of unpaid workers are the people expected to provide the bulk of care necessary after discharge. Families should be provided with basic instructions concerning routine management, and in most instances will have the opportunity to learn gradually how to care for their disabled relatives, by taking them home for progressively longer periods of time before the final discharge.

The responsibility is indeed a daunting prospect. Initially most disabled people feel extremely apprehensive at the prospect of returning home, and of being cared for by close relatives, especially if they are unable to fend for themselves. Homecoming can sometimes be an anticlimax when it is not possible to do the same things as before the injury occurred. This naturally causes frustration, outbursts of temper, tearful spells and indeed extremes of all emotions. The carers' job is not easy and they will have to exercise profound degrees of patience, tolerance and love. To all these carers may I say try not to become over-protective, but remain firm concerning daily management. There is always a tendency to invite hordes of visitors and to throw parties as a 'welcome home' gesture. These can be overpowering, embarrassing and exhausting. Time to settle in and gradually pick up the threads of life is vital before participating in too many social activities.

To avoid back injury, carers must learn correct techniques of lifting, turning and transferring the disabled relative prior to discharge. I would suggest that all carers be given basic training from the physiotherapist, nursing staff or occupational therapist before the first visit home is contemplated, thus preventing injury which could make homecoming impossible.

Throughout the lives of most families there are stress periods when, for various reasons, it is necessary to seek help and advice or just talk to an outsider about problems. Families caring for a disabled member are frequently faced with problems they are unable to resolve. These may range from particular aspects of daily care, to more intricate marital difficulties.

The Spinal Injuries Association recognises this need for a proper counselling service specifically designed to meet the needs of paraplegics and their families. Until such a service is fully established, there are organisations in existence to which paraplegics and families can turn for help and advice during periods of stress.

In the first instance, never feel afraid to contact your spinal centre for advice. Failing that, contact the Spinal Injuries Association who may be able to put you in touch with someone who has lived through a similar problem and can offer help, understanding and advice. Alternatively, there exists an Association of Carers. This association formed in 1981 by Judith Oliver, also married to a tetraplegic, aims at providing information and bringing carers together in order that they may share individual frustrations and generally let off steam. Addresses for some of these organisations will be found on page 162.

MEDICAL CHECK-UPS

Regardless of how much patients hate the thought of re-entering hospital, even as outpatients, it is important to have regular check-ups. This cannot be stressed enough: underlying complications may exist without a patient feeling the slightest effect. Such complications, if discovered in time, can often be treated without subjecting patients to too much inconvenience, but if they are left until permanent damage is done, then patients must not expect hospital staff to perform miracles.

Such a check-up may include blood and urine tests, a neurological examination, a general physical overhaul and occasionally an intravenous urogram (IVU). The latter is an x-ray procedure to assess kidney function as well as the efficiency of the whole urinary system. Individuals will be advised by their spinal specialist if there is a need for IVUs to be done regularly. The responsibility for check-ups rests with each person, and arrangements should be made through his own GP. Whenever possible it is probably better if the IVU is carried out at the spinal centre for they can then compare the results with earlier ones. Blood and urine tests can be done at the local hospital and should be carried out at 6-monthly intervals.

While many paraplegics, particularly those with high lesions, depend on the spinal centres for follow-up treatment, it must be emphasised that general hospitals do an excellent job in caring for spinally injured patients. I am certain that this is in part due to the concern of many specialists, nurses, doctors and paramedicals, who continually educate and teach their fellow professionals about the particular needs of patients who have spinal lesions.

GAMMA CAMERA

The introduction of computerised scanning equipment such as the gamma camera, could greatly aid in check-up examinations. In certain circumstances this equipment can be used instead of conventional urography (IVUs), for example in cases where patients are allergic to iodine.

The procedure involves intravenous injection of a small quantity of a special radiopharmaceutical solution which penetrates the particular organ to be examined releasing energy in the form of gamma rays. Scanning is then a simple, painless procedure with an ultra-sensitive camera that picks up the gamma rays. These are then converted into visual pictures by the computer.

Although patients receive a small radiation dose, this is even less than the radiation from conventional x-ray investigations.

SYRINGOMYELIA

A minority of patients undergoing check-up examinations sometimes show symptoms of a condition known as syringomyelia. This condition is not uncommon in paraplegia.

Syringomyelia is a disease of the spinal cord affecting ablebodied people, as well as those with spinal cord injuries. Its cause is uncertain, but in paraplegia it is probably associated with the injury to the spinal cord. The condition usually affects the cervical spinal cord above and below the level of the original spinal cord injury. Early symptoms show slight neurological changes affecting pain and temperature sense, followed by weakness and wasting of muscles to the upper limbs. In simple terms there is an increase, or worsening, in the degree of paralysis.

Whenever the condition is suspected, a special x-ray examination of the spinal canal (a myelogram) with CT scanning is carried out. If positive it will show a swelling of the spinal cord caused by an enlarged fluid-filled cavity within the spinal cord itself. This swelling causes pressure to other nerves thus accounting for the neurological changes.

Treatment of syringomyelia will be decided by the spinal specialist; should the condition give rise to a severe degree of impaired function to the upper limbs, it might be necessary surgically to drain the cavity within the spinal cord, thus relieving pressure to the nerves involved.

GENERAL HYGIENE

Personal hygiene is all important in the daily battle to prevent complications. Very often regular and adequate washing of paralysed limbs is forgotten. A complete bath or shower weekly, plus the daily washing of the groins and bottom to control skin bacteria is the minimum. This will keep skin free of dry patches and is usually sufficient to prevent septic spots. Many choose to shave pubic hair, and this certainly prevents the collection of skin adhesive where condom urinals are worn. It also reduces infections, particularly for those requiring indwelling catheters.

Particular attention should be paid to the care of feet. The formation of dry, hard skin on the feet is a common problem, and one which can be controlled by regular soaking and washing in warm soapy water. If it persists, the regular application of lanolin ointment after washing will help prevent further formation. Toe and finger nails often become hard and brittle and these should be kept cut short. Toe nails that grow inwards and become infected, usually the big toes, regularly cause problems for the paraplegic. They can account for the sudden increase of spasms and sweating and if ignored can develop into nasty sores. Skilful cutting of nails by a qualified chiropodist, and the wearing of extra wide shoes to relieve pressure will usually correct this problem. Where difficulties are experienced in finding suitably fitting shoes, specially made orthopaedic shoes can be prescribed – these are also prescribed for use with calipers. Normally one pair of shoes will be supplied initially, with a second pair after 6 months. Thereafter one pair a year is permitted for those who require them.

If toe nails continue to grow inwards, become infected and generally cause problems, it may be necessary to have them removed. Occasionally, removal of the nail bed which will prevent any further growth of nail is required. If you have persistent trouble with an ingrowing toe nail do talk to your doctor or chiropodist.

Teeth are of particular importance to tetraplegics, who depend greatly on them for holding various items as well as for eating. Remember, then, to take good care of them. Thoroughly brush them twice daily – an electric toothbrush may make this less difficult. Do remember also that false teeth cannot do the work of real ones, therefore have regular 6-monthly examinations with your dentist.

Hygiene also applies to clothing. Soiled clothes will cause endless skin problems, irritations, rashes and spots. Cushion covers and sheepskins require regular washing otherwise they become hard and matted and a cause of sores and infections. Bedclothing can be a source of skin problems. Sheets and pillow-cases should be changed at regular and frequent intervals. If washable pillows are used to lie on, they should be regularly washed, other types whenever possible should be thoroughly aired in direct sunlight.

WEIGHT AND DIET

In an attempt to keep their weight down, paraplegics should, unless guided otherwise, aim to eat a balanced, low fat, high protein, high fibre diet, not exceeding more calories than they are able to burn off during the course of a normal day. This is sometimes very difficult, because the price of food, particularly high protein foods, coupled with the inability to exercise normally, make it easy to eat the wrong foods and put on weight.

Excessive weight is difficult to lose and life automatically becomes harder for the individual to manage. An overweight tetraplegic, dependent on assistance, can make life impossible for his family, community nurses and others who have to attend him. This often leads to the necessity of moving paraplegics into homes and the break-up of happy family circles.

People vary in how much they can eat and how much weight they put on according to their metabolism. It is impossible to lay down rules, and common sense has to be applied. As a rough guide, a C6 complete lesion would require approximately 1500kcal a day, for with limited movement, it is impossible to burn off more energy than that. Calorie counting booklets can be bought from many bookshops. If problems of overweight do exist, patients should discuss the matter with their doctor who can seek the advice of a dietitian as necessary.

AGEING

It is reported that a 55-year-old paraplegic man who has been paralysed for 20 years is 10 years older than his chronological age in relation to the natural ageing process of the body (Bedbrook, 1981). In other words, paraplegics who survive 20 or more years will in physical terms be 10 years older than a non-paralysed person of the same age.

This fact accounts for a 50-year-old paraplegic man who had been paralysed for over 30 years and once told me – 'I feel that every day I live is equivalent to 48 hours.' In reality that statement was probably an exaggeration, but it does indicate how at the age of 50 he was finding life more difficult.

Life generally becomes physically, and ultimately mentally, harder for the non-paralysed person growing older. For someone suffering various degrees of paralysis, the physical strain on the active parts of the body is likely to be more severe, for the non-paralysed limbs have been overloaded through carrying and moving the whole weight of the paralysed body. Such physical re-strictions experienced as one grows older can very quickly lead to psychological frustrations not dissimilar to those felt when first becoming paralysed.

Many paraplegics, in particular those who have been active sports enthusiasts, may discover they have developed premature arthritis in their hand and shoulder joints caused by the additional activity of sport. As joints wear more rapidly, so other parts of the body show signs of premature dysfunction. The bladder becomes more prone to infection and generally deteriorates in function, requiring increasingly more treatment as one grows older. This ultimately affects kidney function – failure of which accounts for the highest proportion of deaths.

Paraplegics who suffer persistently from pressure sores will shorten their lives. Repeated and chronic infection may give rise to a condition known as amyloidosis which affects both kidneys and the liver – yet another reason to prevent pressure sores. Circulation appears to deteriorate as one grows older, predisposing to pressure sores, frost-bite, swollen and cold limbs.

Many paraplegics discover their bowel action becomes sluggish and that they need to increase their chosen aperient as the years go by. In an attempt to avoid this, it is necessary to maintain a high fibre diet. This is also helpful in preventing haemorrhoids.

In general terms, to combat many of the ageing difficulties, para-plegics have to live more moderate lives. It is essential to have ade-quate rest and to avoid obesity. This may sometimes prove difficult for there is a natural tendency to gain weight in the middle years.

THE GENERAL PRACTITIONER

If the patient is not already registered with a general practitioner, then this is almost the first thing he must do following discharge from hospital. A list of general practitioners can be found in your local post office. Should you have difficulty in finding a doctor, you should contact your local Family Practitioner Committee or Community Health Council, whose addresses will be found at the post office or Citizens' Advice Bureaux, or in the local telephone directory.

Patients are advised to ask their doctor to see them immediately after they are discharged, when they are fit and well, because he may not have seen a paraplegic person before. The doctor will then have a basis for comparison to work on should he be called at other times. It is the policy of spinal centres to teach their paraplegic patients as much about their own management as they can absorb. This is essential to survival after discharge, and consequently patients sometimes know more about themselves than their family doctor. In these circumstances it can be difficult to converse with the family doctor as the patient instinctively dictates treatment previously recommended in hospital. I shall never forget the difficulty I once had in trying to explain the symptoms of autonomic dysreflexia to my family doctor at a time when I had a bladder infection and my blood pressure was sky high. He had never heard of the condition and was adamant that no such thing existed. Patients should exercise tact and discretion at such times, and perhaps suggest to their doctor that they have read about the particular problem or treatment in publications about paraplegia. If that fails you can suggest, diplomatically, that he telephones the consultant who looked after you in the spinal centre or hospital. Perhaps I should add that these incidents should not occur if the GP is put into the picture by the spinal unit when the individual person is discharged.

Paraplegia remains an uncommon condition to many GPs who frankly admit that they have little or no experience in handling such patients.

PRESCRIPTION CHARGES

Certain groups of people do not have to pay prescription charges. These include children under 15 and adults over 65. Exemption also includes people with continuing physical disabilities. Leaflet P 11 from DHSS offices describes how to go about obtaining an exemption certificate.

INSURANCE

Thirty or so years ago it was extremely difficult for the paraplegic readily to obtain insurance of one kind or another. Insurance companies are in business to make money, and in those days most disabled people were regarded as a high risk. This attitude still prevails, but to a much lesser extent.

Motor insurance has improved dramatically over the last 10 years, and unless there are exceptional circumstances most paraplegic and tetraplegic drivers should have little difficulty in obtaining this. The disabled motoring organisations can provide names and addresses of companies specialising in cover for disabled drivers.

There might be more difficulty in obtaining insurance for travel, house purchase and, most certainly, life assurance. Do not be deterred if your local broker declines to help you. There are now brokers who specialise in finding insurance for people with multiple disabilities, and underwriters are looking more favourably at proposals from the disabled. As one broker put it to me: 'I personally put this down to two separate factors: the continuous advances in medical science resulting in cures (or at least controls) for many ailments which would have been unacceptable to insurers only a generation ago and, in addition, insurers are recognising that the disabled, as a group, often produce fewer claims than their able-bodied counterparts. This is clearly because the disabled person is more aware of his vulnerability, and tends to take more care in any given situation.'

Travel insurance is of particular importance to the paraplegic, especially when contemplating travelling in a country not covered by a reciprocal health agreement. Many package holiday offers and motoring organisation travel schemes are ambiguous and include conditions that exclude the disabled traveller. Again there are a few major insurers who provide full cover at normal rates without any exclusions relating to pre-existing medical conditions.

House purchase policies are relatively easy to obtain. Following the introduction of Mortgage Interest Relief at Source (MIRAS), a number of insurers offer mortgage protection or low cost endowment policies to anyone who has not seen a doctor for 12 months.

Life insurance policies are the most difficult to obtain and are the most complex. Naturally the proposer's medical history will be the most significant factor. Nevertheless cover may still be possible, even if, sometimes, the premiums are slightly raised. (See page 164 for addresses.)

PATIENTS' LEGAL RIGHTS

Many patients are often under misconceptions concerning their legal rights in relation to health care. To allay these I suggest they obtain a copy of *Patients' Rights*. This is a guide to the rights and responsibilities of patients and doctors in the NHS and is published by the National Consumer Council, 18 Queen Anne's Gate, London SW1H 9AA. This booklet sets out all information required concerning GPs, hospitals, second opinions, consent, emergencies, etc. It is available also from HMSO offices.

THE SPINAL INJURIES ASSOCIATION

The British Spinal Injuries Association was formed in 1974 at the instigation of Baroness Masham, herself a paraplegic, and several other paraplegics and tetraplegics.

The Association is run by people in wheelchairs, their object being to promote the welfare of all those suffering from spinal cord injury. The Association provides a comprehensive range of help and advice to its members, including: a quarterly newsletter, an information service, welfare service, care attendant agency, holiday information, holiday accommodation in either their own canal narrowboat or adapted caravan, legal advice and help over many other aspects of disability.

In many areas local groups have been formed and their members are willing to give immediate support to newly injured patients and their families.

REFERENCE

Bedbrook, G. (ed.) (1981). *The Care and Management of Spinal Cord Injuries*. Springer-Verlag, Heidelberg.

FURTHER READING

The following titles are textbooks for doctors, nurses and para-medical personnel.

Bedbrook, G. (ed.) (1985). *Lifetime Care of the Paraplegic Patient*. Churchill Livingstone, Edinburgh.

Guttmann, L. (1976). *Spinal Cord Injuries, Comprehensive Management and Research*, 2nd edition. Blackwell Scientific Publications Limited, Oxford.

Hardy, A. G. and Elson, R. (1976). *Practical Management of Spinal Injuries*, 2nd edition. Churchill Livingstone, Edinburgh.

Roaf, R. and Hodkinson, L. J. (1977). *The Paralysed Patient*. Blackwell Scientific Publications Limited, Oxford.

Sutton, N. G. (1973). *Injuries of the Spinal Cord: The Management of Paraplegia and Tetraplegia*. Butterworths, London.

Zejdlik, C. M. (1984). *Management of Spinal Cord Injuries*. Wadsworth Health Sciences Division, Monterey, California.

The following booklets are published from the Spinal Injuries Association, and may be obtained from them.

Nursing Management in the General Hospital: The first 48 hours following injury (1980).

Spinal Cord Injuries: Guidance for general practitioners and district nurses (1984).

USEFUL ORGANISATIONS

The Spinal Injuries Association
Yeoman House, 76 St James's Lane
London N10 3DF   01–444 2121

THE CARERS

Association of Carers
Lilac House, Medway Homes
Balfour Road, Rochester, Kent ME4 6QU   0634 813981

Association of Crossroads Care Attendant Schemes
94 Coton Road
Rugby, Warwickshire CV21 4LN

Franklin 'In Touch' Limited
31 New Inn Hall Street
Oxford OX1 2DH   0865 250585
This is a home nursing advice centre.

FINANCE

The AIDIS Trust
Cornborough, Milton Abbas
Blandford, Dorset DT11 ODA   0258 880240
Gives financial support for the purchase of aids for the disabled
and elderly.
Application must be made *in writing*.

National Association of Citizens Advice Bureaux
115/123 Pentonville Road
London N1 9LZ   01–833 2181
Gives advice on all domestic and financial matters. There are local
offices in all areas and addresses will be found in the local telephone directory.

Disability Alliance
25 Denmark Street
London WC2H 8NJ   01–240 0806
Gives advice and information on social security benefits.

Disablement Income Group (DIG)
Attlee House, 28 Commercial Street
London E1 6LR   01–247 2128
This is a pressure group which fights for better economic and
social status for all disabled persons. Gives advice on social secur-
ity benefits.

HER MAJESTY'S STATIONERY OFFICES

Atlantic House, Holborn Viaduct, London EC1P 1BN

Bankhead Avenue, Edinburgh EH11 4AB

Chichester House, Chichester Street, Belfast BT1 4PS

Ashton Vale Road, Ashton, Bristol BS3 2HN

Sovereign House, Botolph Street, Norwich NR3 1DN

Broadway, Chadderton, Oldham, Lancashire OL9 9QH

RIGHTS

Consumers' Association
14 Buckingham Street
London WC2N 6DS   01–839 1222
Gives advice on all consumer rights.

Association of Community Health Councils
Mark Lemon Suite, Top Floor, Barclays Bank Chambers
254 Seven Sisters Road
London N4 2HZ   01–272 5459
Gives advice about health rights. There are local offices whose
addresses will be found in the local telephone directory.

The Patients' Association
Room 33, 18 Charing Cross Road
London WC2H OHR   01–240 0671
Gives help and advice to patients and their families on all health
matters.

INSURANCE COMPANIES

Tweddle, French and Company Limited
Ibex House, The Minories
London EC3N 1DY
(Also at Lloyds)   01–480 6918

Bolton Associates Insurance Brokers
165 Western Road
Bletchley, Milton Keynes MK2 2PX   0908 72203

M. J. Fish and Company Limited
Insurance Brokers
1–3 Slater Lane
Leyland, Preston PR5 3AL   0772 455111

9. Housing and Living

Local authorities are empowered to provide care for the disabled as laid down in the Chronically Sick and Disabled Persons Act 1970. In theory it is incumbent on the authority to meet the need, but the assessment of need lies entirely within each authority's discretion and will inevitably vary from area to area.

SOCIAL WORKERS

Social workers employed outside specialised spinal units almost always lack general knowledge regarding the needs of paraplegics. In my experience one of the solutions to this weak link in the re-habilitation chain is for patients and their relatives to find out for themselves what is available locally. This information will include facts about the social services, and how they can be applied to individual requirements.

At varying stages after a patient is admitted to a spinal unit, the hospital-based social worker will interview both the patient and his relatives in an attempt to assess their domestic circumstances in relation to the subsequent return home of the paraplegic, probably in a wheelchair. After these meetings, when items such as suitability of housing are discussed, the social worker usually writes to the social services department in the patient's home area, outlining the general situation and arranging a possible visit to the patient's home. This visit is sometimes carried out by the hospital social worker and occupational therapist, but more often it is done by the community social worker and domiciliary occupational therapist and perhaps the community nurse. After the patient's home has been carefully assessed regarding its suitability for wheelchair access; lavatory, bathroom, bedroom, kitchen and living room being carefully considered, recommendations may be put to both the patient's family and the local authority.

These recommendations will vary, depending primarily on whether the property in question is privately or council owned. If it is rented from the local council, any necessary recommendations will be made to the local housing authority either for alterations and adaptations to be made under Section 2 of the Chronically Sick and Disabled Persons Act, or for the disabled person and his family to be rehoused in a more suitable house or bungalow, or for a purpose-built bungalow or flat suitable in every aspect to the disabled person's needs to be provided. This latter will happen in only a minority of cases. The extent to which local authorities are willing to co-operate under Section 2 of the Act varies considerably from one area to another and depends on local finances.

When the property is privately owned, either by the patient or the family, or if it is owned by a landlord and rented, the question of alteration or adaptation is a very different matter. The first consideration to be taken into account is suitability and whether it is a practical proposition either to alter or adapt the property. The second consideration is cost. Many old houses with steps and stairs all over the place are not worth modifying to suit a wheelchair.

If the property is totally unsuitable (this is for the patient and his family to decide regardless of what the social services may say or think) or if the owner or landlord refuses to allow alterations, there are two alternatives. First, to buy or rent another more suitable house, flat or bungalow, or second, to apply to the local housing authority for a suitable council owned property. Whichever option is taken depends on personal, domestic and financial circumstances. It is often very much quicker, and certainly more satisfactory, to move into a new, privately owned property, rather than rely on the local council to find suitable council owned accommodation.

If the privately owned property is found to be suitable, providing suggested alterations are made to accommodate a wheelchair, then the question of cost arises and who is going to pay? Under Section 2 of the Chronically Sick and Disabled Persons Act, local authorities will make all necessary alterations and adaptations to property in order to house a disabled person who qualifies under the Act. There is no reference as to whether the property is privately or council owned. Unfortunately social services departments interpret the Act as being an extension of the 1948 National Assistance Act, which gives them the power to subject applicants for help under the Chronically Sick and Disabled Persons Act to a means test.

I doubt very much if there are many people who would choose to turn to the social services for financial help with house alterations if they could genuinely afford to pay themselves. It is often the average family who are already sacrificing a great deal paying off a house mortgage or paying for their children's education, who, when distressed and not knowing which way to turn next, suddenly find themselves subjected to the humiliation of a means test. Authorities maintain that the means test is the only way of ensuring that help is distributed fairly, yet not all applicants are subjected to such a test. Perhaps in time to come a more efficient method of assessing genuine need will evolve other than the obvious physical needs of paraplegia and particularly tetraplegia.

HOUSE ALTERATIONS

Property whether private or council owned should, whenever possible, be adequately adapted or modified to provide easy access, comfortable sleeping accommodation and suitable toilet and bathroom facilities *before* a paraplegic is discharged from hospital. Not only would this seem common sense for the benefit of the disabled person, it is also vitally important to give families as a whole every possible support in the often difficult task they are undertaking – that of caring for their disabled relative. Only too often one hears of families and marriages breaking up, which can be attributed primarily to unsuitable housing and to inadequate help and advice.

I think most people agree that a ground floor flat or bungalow type of accommodation is most suitable for a wheelchair user. Many wheelchair users do live in ordinary houses and blocks of flats that have been fitted with lifts, and it may prove less expensive to provide this type of alteration to a house rather than rehousing the whole family.

Obvious disadvantages of lifts are the risks of mechanical failure, power cuts, fire, vandalism and difficulty in operation for the more severely disabled, together with the loss of space and major alterations necessary. However, there are a number of firms providing house alterations of this nature which seem to be most satisfactory. Some even provide external lifts and lifts operated on a counterweight principle without the need for electricity.

The most important consideration when assessing whether a property is suitable for a wheelchair user is that of easy access. This means that the person in the wheelchair should be able to enter and leave the property without assistance. It also includes easy access to and from the road and frequently necessitates the construction of a ramp in place of steps and a suitable concrete pathway. Ramps should be of concrete construction; wooden ramps can burn, be removed and are often slippery especially when wet. Ramps should be gradual and wide enough for safety purposes and if possible constructed with side walls and rails (Figs. 9/1 and 9/2).

Whenever possible a property with at least two suitable entrances should be chosen. Ramps may be necessary and I don't think it is unreasonable to ask the social services department to provide these under the terms of the Chronically Sick and Disabled Persons Act. Should they be reluctant to provide a ramp, then you may need to go to the extreme limit by suggesting that you will hold them legally responsible for your safety in the event of fire.

All doors, including the main entrance, should be sufficiently wide to allow free access, eliminating the risk of damaging hands on pushing through. This usually means that doors will require alteration to make them approximately 90cm (3ft) wide. Internal doors of the sliding type are in most cases more suitable. Front doors that open inward may be difficult for the wheelchair user to close on leaving the property. Sometimes the addition of a D-shaped handle fixed to the centre of the door permits the paraplegic to reach back and pull the door shut. Locks and latches may also require alteration, such as lowering them for easy reach.

Specific alterations and modifications will vary enormously depending upon the layout of the accommodation. Obviously all steps should be removed and replaced by ramps. Inside these can

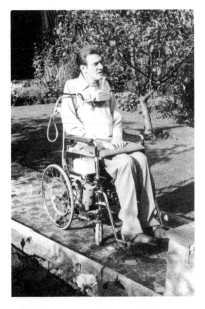

Fig. 9/1 The author manipulating himself in his powered wheelchair up the graded concrete ramp in his garden. *Note* the tiles set into the surface to prevent slipping

Fig. 9/2 As previous illustration, but *note* the raised edges to prevent the chair slipping off

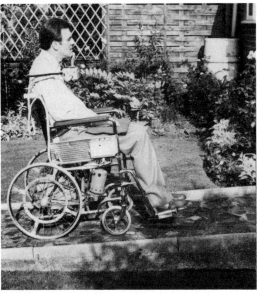

be of wooden construction providing they are fixed securely. Electric light switches may require to be lowered and socket plugs raised to 1 metre (3 feet) from the floor.

Whenever possible a lavatory and bathroom should be accessible from the bedroom and at least one other lavatory provided for other members of the household to use. Conventional bath tubs may be difficult to get in and out of for many paraplegics and a shower unit might prove more satisfactory. This is a personal choice. There are firms who produce specially designed shower units with the disabled in mind. Many such units require the user to transfer out of the wheelchair on to a fitted seat within the unit, which can often prove awkward. Where plenty of space is available, an open tiled and drained area with shower above where the paraplegic can sit in a shower-chair fitted with foot-rests is so much more satisfactory. However, in accommodation with restricted space, I do recommend one of the Inva-dex range of showering systems made by J. W. Swain (Plastics) Ltd (see p. 200). The shower trays sit on top of existing floor levels and require minimal plumbing. They can be used with either a wheelchair-type of shower chair or by a fixed folding shower seat.

Reconstruction of a kitchen, especially for the disabled housewife, is a very important aspect. Not only must the kitchen be functional, but space is of paramount importance (Fig. 9/3). Split-level cooker units are most practical, where the oven opens just above knee level. Some paraplegic housewives prefer oven doors that hinge downwards, they can then rest whatever they are cooking on the door. Others say the door that hinges down prevents them getting close enough to put pots and pans into the oven and they prefer the side-hinged door. Again this is a personal choice. Naturally all cupboards must be accessible from the sitting position. The washing-up sink unit must be placed high enough to allow the knees and a wheelchair underneath. Waste and water supply pipes should be well lagged or strategically positioned to prevent burns to knees.

Kitchen modification for a tetraplegic is even more crucial and great thought must be put into every aspect of design. Unless the tetraplegic has use of triceps (the muscle which straightens the arm) the risk of trying to cook or handle boiling-hot pots and pans should be carefully considered. I suggest that all tetraplegics, and

Fig. 9/3 Paraplegic housewife in her specially converted kitchen. *Note* the eye-level oven, hob, and lowered work surfaces, also the converted sink unit to accommodate the wheelchair

especially those without triceps, stick to handling cold food and drink for their own safety.

Adequate heating is another important consideration when altering or building a house. In the UK central heating is almost essential. The choice of system will depend on circumstances, but with the continuing rise in fuel costs, anybody installing a new heating system would be wise to consider the addition of solar panels. If open fires are used, care should be taken to ensure that coals do not fall from the grate and that the wheelchair user does not sit too close and possibly burn his legs.

Cooling is another consideration. Should excessively hot spells cause distress, as I personally find they do, then the installation of air conditioning to one or more rooms might be necessary. There now exist portable air conditioning plants which can be wheeled from one room to another and which also double as heaters. In the same range of appliances there are also humidifiers for those with chest problems (see p. 229).

Special adaptations, modifications and aids may be necessary for paraplegic children. Examples of equipment available include variable height wash-basins that have telescopic drainpipes. As the child grows the basin can be raised on adjustable brackets. Inserts for toilet seats can be fitted over the standard size toilet seat, thus leaving the toilet basically unaltered. Further examples of these aids and others which help towards greater independence within a house, together with ideal modifications and layouts of kitchens, bathrooms, bedrooms, and electrical equipment are all splendidly displayed in the many aids centres throughout the country, including the Disabled Living Foundation in London. The Foundation also provides a library and an up-to-date information service on practically everything connected with disablement of all kinds.

In theory, all housing alterations and adaptations should be provided for under Section 2 of the Chronically Sick and Disabled Persons Act. In practice this does not always happen. Some social services departments are only able to provide a bare minimum while others are more generous. Some provide interest-free loans to house owners to make their own alterations, while others undertake the alterations themselves and take a lien on your property which entitles them to reclaim their expenses should you decide to sell and move. The degree of help that one can expect to receive appears to depend on where you live, how determined you can be and the extent of your problem.

Personal note

I strongly urge anybody experiencing difficulties in obtaining what they feel is their entitlement not to give in easily, but to seek advice, help and assistance from organisations experienced in dealing with these issues (see p. 162). This is by no means a biased view directed towards the social services; it is merely my wish that patients and their families should receive that to which they are entitled. Time and again some social services departments refuse requests because they themselves do not accurately interpret the many complicated rules and regulations laid down regarding these matters.

It should also be made perfectly clear that in no way are patients compelled to involve the social services departments in their domestic affairs and rehabilitation. Many patients enter and leave hospital managing their own affairs. However, the majority of paraplegics are compelled to rely on the system for at least some degree of assistance, more often than not because of financial limitations.

Before final discharge, and usually about the time patients are ready to go home for weekends, application should be made by the hospital to the local social services for the provision of home nursing aids and equipment. These aids are basic requirements for survival at home and are supplied, if required, regardless of circumstances. Such articles could include a suitable bed; a suitable mattress such as Alpha-Pad, ripple mattress; a hoist; a commode chair with detachable armrests. After final discharge, if further aids are required, these can be obtained through the community nurse or social worker.

COMMUNITY NURSING SERVICE

There are many paraplegics living successfully at home with help from a community nurse. Without the nurse's help they would certainly have to be admitted to hospital or institutional care. Prior to discharge, patients and families who consider they will need help from a community nurse, either on a permanent or temporary basis, can have the service arranged in advance by the hospital. In many cases a community nurse will visit the patient in hospital before his final discharge, to receive instruction regarding his future care. Whenever this is possible, it is a highly desirable arrangement. Like many GPs not every community nurse will have had experience in caring for a spinally injured person. And for them to receive instruction from their own colleagues reduces tension between them and their patient. A community nurse may also visit the patient in his home during a weekend before final discharge to assess further the degree of disability, and to suggest any further aids and equipment which would make her job less difficult while making life for the patient more manageable.

There is an increasingly heavy demand in most areas for the community nursing service, not only from paraplegics, but from elderly people, heart cases, diabetics, postoperative cases, nursing mothers and various other categories of disabled people. All require help. Consequently, it is not always possible for the nurse to attend patients at regular hours. This sometimes makes it difficult for the paraplegic to undertake regular employment and keep appointments outside the home.

Community nurses are more usually requested by tetraplegics and will undertake all nursing duties such as bladder and bowel management, washing and dressing, treatment of pressure sores and injections. Patients who normally manage without help from the community nursing service and then suddenly find they require assistance (perhaps during a period when they themselves or their attendant are ill), should contact their general practitioner who will then make necessary arrangements.

Services provided by the community nurse vary from area to area and often depend on the type of general practice to which they are attached. In the same way as GPs cover off-duty, holidays, weekends and nights for each other, so nurses do likewise. Therefore patients may be cared for by different nurses. Some community nurses will undertake the task of supplying patients with such items as paper sheets and incontinence rolls. Some will bring drugs and medications from the doctor's surgery but others will leave these things for patients to arrange themselves. It is not possible to generalise on the degree of help available.

HOME HELP SERVICE

Another practical form of help for physically disabled people is the home help service. Most local authorities assess the need on physical limitations and will expect those financially able to pay for the service.

Most home helps are friendly, good-natured people who undertake the work for more than merely doing a job. They will undertake light housework, ironing, shopping, collecting pensions, assist in getting the elderly up and taking them to and from the toilet, as well as a little cooking. Again there is an overwhelming demand on the service and applicants cannot expect to have their help more than perhaps a few hours weekly. This varies however from area to area, and full details of the service can be obtained from local social services departments.

LAUNDRY SERVICE

In certain circumstances, local authorities may provide a laundry service. Invariably this service is much sought after by incontinent elderly people. It is, however, of great value to many paraplegics, especially females who, due to the lack of a suitable urine collection device, soil a large amount of personal and bed-clothing. Consequently social services departments frequently provide assistance in the form of either a spin or tumble dryer and sometimes a clothes washing machine. Further information regarding the help available in certain areas can be obtained from local social services departments.

TELEPHONE

One of the facilities which local authorities are enabled to provide for severely disabled people under Section 2 of the Chronically Sick and Disabled Persons Act is a telephone. I think that all people disabled to such a degree that they are prevented from leaving their property in an emergency, such as fire, should be connected to the outside world by telephone.

Most local authorities subject applicants for telephones to a means test and base the requirement more on the period of time the disabled person is left on his own, rather than the physical limitations. What happens to a paraplegic at night may be overlooked. Only in bed is the true impact of not being able to walk fully realised; the wheelchair may roll away from the bed, the patient may be taken ill or the house catch fire – what then?

Installation and rental of a telephone is expensive and it is understandable that local authorities cannot provide all disabled people with telephones much as they might like to. All I can suggest to those who have been refused a telephone is to appeal. If you are still unsuccessful, think very hard about saving and paying for one yourselves. Remember: it is for your own safety.

As from 1st January 1985, it is no longer necessary to pay a rental charge to British Telecom for the telephone receiver. All that is required is to pay rental for the residential line. With this installed, it is possible to purchase your own telephone receiver from a private company if you so wish, and the range of alternative suitable sets might be bigger than those offered by British Telecom. These include cordless telephones with a range up to 700 feet, receivers with their own memory bank of programmed numbers and two-way intercom systems. Under these circumstances it might be possible to come to an arrangement with local authorities who have initially refused an installation.

DOMICILIARY OCCUPATIONAL THERAPY

Most local authorities provide occupational therapy for elderly and disabled people if they require it. This service is normally provided in day centres which the recipients attend. Many tetraplegics requiring additional help to enable them to function effectively, for example in making toys, painting and woodwork, etc., derive great benefit from attending such centres.

Transport to and from the centres is normally provided by the health authority, Red Cross or St John Ambulance. Occupational therapists employed within the day centres may also help disabled and elderly residents within their own homes – to make minor aids and adaptations as necessary so that life becomes more manageable. For example, some while ago the local domiciliary occupational therapist made me a platform for my painting-board on which I can rest my brushes. Such simple extras help to make life more tolerable.

Patients wishing to benefit from the domiciliary occupational therapy service should contact their local social services for further information.

SOCIAL SECURITY FINANCIAL BENEFITS

Entitlement to social security benefits varies considerably and depends largely upon individual domestic circumstances. The system is complex and can baffle even the most ardent legal brains!

There are many benefits to which the spinally injured victim may become entitled, most of which will depend on the circumstances of the injury and whether the requisite number of contributions to the National Insurance Scheme have been paid. At present there are four basic avenues of entitlement: the Industrial Injury scheme for injuries that occurred at work; the Sickness Benefit scheme for injuries that occurred in your own time; Injury Benefit for serving members of the armed forces; and for those not in any of those categories, entitlement to supplementary benefits may be possible.

The DHSS produces leaflets covering all benefits. Leaflet HB1 *Help for Handicapped People* is a booklet which gives basic information about most benefits available to various groups of people. Leaflet NI 146 is a catalogue of social security leaflets and leaflet NI 196 gives full details of social security benefit rates. The leaflets may be obtained from post offices or the local DHSS office. In case of difficulty they may be obtained from the DHSS Leaflets Unit, PO Box 21, Stanmore, Middlesex HA7 1AY.

VALUE ADDED TAX (VAT)

Many disabled people are unaware that they are automatically exempt from paying VAT on a number of items under the VAT (Handicapped Persons and Charities) Order 1981 and 1982.

Exemption from VAT applies to:

a. Electrically or mechanically adjustable beds; commode chairs and similar sanitary appliances; wheelchairs and carriages (not road vehicles); haemodialysis units; artificial respirators and similar appliances; stair lifts or chair lifts for wheelchairs; and other hoists and lifts for the domestic or personal use of the disabled or chronically sick person.

b. Other aids and equipment for the domestic, personal use of a disabled or chronically sick person, including clothing, footwear, wigs, dentures, spectacles and contact lenses.

c. Adaptations, maintenance, repairs and spare parts for the above items (Matthewman and Lambert, 1982).

VAT is also exempt on cars or vans which are significantly adapted to carry a disabled passenger in a stretcher or wheelchair.

VAT is exempt on some building alterations such as the widening of doorways and corridors, construction of ramps and the installation of a toilet and bathroom on the ground floor specifically required by a disabled person. The VAT relief only applies to a new installation and not the conversion of existing bathrooms.

RATES RELIEF

A reduction in the rates charged on property that has been adapted or includes special facilities for a disabled person is permitted under the Rating Disabled Persons Act 1978.

Relief is allowed on a garage, carport or land on which the disabled person parks his car; central heating in two or more rooms; specially adapted or provided bathroom facilities; rooms specifically used for the benefit of the disabled person.

A disabled person who is registered with the local authority automatically qualifies for rate relief; others will have to apply to the finance department of their local rating authority, who may seek medical confirmation of the applicant's disability. Before granting rate relief the local authority usually require to inspect the applicant's property.

VOTING

Physically disabled people are entitled to postal voting; apply to your local electoral registrar for full details.

REFERENCES

Matthewman, J. and Lambert, N. (eds) (1982). *Social Security and State Benefits*, p. 58, 5.2. Tolley's, Croydon, Surrey. (Regularly up-dated.)
Chronically Sick and Disabled Persons Act 1970. HMSO, London.
National Assistance Act 1948. HMSO, London.
Rating Disabled Persons Act 1978. HMSO, London.

FURTHER READING

Oliver, M. (1983). *Social Work with Disabled People*. Macmillan Press, London.

COMPASS (Direction Finder for Disabled People). Published by DIG, Attlee House, London E1 6LR. (Regularly updated.)

Disability Rights Handbook. Published by the Disability Alliance, 25 Denmark Street, London WC2 8NJ. (Regularly up-dated.)

National Welfare Benefits Handbook. Published by the Child Poverty Action Group, 1 Macklin Street, London WC2B 5NH. (Regularly up-dated.)

10.   Aids and Equipment

The manufacture and supply of aids and equipment for people with various disabilities has become a large and competitive business over the past decade. Many of the aids and equipment are available free of charge to the spinally injured person. This chapter is designed to outline some of the aids and equipment that have been found satisfactory for the paraplegic's use and to indicate from which DHSS department they may be obtained.

AVAILABLE FROM ARTIFICIAL LIMB AND APPLIANCE CENTRES (ALAC)

WHEELCHAIRS

To the paraplegic the most useful single item of equipment supplied by the National Health Service is undoubtedly the wheelchair. These are issued to those who require them, but they remain the property of the National Health Service. The Everest and Jennings folding wheelchair has been found to be the most satisfactory chair for patients with spinal cord injuries and the DHSS will issue this type to continuing long-term physically disabled patients. These chairs are produced in different sizes to accommodate individual needs. For the more severely disabled person who has limited or no arm movements electrically-powered chairs of different types can be supplied.

Regardless of the type of chair supplied, its value must be appreciated not only in terms of cash, but as an aid to mobility. Without a wheelchair, the paraplegic will either be confined to bed, or at least to an armchair inside the house. A wheelchair can dramatically broaden the horizons of your life, and – as all chairs are supplied on the understanding that users are responsible for their maintenance, cleaning and oiling – look after them well.

In most cases it is possible to supply only one wheelchair per person (on the NHS); those supplied with an electrically-powered chair are also able to have an ordinary wheelchair to enable them to be taken out and to travel. Remember, *never* travel in a car without a wheelchair, in case of a breakdown.

Patients who are financially able to purchase a second (or third) chair of their own (perhaps with a compensation claim) are well advised to do so. Thus if one chair breaks down, mobility is not impaired while repairs are being carried out. Wheelchairs *are* expensive, but when one considers emergencies such as fire there can be no price placed on mobility. Wheelchairs are exempt from VAT.

Following discharge from hospital, the DHSS Artificial Limb and Appliance Centre (ALAC) in the paraplegic's home area becomes the centre responsible for all problems and repairs to NHS-supplied wheelchairs. Their address can be found in the telephone directory under 'Health and Social Security, Department of'. A technical officer from the centre will visit in their own homes those patients who have been issued with electrically-powered wheelchairs and arrange for any necessary repairs. Between his visits, if minor repairs costing a maximum of £6.00 are required, they can be carried out under the orders of patients and receipts sent to the ALAC, for reimbursement. This same rule extends to patients who have been issued with hand-propelled chairs. More expensive repairs required must be notified to your ALAC, when their official repairer will be responsible.

Wheelchairs should be inspected regularly at monthly intervals. Nuts and bolts should be tightened and in particular the screws holding the backrest should be checked. The backrest material is inclined to be torn by the top fixing screw, particularly when patients drape their arms over the backrest. During hot weather and in central heating conditions, the bearings soon dry out. These should be well oiled or greased as recommended. Tyres should always be kept well inflated as soft tyres wear out more easily and make the job of pushing the chair considerably harder. The manufacturers supply a small tool kit and pump, together with maintenance instructions. These should be read carefully and the instructions followed.

Powered wheelchairs

The more severely disabled are, under certain circumstances, supplied wth electrically driven wheelchairs for indoor use. These chairs are supplied on the same terms and conditions as ordinary chairs; namely that the user is responsible for maintenance, cleaning and oiling.

All recipients of powered wheelchairs from the DHSS are required to sign an undertaking that they will not use the chairs outdoors. The DHSS claims that none of the electrically driven wheelchairs issued is suitable for heavy outdoor use and that none matches up to the specifications laid down in the regulations made under Section 20 of the Chronically Sick and Disabled Persons Act. Despite this Act and the written undertaking, DHSS officials agree that their chairs may be used outdoors with care 'within the curtilage of the residence'; and to save you looking that up in your dictionary it means a 'small courtyard attached to a dwelling house'.

Powered wheelchairs need not be registered or display number plates; they are also exempt from excise duty and from compulsory insurance requirements of the Road Traffic Act 1960. However users must consider suitable third-party insurance if the chair is to be used at regular times on pavements and crossing roads.

The Everest and Jennings powered wheelchair fitted with 'Dudley Controls' is the make usually issued to the tetraplegic at the National Spinal Injuries Centre. Some spinal centres prefer to issue the BEC powered wheelchair made by BEC Mobility Ltd. Both chairs can be fitted with different types of control, placed in whatever position allows the use of any remaining movements that the individual may have. Chairs have been adapted to electromechanical, electropneumatic, breathing, voice and even optical controls. For the majority, the electromechanical control, where the control box can be mounted either for hand, foot, chin or head use appears to be the most suitable.

Whatever type of powered wheelchair patients may have, reliability and safety are *essential*, more so if the user is left on his own for any length of time. Many of the problems concerning failure of these chairs can be attributed to a poor understanding of basic maintenance. Chairs need to be inspected weekly and the nuts and bolts tightened at regular intervals. Particular attention should be paid to the pulleys on the motor drive shafts, as these sometimes wear loose. Care should be given to the vertical bolt that locates the motor mounting on the chair frame. This should be maintained in a 'pinched tight' position, thus ensuring that the spring or fibre locking nuts are secure. They should not be overtight, for the slight movement of the motor allows the drive pulleys to align when the drive belt is under tension. The drive belts require adjustment from time to time and should be regularly checked for wear. Adjustment is made by turning the bar nuts on the motor mountings, having first released the locking nuts. Drive belts that are adjusted incorrectly are often the cause of excessive wear and are responsible for the chair's veering to one side when travelling. Later models of this chair which are gear-driven have eliminated most of these problems.

Batteries: The Everest and Jennings powered wheelchair is fitted with lead acid type batteries. These are filled with dilute sulphuric acid, which if allowed to come in contact with the skin or clothing will burn. Therefore *great care* must be taken when handling them. The acid level should be checked every second week. If it is found to be below the level of the plates, as seen through the filler caps, it should be topped up with *distilled water*. The plates should be covered by about 3mm ($\frac{1}{8}$in) of distilled water and no more. Over-filling will result in spillage when charging or handling. A proper battery filler spout can be obtained from most motor accessory shops. This fits to a bottle and will only allow 3mm of water to cover the plates. Distilled water can be purchased from most garages and accessory shops.

Where corrosion is found on terminals, the clamps should be removed and all traces thoroughly cleaned off. This is best achieved by soaking in boiling water, or thoroughly scrubbing with detergent. Before refitting the cleaned clamps, cover them and the battery posts with a light coating of lanolin ointment.

Charging batteries: New batteries should last three days or more without being re-charged if the chair is used under normal domestic circumstances. During the summer months and if the user lives in a hospital or institutional home, when the chair will be used more, charging will be required more frequently. Best results are obtained if the battery is allowed to run almost flat before charging. With the issued 5-amp charger, a charge for 12 hours from flat will be required. Overcharging will not extend the running time of the chair, it will only result in damage to the batteries. As batteries get older they will absorb less charge and will require more frequent topping-up with distilled water. Under normal conditions the average life span of batteries should be between 2 and 4 years, but this varies according to the make.

When the charger is connected to the chair, the needle of the ammeter should show a reading. If it remains at zero, there is a fault and the battery is not being charged. When this happens switch off the electricity supply immediately and check that the chair is switched to the top speed and the charging position, and that the terminals of the batteries are clean and making good contact. Check that the fuses of the plug, chair and charger are not blown (chair and charger fuses might be of the make-and-break contact type; the red buttons then only need to be pushed in), and check that the mains output socket is working.

If all these points are satisfactory, then something more serious may be wrong, requiring the attention of someone familiar with electrical circuits. Other faults with chairs might be connected with the motors or controls. These are complicated and should not be tampered with by an amateur. Contact your ALAC.

In the process of charging lead acid batteries, gases are given off which could be harmful in very confined spaces. To avoid this possible hazard, always ensure there is adequate ventilation when charging is in progress. It is also advisable to position the wheelchair where floor coverings will not be damaged in the event of acid spillage from the batteries.

As with ordinary chairs, patients having to use electrically powered chairs and who are in a financial position to purchase a second chair of their own would be well advised to do so. There are now many different makes to choose from, some of which are superior to those on issue through the NHS. Most other makes of powered wheelchairs can be purchased through the 'Motability

Scheme' by recipients of the Mobility Allowance (see p. 213).

While still in hospital, patients requiring a wheelchair of whatever type will have been assessed by the hospital's rehabilitation team for the most suitable make and model and this will have been prescribed initially by the consultant in charge. After discharge, if a new chair is required, it is not necessary to contact the consultant as general practitioners can prescribe chairs. In reality most ALACs will replace chairs if necessary, following inspection by their technical officer.

Wheelchair seat cushions

As an aid in the prevention of pressure sores, patients issued with wheelchairs are also supplied with a cushion on which to sit. These are supplied from your local ALAC. Cushions are produced in many different forms, and like wheelchairs, are supplied free of charge on the NHS but remain its property.

Regardless of the type of wheelchair cushion used, and there are some very sophisticated makes available, *no* cushion will totally eradicate the need to lift, or be lifted at regular intervals to relieve pressure. This point *must* be remembered.

The majority of patients who are fully able to lift themselves and who have sound pressure areas will normally be supplied with the standard latex foam sorbo-rubber cushion, measuring 45cm (18in) square by 10cm (4in) thick. The junior model is 40cm (16in) square by 10cm thick. Patients are advised not to sit on cushions of this type that are less than 10cm (4in) thick unless they are under medical supervision. Most will find this type of cushion satisfactory for normal daily use. But *beware*: ensure that you ask for *latex foam sorbo-rubber*. Some appliance centres have been issuing inferior synthetic foam-rubber types which are not so effective.

With regular daily use the sorbo-rubber cushion soon deteriorates, the rubber becomes soft and eventually compresses to a solid state under very little weight, thus increasing the risks of pressure sores forming. To reduce this risk cushions should be examined at regular weekly intervals and when they are found to be soft, they should be replaced. Under normal circumstances and providing care has been taken of cushions, they should last approximately 6 months. Their life can be extended by preventing them from getting wet and by removing them from wheelchairs overnight. This allows them to air, for they do tend to absorb moisture from the skin. When replacing a cushion in a wheelchair, turn it the other way about to ensure even wear.

Cushions should not be placed on hot pipes or close to open fires. Excessive heat will result in the rubber perishing. Minor wetness should be dried in sunlight, which also sterilises the cushion, or by leaving it in a drying room or airing cupboard. Should the cushion become soiled through a bowel accident it is best destroyed, for any attempt to wash it only rots the rubber.

There is often considerable delay in the supply of new cushions and they should therefore be ordered well in advance. In any case, a reserve cushion should always be available.

Gel-cushions

Tetraplegics and others unable to lift themselves, or those with pressure problems, may have to depend on alternative wheelchair cushions for the prevention of pressure sores. There are numerous different types of gel-cushion available. These are filled with a synthetic gel-type material designed to represent body fat. One such cushion, the Spenco Omega 5000 has been found to suit some patients and not others. Some patients prefer to sit on the gel-cushion by itself, while others find a 5cm (2in) thick foam-rubber cushion underneath more satisfactory.

Other makes of gel-cushion which are available from the ALAC, either on the recommendation of a hospital consultant or on prescription from the family doctor, include the Sumed, Seabird, Western Medical and the Aberdeen. I advise patients to try out the various types thoroughly whenever possible, before finally having one supplied.

Roho wheelchair cushion

To date I have not discovered a better cushion designed to prevent pressure sores than the American-made Roho. Made of a flexible but hard wearing rubber and formed into numerous individual interconnected yet free standing air cells, similar to 'bulb-like' inflatable balloons, the Roho cushion supports a patient evenly and comfortably by distributing the weight. I regularly sit for between 5 and 8 hours daily without being lifted and without adverse skin problems.

Unfortunately the Roho cushion is expensive as its cost is linked to the rate of exchange with the American dollar. Nevertheless, a limited number of cushions is available on a consultant's recommendation and these are obtainable from the DHSS at Blackpool via your own ALAC. The Roho may sometimes be obtained through local social services and the Manpower Services Commission.

With careful use Roho cushions should last for 4 years. The disadvantage of them is the fact that they can quite easily puncture, as has been discovered by patients who make several transfers during the course of a day. They do also tend to make the skin sweat.

New types of cushion are constantly being invented, the latest to appear in this country is the Jay cushion. Marketed by Tendacare, this cushion has a moulded base and includes a pad filled with fluid. The pad detaches from the base for individual use, perhaps in bed, in a car, or in an armchair. Like the Roho, the Jay cushion is expensive, but it may be prescribed on recommendation of a hospital consultant.

No matter what kind of cushion is used, there will, I repeat, always be pressure problems caused by body-weight. Some cushions may help reduce pressure to a minimum and when the individual is well padded with normal body fat and tissue, and has a good circulation, he might be under the impression that the particular type of cushion he is using is working efficiently for him. In actual fact it is his own natural bodily functions doing the work under ideal conditions. *So, always be on guard for signs of pressure.*

Sheepskins

Sheepskins continue to be successfully used by numerous patients in aiding the prevention of pressure sores. They also provide additional comfort for those patients with hypersensitive skin areas. Basically all they do is absorb moisture from the skin, which otherwise promotes redness, chafing and ultimate cracking of the skin. They also encourage circulation of air through the fleece which helps dry and cool the skin. Sheepskins can be used on top of a 10cm (4in) sorbo-rubber cushion when sitting, or, as many patients do, behind their backs to relieve pressure over prominent bones of the vertebral column. Sheepskins are also used successfully for lying on directly in bed.

Those who find them of benefit should remember that they do require regular washing as instructed by the suppliers, otherwise they soon become hard and matted and can only result in causing additional pressure. Sheepskins are available on the recommendation of a hospital consultant or general practitioner and are supplied through an appliance centre.

CRUTCHES, ORTHOSES (CALIPERS) AND WALKING STICKS

As part of medical rehabilitation, some patients, usually those with mid-thoracic and lower lesions, are taught to walk with the aid of orthoses (calipers) and crutches or walking sticks. The style of walking will vary depending on the level and extent of injury, but basically orthoses are worn to lock the knees and to keep the legs straight. Walking is then achieved by using the upper limbs together with the crutches or walking sticks which support and steady the trunk. This enables weight to be lifted off the legs either by tilting the pelvis and allowing alternate legs to move forward, or by swinging both legs through together.

Patients requiring orthoses and crutches or walking sticks, will have them measured to fit while in hospital. Crutches and sticks are frequently of the telescopic adjustable type and are a standard issue. Orthoses for paraplegics will be individually made. If difficulties are experienced, patients will need to have them adjusted by the original maker. The same applies to spinal braces, which may or may not include leg orthoses; these are often required by children and will require frequent and regular adjustment as the child grows up. If it is not possible to be seen by the original maker, then ask your ALAC for help and advice. Appliance centres should be contacted for all problems connected with crutches and walking sticks.

AVAILABLE FROM LOCAL SOCIAL SERVICES

BEDS

It is of prime importance for a paraplegic, and especially a tetraplegic, to have a suitable bed, not just for their own personal comfort and for the prevention of pressure sores, but also to facilitate easy access for attendants providing care. Social services departments are able to supply many different types for patients requiring a bed of the hospital type.

At the time when I was first discharged from hospital in 1965, spinal units generally suggested that paraplegics should sleep on a latex foam sorbo-rubber mattress at least 10cm (4in) thick. This was the standard type used on the old-fashioned spring-based hospital bed. Similar beds were, and I suspect still are, used in many boarding schools, army barracks and other institutional establishments.

In recent years hospitals have been equipped with modern sophisticated beds equipped with features such as variable height adjustment, which is of great value in transferring. Head-up or head-down positions for postoperative management; wind-up head sections for sitting up in bed; cot-sides to prevent falling out, plus a number of additional features. There also exist more elaborate electrically operated beds which will turn a patient from the back to the side at the touch of a button and will sit a patient up in the normal sitting position with the feet down. Besides this range of now almost standard hospital beds, there are others designed to nurse patients with specific problems such as severe pressure sores.

Personally, I consider that modern hospital beds are extremely hard and uncomfortable to lie on! Because of fire regulations (or so I am informed), the latex foam sorbo-rubber mattress was replaced by a synthetic rubber mattress, and the bed has a solid base. As a result of this they are not so effective in the prevention of pressure sores. To combat this the vast majority of paralysed people using a modern type of hospital bed, combine their use with either pillows, sheepskins, Roho mattress sections, a Ripple-mattress or Alpha-Pad.

Although all these beds are available through the local social services, a visit to the Disabled Living Foundation or one of the aids centres will give individuals the opportunity of seeing and trying the many different beds available.

In extreme cases where a paraplegic is very large and heavy to turn, or having problems with pressure sores, the Stoke

Mandeville Egerton electric turning bed can be supplied. This is usually done on the recommendation of a hospital consultant or the GP. These beds are large and require a big bedroom.

Many patients do not need to borrow a bed from the social services department, because they find their own to be quite satisfactory. Provided no problems are experienced regarding pressure, an ordinary bed with a good quality interior spring mattress is perfectly acceptable and often more comfortable. Tetraplegics purchasing their own bed, should choose one which will enable the legs of a hoist to go under it.

Couples wishing to sleep in a double bed, may, under certain circumstances, have one supplied by the social services. They might, however, be expected to contribute half the cost. Double beds are available in an assortment of designs, some providing electrically operated sit-up facilities (p. 199).

MATTRESSES

There are several additional mattress aids available which are specifically designed to reduce the effects of pressure, and the formation of sores. Whereas many patients train themselves to wake and turn over every three or four hours, many paraplegics and tetraplegics have difficulty in doing this and rather than call for help during the night they sleep on an additional mattress which is placed on top of their existing one. The large cell Ripple-mattress and the Alpha-Pad are both effective in the relief of pressure. Both have mains-operated electric pumps. (This should be remembered in the event of power failures.) One disadvantage of these mattresses is that they can puncture. Cells of the Ripple-mattress can be replaced; the whole Alpha-Pad has to be replaced should it become punctured – yet the Alpha-Pad is considerably less expensive. Those using an Alpha-Pad should always have a spare one available.

In recent years some of the spinal units have started to use the Vaperm mattress as the standard one on which to nurse their patients. This mattress should be used without a draw sheet or additional pillows on which to lie but it does *not* eliminate the need for regular turning. The mattress has proved to be most successful and is also available through the social services. The Vaperm mattress is manufactured by Beauvale Medical, Hallam Fields Road, Ilkeston, Derbyshire DE7 4BO.

HOISTS

In many cases, particularly when the patient is tetraplegic, very heavy or spastic, it may be necessary for relatives or attendants to use a hoist to transfer the patient in and out of his chair, bed, bath or car (Figs. 10/1 and 10/2). Hoists are also of great value in lifting someone off the floor should he accidentally fall from his wheel-chair or bed.

There are many different makes available, either mechanically, hydraulically or electrically operated. Choice of type will depend on circumstances. Many disabled people are able to live on their own with the aid of an electrically operated hoist such as the Wessex. This hoist can be fitted to an overhead rail system for carrying the patient suspended, from bathroom to bedroom for example. Other smaller mechanical or hydraulically operated hoists can be wheeled from one room to another with the patient suspended in it, which is useful for getting in and out of the bath and returning to bed. This type of hoist requires an attendant to operate it.

There are no hard and fast rules regarding the type of hoist, other than those which use a sling. The correct sling should be of the one-piece hammock type. The two-piece sling is dangerous: the patient might be unable to hold on, may spasm and then fall out. The inherent disadvantage of the one-piece hammock sling is that, on being lowered into the wheelchair, it has to be left under the buttocks, tucking it around the sides of the cushion. Users tell me that this causes no problem. Alternatively, I believe a more completely satisfactory sling to use is the divided-leg sling. This sling is in one piece but can be removed from under the patient after he is lowered into the wheelchair. I have one of these slings which I use with the Oxford hoist as an emergency back-up to doing standing transfers.

Patients requiring a hoist should contact their local social ser-vices or community nurse who will then make the necessary arrangements to obtain a suitable model. Tetraplegics unable to transfer unaided should always have a hoist, regardless of whether

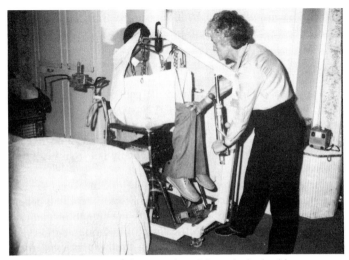

Fig. 10/1 The author being transferred from the bed to his wheelchair, by his wife. *Note* she pushes him backward on the knees while lowering him into the chair

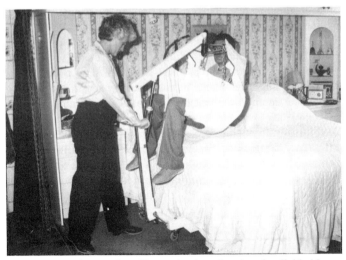

Fig. 10/2 As the previous illustration but showing the divided leg sling which can be removed once in the chair

or not it is normally used. In the event of an emergency, when for example your attendant has strained her back, it will prove invaluable.

Special hoists which are fixed to the roof of the car, such as the Burville car top hoist, may also be used to transfer patients in and out of the vehicle. There are several models commercially available. The Disabled Living Foundation and other aids centres display numerous hoists, ready for patients and relatives to try.

COMMODES AND SHOWER-CHAIRS

In circumstances where toilets are inaccessible, or when there is difficulty in using a lavatory, many paraplegics find that a commode chair in the bedroom or bathroom is of great benefit. One young lady I know keeps a commode in her parents' garage to use when she is visiting because their toilet is totally inaccessible to her. Many commode chairs can also be used as shower-chairs, such as the one produced by Everest and Jennings. These may prove more satisfactory than many normal shower-chairs which often have no footrests making it difficult for those with spasms (Fig. 10/3).

Commodes are available through the social services and further information about them can be obtained from your spinal centre, Disabled Living Foundation or nearest aids centre.

AVAILABLE FROM COMMUNITY NURSING SERVICES

Besides the personal help and advice which the community nurse is able to provide to patients and their families, she is also able to supply patients with numerous items as part of daily care. Services do vary from area to area, but generally the community nurse can supply the following: paper incontinence sheets, incontinence padding rolls, plastic pants and incontinence liners, bladder washout and catheter changing packs, urinals, dressing and indeed most other nursing aids. Community nurses may offer advice over the type of bed, mattress and hoist that patients use, and will often

Fig. 10/3   The specially built shower unit in the author's home. *Note* the fall of the floor to take water away via the central drain. The chair was made by Linido and supplied by Amilake Ltd through the social services

make representation to the GP, social services, or hospital authorities on their patient's behalf.

AVAILABLE FROM GENERAL PRACTITIONERS (GPs)

The GP prescribes all drugs, medications and other aids listed in the drug tariff. A family doctor suddenly confronted with the requirements of a paraplegic may not always be familiar in prescribing many of the listed items. It is, therefore, essential for patients to be aware of what they are entitled to, and one way of finding this out is by talking to your local pharmacist. Alternatively make a point of learning about your entitlements before leaving hospital and through joining the Spinal Injuries Association who will keep you updated through their regular newsletter.

The GP is able to prescribe all equipment necessary for bladder and bowel management including catheters, urine collecting bags, condoms, disposable plastic gloves, cotton wool (hospital quality) and cellulose wadding. Interestingly, they are the only prescribers of skin adhesives for condom application.

As has been indicated previously, the GP can prescribe elastic stockings wheelchairs and seat cushions. He may also be required to issue medical certificates and carry out examinations for insurance purposes in relation to driving and other domestic requirements.

AVAILABLE ON RECOMMENDATION FROM A HOSPITAL CONSULTANT

Hospital consultants have considerable powers to recommend special items of equipment to patients with special needs. One example is the Roho wheelchair seat cushion. To obtain one of these cushions on the NHS a letter of recommendation from a hospital consultant must be sent, with your request, to your local ALAC. This is then processed and forwarded to DHSS Blackpool. Hospital consultants may also recommend specially adapted and powered wheelchairs, as well as beds not normally available. They are also able to recommend sophisticated electronic environmental control systems, such as POSSUM, communication systems, reading equipment and indeed many computerised electronic aids that are now commercially available.

Consultants can recommend almost anything on health grounds for their patients that are commercially made, which then automatically exempts the purchase from VAT. Such items could include air-conditioning, extra heating appliances, electric fans and indeed many other items not listed under VAT exemption.

Consultants are asked to represent patients over medical insurance compensation claims, which will require them to carry out examinations and prepare medical reports for counsel. A fee is normally charged for this work.

AIDS AND EQUIPMENT AVAILABLE FROM
THE PRIVATE SECTOR

The whole subject of aids and equipment to help disabled people gain greater independence is now big business and quite outside the scope of this book. Aids vary from the simple walking stick to extremely expensive computerised and electronic equipment for the more severely disabled like POSSUM as previously mentioned.

Being suddenly confronted with physical disability, either as a patient, friend or relative, there is a natural desire to look around for aids and gadgets that might widen the disabled person's horizon. Long before the stage of getting out of bed into a wheelchair is reached, many families blindly consider buying this and that, changing their cars, altering their houses, believing their disabled relative will need all these things for survival. I can even recall one family who went to the length of having electrically-operated doors fitted to their house within 10 weeks of their 20-year-old son's becoming paraplegic. All they really required was to have the doors made wider and the latch and lock lowered. That particular family could have saved themselves a lot of money if only they had waited until their son had got up in his wheelchair and discovered what he could or could not do.

This is precisely the key to the whole problem and much private and NHS money could be saved on aids and equipment that are totally unnecessary and never used. And here I must say how amazed I am when I hear of the totally unnecessary amount of equipment prescribed to patients by their doctors. Examples ranging from a general practitioner who prescribed a new GU suprapubic bag ('kipper') for his paraplegic patient every week, to another paraplegic with perfectly normal strong arms and sound pressure areas, who persuaded his GP to get a local consultant – who had never seen the patient – to prescribe a Roho seat cushion just because the man felt it would be better than his usual cushion.

Apart from making basic house alterations and providing essential aids such as a suitable bed, my advice is to postpone buying extra aids and equipment until after the disabled person has been discharged and has had time to explore his limitations.

Fig. 10/4   The author's desk! Everything visible: Apple computer, Olivetti Praxis 35 daisy-wheel printer, telephone connected to the tape recorder, the light and the fan can be controlled fully with various mouth sticks

When it comes to the purchase of high technology and expensive equipment such as computers, communicators, page-turners, specialised environmental control systems, families would greatly benefit by seeking help and advice from someone highly recommended and experienced in assessing the capabilities of disabled people (Fig. 10/4). One such person, Roger Jefcoate, is the

only independent consultant adviser for aids and equipment in the
UK. He has had many years of experience in assessing patients
with numerous disabilities and offering practical advice and assistance on specific needs to handicapped people from all walks of life.

FURTHER READING

The Directory for the Disabled. This is a wide-ranging reference
   book which is up-dated annually. Edited by Derek Kinrade and
   Ann Darnbrough, it is published by Woodhead-Faulkner
   Limited, Cambridge.
REMAP Yearbook. Published by RADAR, 25 Mortimer Street,
   London W1N 8AB. Up-dated annually.
Equipment for the Disabled: Personal Care, 5th edition. Published
   by Mary Marlborough Lodge, Nuffield Orthopaedic Centre,
   Oxford.
Jay, P (1983). *Choosing the Best Wheelchair Cushion for Your Needs,
   Your Chair and Your Lifestyle*. Royal Association for Disability
   and Rehabilitation, London.
Jay, P. (1983). *Wheelchair Cushions*. Report to the DHSS Aids
   Assessment Programme. HMSO, London.

USEFUL ADDRESSES

Roger Jefcoate
Willowbrook, Swanbourne Road
Mursley, Milton Keynes MK17 0JA   (Mursley) 029672 533

Disabled Living Foundation (DLF)
380–384 Harrow Road
London W9 2HU   01–289 6111

The following is a selection of manufacturers of aids and equipment, most of which have been mentioned in the chapter. There
are many more, and the interested reader is advised to contact the
DLF (address above) who will be able to advise further. They can
also put paraplegics and/or their families in touch with the nearest
aids centre to their home.

BEDS AND MATTRESSES

Egerton Hospital Equipment Limited
Tower Hill, Horsham,
West Sussex RH13 7JT
0403 53800
> *Produce a number of electrically operated beds, including a turning, stand-up and sit-up bed. Equipment can be hired or purchased*

J. Nesbit Evans & Co. Limited
Unit 8, Woods Bank Trading Estate
Woden Road West, Wednesbury
West Midlands WS10 7BL
021–556 1511
> *Electrically operated sit-up or lie-down 'Home Care Bed'*

Hoskins Limited
Upper Trinity Street
Birmingham B9 4EQ
021–773 1144
> *Produce the K.F. International bed and other hospital furniture*

Huntleigh Medical Limited
Bilton Way, Dallow Road
Luton, Bedfordshire LU1 1UU
0582 413104
> *Makers of the Alphabed Bubble Pad*

HOISTS

The Wessex Medical Equipment Company Limited
Unit Two, Budds Lane Industrial Estate
Romsey, Hampshire SO5 0HA
0794 518246
> *Produce the Wessex electrically operated hoist, internal lift and electrically operated door-opening device*

F. J. Payne (Manufacturing) Limited
Stanton Harcourt Road
Eynsham, Oxford OX8 1HY
0865 881881
> *Produce the Oxford and Isis hoists*

SHOWER UNITS

J. W. Swain Plastics Limited
Byron Street, Buxton
Derbyshire SK17 6LY
0298 2365
> *Makers of the Invadex showering system which fits to existing*
> *floor levels*

TOILET AIDS

Clos-O-Mat (Great Britain) Limited
2 Brooklands Road
Sale, Cheshire M33 3SS
061–973 6262
> *Suppliers of the excellent Samoa automatic WC. Combines*
> *facility of WC and bidet. Of great value to the female paraplegic*
> *and tetraplegic*

Southern Sanitary Specialists Limited
Cerdic House, West Portway
Andover, Hampshire SP10 3LF
0264 24131
> *Manufacture an excellent wide range of grab and handrails for*
> *any application – bath, toilet, shower, etc*

WHEELCHAIRS

Carters (J & A) Limited
Alfred Street, Westbury
Wiltshire BA13 3DZ
0373 822203
> *Makers of E & J wheelchairs supplied by National Health*
> *Service*

Everest and Jennings
Princewood Road
Corby, Northants NN17 2DK
0536 67661
Suppliers of a wide range of powered and self-propelled wheelchairs

Myera-Rehab UK
Millshaw Park Avenue
Leeds LS11 0LR
0532 776060
Manufacturers of powered and self-propelled wheelchairs

SML Aids Limited
Bath Place, High Street
Barnet, Herts EN5 5XE
01–440 6522
*Produce the 'Levo' stand-up wheelchair. Expensive, but excellent
to widen your range of action, and of great value in relieving
pressure areas. Also supply a wide range of other aids, hoists and
commodes*

Vessa Limited
Paper Mill Lane
Alton, Hampshire GU34 2PY
0420 83294
Provide a wide range of powered and self-propelled wheelchairs

Falcon Research and Development Co
109 Inverness Drive East
Englewood
Colorado 80112 U S A
*Manufacture powered reclining wheelchair systems that enable
users to recline themselves automatically*

WHEELCHAIR SEAT CUSHIONS

Tendercare Products Limited
London Road, Ashington
West Sussex RH20 3JP
0903 892825
Suppliers of the Jay wheelchair cushion

Raymar, Hodgkinson and Corby Limited
PO Box 16
Henley on Thames, Oxon RG9 1AG
0491 578446
  Distributors of Roho wheelchair cushions and mattresses

IMPORTANT NOTE: At the time of going to press Roho wheel-chair cushions were no longer available for NHS prescription. The matter was under view and it is suggested that any reader wishing to know the up-to-date position should contact the Spinal Injuries Association (p. 162).

11.   Work, Play, Education and Holidays

Employment for both paraplegic and tetraplegic patients is not always easy to find. Frequently further education and training in a new occupation are necessary. To help patients find suitable employment, a disablement resettlement officer (DRO) is available to give advice and possibly to arrange special training courses. In most cases the DRO will visit patients before they are discharged from hospital, otherwise full details of this service can be obtained from the local employment office or job centre.

Employment for paraplegics is obviously less difficult to obtain than it is for tetraplegics. During a research project into employment for tetraplegics in which I was involved during the early 1970s, however, we were delighted to discover the wide range of full and part-time occupations being undertaken. Naturally present-day circumstances have changed, yet many of the jobs people were doing were the result of their own determination and ingenuity, and with the advent of the computer together with all the other modern sophisticated electronic wizardry currently available – if patients are really determined – then somewhere there is something most patients can undertake. The report on this research project, *Employment for Tetraplegics*, was published by the National Fund for Research into Crippling Diseases, who were sponsors for the research.

The late Sir Ludwig Guttmann has been quoted as saying that his interpretation of fully rehabilitated paraplegics was to see them again as taxpayers. How appropriate his words were when you consider the vast sums of taxpayers' money spent on health care.

Naturally not every spinal injury patient will be capable of, or need to, return to employment. Much depends upon age, extent and location of injury, domestic circumstances and financial requirements. Nevertheless, employment is not just a means of earning money. Indeed quite often this is the last consideration. Employment provides a feeling of self-satisfaction and independence, of being able to compete with able-bodied members of society, of responsibility, pride and social status.

RECREATION

Recreational activities, both within the home and hospital, are important to prevent the boredom which frequently arises through restricted physical activities. During a patient's stay in hospital, the daily routine is often so demanding that little consideration is given to recreation after discharge. Most patients will admit that after discharge there is a period of inactivity when sheer boredom is experienced. This is due to the sudden switch from a very active and busy hospital routine filled with physiotherapy, swimming, sport, occupational therapy and social functions to days at home when all one has to consider is personal management.

Recreational activities are of course restricted to a certain degree, and more so for tetraplegics. There are, however, many activities that can be carried out from a wheelchair with ease. Gardening, bird watching, fishing and photography are varied examples of outside activities which are popular among disabled people. Expeditions to concerts, theatres, museums, art galleries and cinemas are possible; and active participation in amateur dramatics, a choir or playing a musical instrument can also be enjoyed from a wheelchair. But perhaps after a prolonged hospital stay, the younger generation of patients will prefer their recreation in a pub or disco, whereas others may enjoy the luxury of fine restaurants. At home there are numerous sedentary pursuits to keep a patient occupied. In the first instance the home micro-computer provides a vast range of video-games. There is further education and study, carpentry and metal-work, painting or craft work, chess or draughts. The possibilities are too many to list here (see p. 233).

SPORT

Sport as an extension to the medical rehabilitation of paraplegic patients was introduced by Sir Ludwig Guttmann during his early pioneer days at Stoke Mandeville Hospital. His aim was to use the medium of sport to strengthen non-paralysed parts of the body and to create comradeship between disabled people. In countless cases the sporting medium has played an important role in social acceptance, adjustment and resettlement for all kinds of disabled people (Fig. 11/1).

Fig. 11/1   Two paraplegic fencers in combat. *Note* how the wheelchairs are retained in a specially constructed frame, which also allows them to be correctly adjusted apart via the central adjusting gear

Since those early days, sport for the disabled has become recognised the world over as being a first class method of keeping fit, promoting understanding between disabled people, and encouraging medical and paramedical staff to improve standards of care for the disabled.

Today there is a world-wide paraplegic sports movement which meets and partakes as part of the Olympic Games. Throughout the UK, and indeed most other countries, sports clubs and holiday centres are now able to offer a wide range of sporting activities including archery, table-tennis, basket-ball, fencing, shooting, snooker and billiards, swimming, sailing, field events, and track and road racing just to mention a few. There are many organisations offering paraplegics further information (see p. 234).

EDUCATION

The interruption of education through spinal injury sometimes creates extreme difficulties for patients trying to catch up with their studies. Children below the compulsory school leaving age will be provided with educational facilities during their hospital stay and whenever possible after discharge will return to their former school. A free leaflet *Should I Be In a Special School* and available from the Advisory Centre for Education (ACE), 18 Victoria Park Square, London E2 9BP, explains the rights of children, who are already in special schools, to be educated in ordinary schools under the Education Act 1981.

Further, and advanced, education, which may be necessary for the paraplegic to gain employment, is available throughout the country for disabled people generally. Many universities, technical colleges, polytechnics, art colleges, etc, offer special accommodation to disabled students and indeed have provided infinite facilities for their general well-being. But perhaps the most uncomplicated way to continue studying after becoming disabled, is from the comfort of one's own home. Many educational establishments, including the Open University, offer excellent correspondence courses (see p. 230).

HOLIDAYS

Finding a suitable place to go on holiday can sometimes be a nightmare for disabled people, with or without a family. There are so many considerations involved, most of which revolve around the degree of disability. Nowadays there are many organisations offering advice and information on a wide range of alternative holidays both in the British Isles and overseas. In addition many paraplegics write about their experiences of particular holidays in the Spinal Injuries Association's newsletter for general information (see p. 162).

Taking a holiday in one's own country may prove less traumatic should there be medical problems. Overseas travel does demand good health, for it may prove impossible to obtain health insurance, although this should not prove a problem in a European country that has a reciprocal health agreement. Full details of obtaining reciprocal health treatment in an EEC country can be found in the leaflet *Medical Costs Abroad* which is available from DHSS offices. All the same, a thorough medical and dental check-up is advised before venturing abroad.

For a holiday overseas, items involving electrical voltage must be considered, especially if Ripple or Alpha mattresses are being taken, and in particular for re-charging the batteries of radio-linked bladder implants and shavers, etc. I do advise any paraplegic travelling abroad to contact his spinal centre in advance to find out the whereabouts of the nearest *specialist* spinal unit in the country to be visited. Some general hospitals overseas are not adequately equipped to provide specialist care and, particularly if you cannot speak the language fluently and are paralysed, there may be problems.

Since becoming paralysed I have been abroad four times on holiday with my wife. We have visited France twice, Switzerland and Holland. On each occasion we have motored, stopping off at motels en route whenever necessary. In 1985 we made our most adventurous trip by motoring 850 miles to the south of France with only one overnight stop at Auxerre, a very exhausting journey especially for one driver.

On two previous visits we had stayed with friends, but on this occasion we reserved accommodation in a complex of self-catering apartments in Hyères, near Toulon. Bookings were arranged through a British travel agent – Westbury Travel of Wiltshire, who were most helpful in establishing the suitability of the apartment for a wheelchair. The agents assured us that many wheelchair dependent people had stayed in these apartments; even with such assurance it is advisable to obtain a detailed floor plan to ensure reasonable access. Travel by road in France and indeed most other European countries is relatively simple for the disabled visitor providing careful research and planning are carried out well in advance. French tourist offices, found in all towns, have brochures which mark all hotels suitable for a wheelchair. Their definition of suitability may not tally with yours, but at least the field is narrowed when looking about for a place to stay.

Travel by road for the dependent tetraplegic is usually the most convenient mode of travel especially when considering the volume of luggage and equipment that it is necessary to take, yet many tetraplegics successfully fly with scheduled airways and hire a car at the other end. When travelling by road it is *essential* that your car is thoroughly serviced before departure. Take an adequate selection of tools to make minor repairs to both car and wheelchair, including a tyre pressure gauge – some French gauges are not always very accurate. A spare fan belt plus a spare set of light bulbs, which are compulsory in France, should also be taken.

Although fully comprehensive motoring insurance policies provide minimal insurance cover when visiting EEC countries, visitors are advised to take out 'Green Card' insurance cover, so should contact their insurance company well in advance for advice. I strongly recommend anybody motoring in Europe also to take out adequate motoring insurance through either the Automobile Association or the Royal Automobile Club. Both organisations provide similar schemes that provide comprehensive cover in the event of accident, breakdown and illness that will either get you back on the road or safely home. Membership of either organisation is not mandatory to obtain cover. The information concerning the various countries to be visited, which is provided when joining such schemes, is invaluable.

The next consideration when visiting Europe is how and where to cross the Channel. This is mainly dictated by the country to be visited and the geographical point of access. Various companies operate similar car ferries and there is also a hovercraft ferry. All ferries require passengers to travel on an upper deck thus making it necessary to transfer out of the car into the wheelchair. In previous years we have crossed with Sealink from Newhaven to Dieppe and from Harwich to the Hook of Holland. This year for a change we elected to go from Dover to Calais with Townsend Thoresen. The other alternative was the hovercraft service, but for the high lesion tetraplegic this is not suitable because it necessitates being carried up narrow stairs from the car deck and to sit in an ordinary passenger seat.

The cost of crossing the Channel varies enormously and is frequently included with the travel agent's charges for accommodation. Disabled drivers who are members of one of the disabled drivers organisations may well qualify for free Channel crossings provided that bookings are made through the disabled drivers' organisation and not the travel agent. The majority of ferries operating are equipped with adequate lifts to take the wheelchair user from the car deck to the passenger decks. However it is always a wise precaution to write directly to the ferry company concerned to confirm the availability of suitable lifts and to confirm that a wheelchair user will be travelling. For example, the lift as fitted to one of Sealink's ships on the Newhaven to Dieppe crossing is so small that it is necessary to remove the wheelchair's footrests and tuck the legs underneath. My wife has then to stand on the wheelchair's armrests before there is room for the door to close. The lift finally exits in the ship's galley. The French ship on the same crossing has no lift at all – thus making it necessary to be carried up three flights of steep stairs by brawny French sailors!

The Newhaven crossing takes 3 hours compared with 75 minutes from Dover. Yet it was our experience that the Dover crossing was too quick. There was insufficient time to eat, visit the bank and duty-free shops amid the stampede of day trippers and other passengers fighting to get their duty-free benefits. Loading arrangements on both crossings were excellent and the ships' crews most helpful. A final note of warning – do not take laxatives until you have safely docked – quite often sailings are delayed, which could prove embarrassing.

Throughout Europe and indeed many other parts of the world various chains of motels and hotels exist, the majority of which have accommodation specifically set aside for disabled travellers. The accommodation includes a fully accessible toilet and bathroom with suitably fitted wash-hand basin and handrails. Bedrooms comprise a double as well as a single bed, although they tend to be slightly low for easy transfers, but not impossible. Two such chains that we have stayed in – Novotel and Mercure – provide extremely comfortable accommodation, first class food and a degree of luxury. They are slightly expensive but most certainly good value knowing that they are accessible. Within the hotels there are ramps to all facilities. Brochures listing the vast range of Novotel and Mercure motels and hotels throughout the entire world can be obtained by writing to 55/57 Harrow Road, London W2 1JH, or by telephoning 01–724 2140.

Regular and frequent stops are necessary for both the able-bodied as well as the disabled traveller. The prevention of pressure sores and the intake of fluids must not be overlooked. Consequently we always stop every 3 hours to empty my urinal and stretch across the front seats to relieve pressure. The movement of the car itself greatly reduces the likelihood of pressure sores forming, and as a result of this I have found it totally unnecessary to sit on anything other than a sheepskin.

A comprehensive medical kit and an ample supply of drugs and equipment to treat unexpected problems is advised when travelling overseas. It was June when we visited the south of France and the temperature was 76°F (25°C). The direct sun combined with the sea breeze easily burned the skin. Suntan oil and a straw hat were essential, as was my water spray to keep cool. It was also necessary to keep my hands covered from direct sunlight – they did in fact get burnt. The mosquitoes were plentiful and a repellent as well as antihistamine drugs were essential. Although we were assured the tap water was suitable for drinking, it is advisable to stick to bottled drinking water. In any case, a suitable drug for the treatment of diarrhoea should also be taken. Besides the normal range of medications an individual person might be taking, it is advisable also to take an antibiotic which might prove suitable in the event of urinary or respiratory infection. It should also be mentioned that when visiting hot climates, glycerol suppositories melt quite easily, consequently they are best kept in a cold box or refrigerator. Before going abroad your family doctor is the best person to consult concerning the drugs and medications that should be carried.

Prevention of pressure sores is a vital consideration when sleeping in unfamiliar surroundings. Fortunately on this occasion I took my Roho mattress and levelling pad, for the bed provided was far from ideal. I also had taken two extra double pillows and a spare 4-inch sorbo-rubber wheelchair cushion as a back-up for the wheelchair Roho, all of which proved essential in obtaining a comfortable and pressure free position in which to lie.

A comprehensive understanding of the language is an obvious asset when holidaying abroad. To supplement any shortcomings a phrase book or dictionary is essential, as was our short wave radio receiver with which we could tune into the BBC World Service in English. Another vital aid is an international power point adaptor which can be adjusted to fit foreign sockets. Another useful but non-essential aid was an individual cup boiler. This proved most useful to boil mugs of water for tea or coffee especially when staying in the motels.

Naturally anybody visiting a foreign country immediately wants to eat the local foods. In most instances no harm will result. Yet a large number of people do go down with gastric upsets, which can be disastrous for the paraplegic. My advice therefore is to choose restaurants carefully, thus ensuring the food is well cooked, and to introduce the local specialities into your diet gradually. When buying food, ensure it is bought from a reputable shop rather than the street vendors – foodstuffs 'go off' very quickly in hot climates. By following these simple guide-lines I have avoided problems.

Always inform as many people as possible where you will be staying. And it's not a bad idea to inform your local spinal centre of your movements. Rescue services are very efficient in the event of accident or illness; these will be greatly enhanced if people know your whereabouts. It is also a good idea to wear an SOS bracelet (available from most jeweller's shops) which holds all your personal details, in case of emergency. Finally, always leave your wheelchair easily accessible when packing the car.

FURTHER READING

Adaptations of Jobs and Employment of the Disabled. Published by, and obtainable from, International Labour Office, Marsham Street, London SW1 4JG.

Fallon, B. (1979). *Able to Work*. Spinal Injuries Association, London.

Johnson, J. *Working at Home*. Penguin Books, Harmondsworth.

Lansdale, S. and Walker, A. *A Right to Work. Disability and Employment*. Low Pay Unit and Disability Alliance, London.

Saunders, P. (1984). *Micros for the Handicapped*. Helena Press, Whitby, Yorkshire.

Guttmann, L. (1976). *Textbook of Sport for the Disabled*. (H.M. & M. Publishers) John Wiley, Chichester.

Water Sports for the Disabled. (1977). The Sports Council Advisory Panel on Water Sports for the Disabled, London.

Croucher, N. (1981). *Outdoor Pursuits for Disabled People*. Woodhead-Faulkner, Cambridge.

Holidays for the Physically Handicapped. RADAR, London. This book is up-dated annually. It is available through W. H. Smith bookshops.

12. Transport

The ability and freedom to travel from A to B, either for business or pleasure, are equally important, but often very much more difficult for the disabled traveller than for the able-bodied person. In most cases the disabled are able to travel in exactly the same transport as that provided for the general public, although special thought may need to be given to suitability, adaptations and modifications, time of journey and advance bookings.

Transport can be divided into two groups, public and privately owned. In relation to transport and travel for the paraplegic, transport includes travel by road, rail, air and to a lesser extent sea. This chapter relates to the more common methods of transport suitable to paraplegics, and because there are so many organisations and publications specifically concerned with this subject, it is intended only to provide guidance.

PRIVATE TRANSPORT

The privately owned motor vehicle is undoubtedly the commonest and most satisfactory method of transport for the paraplegic. It is an almost essential, if not vital, part of the basic necessary equipment required.

In an attempt to provide a wide range of help to all disabled people, the DHSS has introduced a tax free Mobility Allowance linked with the cost of living. How the recipient of the Mobility Allowance uses the cash benefit (paid at 4-weekly intervals in arrears) in relation to transport, is entirely up to the individual concerned. It can be used to purchase a train or bus ticket, pay a taxi fare, or saved up to purchase an air or sea ticket to the other side of the world. Most people use the benefit towards the purchase and running expenses of a motor vehicle.

To obtain the Mobility Allowance, application has to be made on Form No. NI 211 available from the DHSS. The basic criterion in qualifying for Mobility Allowance is the inability to walk, or being virtually unable to walk. You must be aged between 5 and under 66, yet the allowance continues to be paid until the age of 75. The applicant must be able to go out, that is to say, you must be sufficiently physically fit to make use of the allowance. This in reality prevents a newly injured person from qualifying for the allowance before they reach the stage in rehabilitation of being able to go out of hospital, if only for daily outings. Full details concerning qualification are included with the application form.

To help recipients of a Mobility Allowance to gain maximum value for money, a voluntary organisation has been set up at the initiative of the Government called Motability. It has negotiated special terms and conditions with the manufacturers of certain motor vehicles and wheelchairs, insurance brokers and in addition banks have agreed to finance special hire purchase and leasing schemes through a finance company specially established for the purpose. The company is Mobility Finance Limited, Tabard House, 166 Southwark Street, London SE1 OTA.

The Motability organisation assists people in receipt of the Mobility Allowance to lease, or buy a new car on hire purchase. Hire purchase can be arranged over a four-and-a-half-year period, and paid for by assigning the Mobility Allowance to Motability. The choice of car is limited; whenever possible Motability will endeavour to obtain a vehicle not normally supplied. Advantages of purchasing a vehicle are that at the end of the hire purchase period you will own the car. There are no mileage charges, but you are required to pay for your own maintenance and servicing. Leasing a vehicle also requires the Mobility Allowance to be assigned to the Motability company and the lease is for a three-year period. Leasing has the advantage that the company is responsible for maintenance and servicing, but there are additional mileage charges for each mile over 10,000 a year. The disadvantages are that you will never actually own the car – it must be returned after the three years, also the range of cars available is limited. In both cases insurance is an extra cost which individuals have to pay.

Motability also offer a scheme for the purchase of a used car, subject to many regulations. Basically the used car must be under four years old, have done less than 40,000 miles and it must be inspected by the Automobile Association.

In addition to the purchase or the leasing of motor vehicles, Motability offer a hire purchase scheme run on similar lines which enables recipients of the Mobility Allowance to purchase one of a wide range of powered and other wheelchairs. Full details of this and the complete range of help available from Motability can be obtained by writing to: Motability, Boundary House, 91–93 Charterhouse Street, London EC1M 6BT (01–253 1211).

VEHICLE EXCISE DUTY

Normally, recipients of a mobility allowance are automatically exempt from paying Vehicle Excise Duty (Car Road Tax), and will be sent an exemption certificate by the DHSS. When in receipt of this, it should be sent to your vehicle licensing office together with registration documents, certificate of insurance and excise duty renewal form. Certain groups of people not in receipt of Mobility Allowance may also be entitled to exemption from Vehicle Excise Duty; full particulars may be obtained by writing to: Disablement Services Branch, Department of Health and Social Security, Block 1, Government Buildings, Warbreck Hill Road, Blackpool FY2 0UZ.

DRIVING LICENCE

Anyone who held a driving licence before injury and wishes to continue driving following rehabilitation, must notify the Driver and Vehicle Licensing Centre if the disability is going to last for more than three months and if it is likely to affect their ability to drive. The Licensing Centre will then review the position and will probably require a medical report; they will not necessarily withdraw your licence, but since October 1984 regulations exist which require you to take another driving test.

DRIVING TUITION

The British School of Motoring (BSM) offer driving instruction to people with all kinds of disability. To make an appointment at their centre, to arrange for their consultant to visit you at your home, or for further information, write to: The Disabled Driver Training Centre, BSM Specialist Services Ltd, 81–87 Hartfield Road, Wimbledon, London SW19 3TJ (01–540 8262).

An alternative to the BSM is Banstead Place Mobility Centre, Park Road, Banstead, Surrey SM7 3EE (07373 56222) who offer driving instruction and assessment, plus specialist conversion facilities to suit the more severely disabled driver.

HAND CONTROLS

Practically any type of car, be it sports or saloon, can be converted to hand controls to suit the paraplegic driver. Tetraplegic drivers will obviously have a more limited choice and in most cases will have to depend on vehicles fitted with automatic transmission. Tetraplegics with spinal cord lesions above the level of C6 will have great difficulty in driving vehicles fitted with internal combustion engines, a few have managed to drive electrically-powered vehicles, but generally speaking it is the level of injury which is the deciding factor as to whether a person can or cannot learn to drive.

There are specialist companies producing hand controls of various types to suit different disabilities and types of motor vehicle. Some of the larger firms offer nationwide and overseas service. I suggest that potential drivers contact these firms for their advice before purchasing a particular car that requires conversion (see p. 226).

CAR BADGE SCHEME (ORANGE PARKING BADGE)

The car badge scheme for disabled drivers and passengers was introduced in December 1971 and entitles people with defects of the spine or central nervous system, or those dependent on the use of wheelchairs, or those who have difficulty walking, to certain parking concessions. These include indefinite periods of free parking at meters and in areas where time limits apply, but the holder of a parking badge cannot park somewhere that might cause an obstruction and expect the authorities not to take action. Details of the scheme can be found through application to local social services departments. The scheme is valid throughout England, Scotland and Wales except the following areas of central London: the City of London, the City of Westminster, the London Borough of Camden south of and including Euston Road, and the Royal Borough of Kensington and Chelsea. If you live in one of these areas, you can apply for an orange badge for use elsewhere, as well as the special local badge. Local badges are only valid in the borough where they are issued. A nominal charge for the orange and special local badges will be made.

MOTORING ORGANISATIONS

All disabled people, whether drivers or passengers, would be well advised to join one or more of the motoring organisations who can offer assistance in the event of accidents, breakdowns, or simply general information about all aspects of motoring. Membership of organisations specialising in the needs of disabled drivers and passengers makes available a considerable range of concessions, including reductions when crossing the English Channel with most ferry operators. The full range of benefits obtained by joining one or more of the motoring organisations can be obtained by writing to them direct (see p. 225).

CAR HIRE

In America it has been possible to hire cars specially fitted with hand controls for the disabled traveller for some time. In Great Britain, Hertz have become the first international car rental company to provide this service. Given at least seven days' notice, Hertz will fit hand controls for right-hand use in Vauxhall Astra 1.3L automatics free of charge.

Rental charges for disabled drivers are the same as for able-bodied renters. Rentals for longer than two days come with unlimited mileage. Full information can be obtained by telephoning any one of their regional offices in either London (01–679 1799); Birmingham (021–643 8991); Manchester (061–437 8321); or Glasgow (041–248 7733).

A similar service is provided by Kenning Car Hire. Like Hertz they require a week's notice and have depots throughout the country. Telephone their London office (01–882 3576) for full details.

The choice of vehicle becomes even more important when the disabled person is a passenger because of severe disability. The disabled passenger is also entitled to the Mobility Allowance, and this can be used to purchase and convert a vehicle if so required. Most disabled passengers manage to travel quite successfully in an ordinary car driven by a friend or relative. Much depends on the attendant's ability to transfer the disabled person from wheelchair to car. This can be achieved by using either a sliding board, standing out of the chair into the car (standing transfers) (Figs. 12/1–12/4) or a car hoist (see p. 228). The need for adequate safety straps in addition to the normal seat belts cannot be stressed enough for the more severely disabled person, who might not be able to hold on (Fig. 12/5).

An alternative method of transporting the more severely disabled person, is in the wheelchair carried in a specially converted vehicle. Many such vehicles are now commercially available (see p. 227). This mode of transport does have the advantage that transfers are eliminated and that any person capable of driving can take the disabled person out. Nevertheless, from my own experience of travelling in a specially converted vehicle and remaining in the wheelchair, I was extremely uncomfortable for anything but a short journey.

PUBLIC TRANSPORT

BRITISH RAIL

Travel by British Rail for the wheelchair user can present problems and British Rail recommend all disabled people to advise them well in advance of any intended journey. When regular journeys are made, staff employed at the stations concerned soon learn of the disabled person's needs and are most helpful in every way

Figs. 12/1 – 12/4　The author being transferred standing from his wheelchair to the car by his wife. *Note* the position of her feet and hands throughout

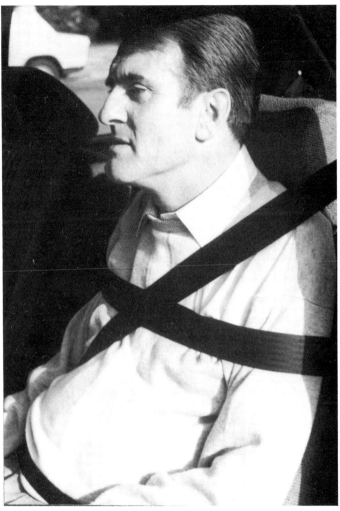

Fig. 12/5   Additional safety straps as fitted for use in the author's car

possible. For the occasional journey it is reasonable to ask that station staff are informed when a disabled person will be travelling on a certain train. British Rail have issued the following instructions to disabled travellers: 'Please write to the Area Manager at the departure station giving the following information.

1 Date and time of intended journey.
2 To where you are travelling and list of stations where changes have to be made.
3 Whether you are totally dependent on your wheelchair.
4 Whether you will be alone or with a travelling companion.
5 Whether you wish to travel in the guard's van or whether you are able to transfer out of your wheelchair and sit in an ordinary passenger seat. (To do this it might be necessary to be transported in a special narrow transit chair along train corridors.)'

Facilities available at local stations and on local trains compared with Inter-City stations and lines, vary enormously for the wheelchair user and I strongly advise people to make extensive enquiries before undertaking a journey.

Fare concessions

Under certain circumstances British Rail allow reductions in the fare normally charged. Those travellers who elect to travel in the guard's van, either because they cannot transfer or because they do not wish to, are charged half the normal second class single fare for each journey made and this also applies to one travelling companion. Written permission is required to do this and there are two different application forms and permits, one for regular travellers (form BR 25559/1), the other for single journeys (form BR 25559/2). They enable any passenger, disabled or not, to travel in non-passenger vehicles.

If you qualify for mobility, or attendance allowance, you can purchase at a nominal price a Railcard which entitles holders to buy Ordinary Single, Ordinary Return or Awayday tickets at half the adult fare for themselves as well as a travelling companion. For more details and application form see the leaflet – half price train travel for the disabled – obtainable at post offices, travel agents and stations.

Access to trains

The modern Inter-City coaches are constructed with wider doors than the older coaches, corridors are also wider. If the wheelchair is no wider than 65cm (25.5in), then the wheelchair can be lifted on board and wheeled to a suitable seat where the occupant has then to transfer and the wheelchair to be stowed in the guard's van. British Rail's Mark III first class coaches are constructed with a seat and table that can be removed and the traveller can remain sitting in the wheelchair, providing it is not more than 63cm (24.5in) wide. Although these are first class coaches, British Rail charge a second class fare for the wheelchair user and for his companion.

The majority of mainline stations are accessible to wheelchairs, but difficulty may be experienced in getting from platform to platform and routes used for baggage and mail may have to be taken. Toilets are usually accessible, but not all are 'unisex' and some might require access via the 'National Key System'. Toilets on trains however are all unsuitable for wheelchair users and, in circumstances where a journey cannot be made without toilet facilities, then it is probably wiser to travel by road.

Other services which might be of benefit to the disabled traveller include Motorail and Sleeper services; complete information on these and other services can be obtained from most British Rail stations.

TRAVEL BY BUS

Except in the case of patients with very incomplete lesions who are able to walk fairly well, travel by public bus service is, for obvious reasons, quite unsuitable for the wheelchair user. (I do know of one paraplegic woman who travels regularly on buses with her able-bodied husband. He carries her to a seat, then folds and stores her wheelchair in the luggage compartment.) In theory this is possible, but in practice buses are not provided with much luggage space and the conductor has the right to refuse entry to any passenger. And as fewer buses carry conductors, it is unlikely drivers would tolerate the inconvenience.

Nevertheless, one bus company in the UK, the West Yorkshire Passenger Transport Executive, will provide help for people in wheelchairs – particularly if arrangements are made in advance. In certain parts of America, California for example, buses on regular services have been ingeniously converted so that the steps up into the bus double as hydraulic lifting platforms thus allowing easy access for anyone in a wheelchair.

There are several privately owned buses belonging to hospitals, charities or disabled associations, which have been specially adapted to carry wheelchairs. This usually requires the removal of the ordinary seats, the addition of wheelchair locking devices and special safety straps together with either an electric or hydraulic operated side or tail lift.

TRAVEL BY TAXI

Travel by taxi is perfectly possible and is frequently used by many wheelchair users. It would be wise to seek a regular taxi firm or driver if many journeys are anticipated, as they will then learn some of the problems of wheelchair users. Tetraplegics who are unable to transfer themselves, cannot expect the taxi driver to be willing to lift them in and out of their wheelchairs. Previous arrangements should always be made under these circumstances and an assistant taken. Most taxi drivers are very generous and willing to lift/help disabled people in and out if necessary.

Paraplegics who use Roho wheelchair cushions are advised to hold on to them when travelling by taxi and not let the driver pack them in the car's boot with the wheelchair. So many cushions have been accidentally punctured by drivers who have inadvertently thrown them into the car's boot.

TRAVEL BY AIR

Paraplegics who anticipate travelling by air are advised to write to the Air Transport Users Committee, who produce a booklet *Care In The Air*. This outlines all the problems and difficulties likely to be experienced.

The larger airports, such as Heathrow, Gatwick, Stansted, Glasgow, Edinburgh, Prestwick and Aberdeen, produce their own booklets about care for disabled travellers. Your local travel agent is the best person to give advice.

Under normal circumstances paralysis does not prevent air travel, from a medical point of view, although a check-up before a journey is always a wise precaution. The more severely disabled, who are unable to care for themselves completely, will in most circumstances require an assistant to travel with them.

In recent years many paraplegic travellers have been refused travel on various airlines because of difficulties in using the toilets on board. In most aircraft, disabled passengers are transported to their seats and their wheelchairs stowed in the baggage compartment, so unless a urinal is worn it is impossible for you to empty your bladder until your destination is reached. This certainly presents problems for women travellers, who may have to have a catheter inserted for the journey.

Travellers who have had radio-linked bladder implants should inform the airline before embarking, because similar radio-transmitter devices have been reported to have interfered with the aircraft navigational equipment.

Doctors caring for paraplegics can obtain a booklet, *Your Patient and Air Travel*, for guidance concerning health care.

TRAVEL BY SEA

Many large shipping companies cater for wheelchair passengers and your local travel agent is the best person to turn to for initial advice.

As with many other modes of transport for the disabled, difficulties arise over access to toilets. Having travelled on several cross Channel ferries myself, it has always proved a problem to gain access to toilets even in specially adapted cabins for disabled people. Most ships are constructed with high sills of about 10cm (4in) between compartments, designed to prevent water splashing around during rough weather, making access difficult. A limited number of modern cruising ships, including the *Queen Elizabeth II* do, however, have a number of en-suite cabins fully accessible for wheelchairs.

SUGGESTED READING

Door to Door. A guide to transport for disabled people. This is produced by the Department of Transport

Disabled Drivers' Motor Club Yearbook. Available from 1A Dudley
Gardens, London W13 9LU

RAC Guide and Handbook. Available from the RAC, RAC House,
Lansdowne Road, Croydon CR9 2JA

Travellers Guide for the Disabled. Available from the AA, Fanum
House, Basingstoke, Hampshire RG21 2EA

Equipment for the Disabled: Outdoor Transport. Available from 2
Foredown Drive, Portslade, Brighton BN4 2BB

The following books are available from RADAR, 25 Mortimer
Street, London W1N 8AB:

British Rail – A Guide for Disabled People
British Rail and Disabled Travellers
Motoring and Mobility for Disabled People, edited by Ann Darn-
brough and Derek Kinrade
Cars for Disabled People

USEFUL ORGANISATIONS

MOTORING ORGANISATIONS

The Disabled Drivers' Association
Ashwellthorpe,
Norwich NR16 1EX
(Fundenhall) 050 841 449
All information relating to driving

The Disabled Drivers' Motor Club
1A Dudley Gardens
London W13 9LU
0559 370701 (for brochure)
*All information relating to driving. They will send a brochure if
you telephone*

Automobile Association (AA)
Fanum House, Basingstoke
Hampshire RG21 2EA
0256 20123
All information relating to able-bodied and disabled driving

Royal Automobile Club (RAC)
RAC House, Lansdowne Road
Croydon CR9 2JA
01–686 2525
All information relating to able-bodied and disabled driving

DRIVING ASSESSMENT

Mobility Information Service
Copthorne Community Centre
Shelton Road, Copthorne
Shrewsbury SY3 8TD
0734 68383
Provide a mobile trailer housing a specially designed static driving simulator

Banstead Place Mobility Centre
Park Road, Banstead, Surrey SM7 3EE
Driving assessment and tuition

HAND CONTROLS

Alfred Bekker
'The Green', Langtoft
Nr Driffield
North Humberside YO25 0TF
0377 87276
Provide a 'while you wait' service, or you can stay for a mini-weekend while controls are fitted

Automobile and Industrial Developments Limited
Queensthorpe Road
London SE26 4PJ
01–778 7055
Hand controls for most makes of car

Cowal (Mobility Aids) Limited
32 New Pond Road
Holmer Green, Bucks HP15 6SU
0494 714400
Hand controls for most makes of car

Midland Cylinder Rebores (Coventry) Ltd
Torrington Avenue, Coventry CV4 9BL
0203 462424
*Specialists in mobility – hand controls, wheelchair sales and
maintenance*

Reselco Limited
262 King Street, London W6 9BE
01–748 5053
Hand controls for most vehicles

Feeny and Johnson Limited
Alperton Lane, Wembley
Middlesex HA0 1JJ
01–998 4458
Hand controls for most vehicles

CAR CONVERSIONS

Mobility International (Gowerings)
The Grange, Lower Way
Thatcham, Berks RG13 4PH
0635 64464
*Convert a wide range of vehicles enabling people to be transported
while remaining in wheelchairs*

Stoke Mandeville Mobility Centre
69 Lower Road, Stoke Mandeville
Aylesbury, Bucks HP22 5XA
0296 61 2797
*A young enthusiastic firm converting vehicles at highly competitive
rates*

HOISTS AND CARRIERS

S. Burvill and Son
39 Primrose Road, Hersham
Walton-on-Thames KT12 5JD
0932 21124
Roof mounted hoists

Mobility Techniques Limited
The Croft, Great Longstone
Bakewell, Derbyshire DE4 1TF
062987 278
Manufacturers of the Autochair, an automatic car-top wheelchair carrier

Useful Organisations

In addition to the addresses given in individual chapters, the following is only a selection of the many useful organisations available to help disabled people. Also included are a number of manufacturers of specific items.

AIR CONDITIONING AND HUMIDIFIERS

Air Conditioning Equipment (International) Ltd
Ace House, Cedar Way Industrial Estate
Camley Street, London NW1 0PD

ALTERNATIVE MEDICINE

Hydes Herbal Clinic
68 London Road
Leicester LE2 0QD   0533 543178

The British Acupuncture Association and Register
34 Alderney Street, London SW1V 4EU   01–834 1021

British Homeopathic Association
27A Devonshire Street
London W1N 1RJ   01–935 2163

CRISIS COUNSELLING

Alcoholics Anonymous
PO Box 514
11 Redcliffe Gardens, London SW10 9BQ   01–352 5493/9779

Gamblers Anonymous and Gam-Anon
17–23 Blantyre Street
London SW10 0DT   01–352 3060

The Samaritans
17 Uxbridge Road
Slough SL1 1SM   Slough 32713/4

Gingerbread
35 Wellington Street
London WC2E 7BN   01–240 0953
Self-help organisation for one
parent families

EDUCATION

Department of Education and Science
Elizabeth House, York Road
London SE1 7PH   01–928 9222

National Bureau for Handicapped Students
336 Brixton Road
London SW9 7AA   01–274 0565

Open University
Office for Students with Disabilities
Walton Hall, Milton Keynes MK7 6AA
Home study and suitable courses for disabled
students

ELECTRONICS AND COMPUTERS

Possum Controls Limited
Middlegreen Road, Langley
Slough, Berks SL3 6DF   Slough 79234
Produce electronic environmental control
systems, page turners, computer systems,
learning and communication aids,
typewriter controls

Neath Hill Professional Work Shop
One Fletchers Mews, Neath Hill
Milton Keynes MK14 6HW   0908 660364
Organisation backed by the Spastics Society
and specialising in computer technology for
people with a disability. They adapted my
own Apple computer

SEQUAL (formerly Possum User's Association)
The Bungalow, 31A Northfield Close, West End
South Cave, North Humberside HU15 2EW
Supplies and maintains a wide range of
microprocessors and communication aids

EMPLOYMENT

Department of Employment
Caxton House, Tothill Street
London SW1H 9NF   01–213 3000

Employer Division
Manpower Services Commission
Moorfoot, Sheffield S1 4PQ   0742 753275

Opportunities for the Disabled
1 Bank Building, Princess Street
London EC2R 8EU
Employment service for job seekers

British Computer Society
13 Mansfield Street
London W1M 0BP   01–637 0471
Employment opportunities in computing

GENERAL

Association of Disabled Professionals
The Stables, 73 Pound Road
Banstead, Surrey SM7 2HU   (Burgh Heath) 07373 52366

Royal Association for Disability and Rehabilitation (RADAR)
25 Mortimer Street
London W1N 8AB   01–637 5400

HOLIDAYS

Threshold Travel
2 Whitworth Street West
Manchester M1 5WX   061–236 9763
Travel agent specialising in holidays for
the disabled

Holiday Care Services
2 Old Bank Chambers, Station Road
Horley, Surrey RH6 9NW
Specialise in organising holidays for the
disabled

John Grooms Holidays
10 Gloucester Drive
London N4 2LP   01–802 7272
Holiday facilities for the physically
handicapped and their families/escorts

The Jubilee Sailing Trust
Cherry Cottage, Queen's Road
Crowborough, Sussex TN6 1EJ   08926 3757
For physically handicapped and able-
bodied to share the challenging
experience of crewing a ship at sea

Stoke Mandeville Paratravel Society
c/o Tullaquin, 113 Tring Road
Aylesbury, Bucks HP 20 1LE
Provides holidays for people confined to a
wheelchair as a result of spinal injury.
Also provide nursing and medical care

Winged Fellowship Trust
Angel House, Pentonville Road
London N1 9XD   01–833 2594
Holidays for severely disabled people

Across Trust
Crown House
Morden, Surrey SM4 5EW   01–540 3897
Provides Jumbulances for disabled holidays

RECREATION

The CRYPT Foundation
21 Plover Close, East Wittering
Chichester, West Sussex PO20 8PW   0243 670000
Creative Young People Together – will help
to develop creative talent

Photography for the Disabled
190 Secretts House, Ham Close
Ham, Richmond, Surrey TW10 7PE   01–948 2342

Society for Horticultural Therapy
Goulds Ground, Vallis Way
Frome, Somerset BA11 3DW   0373 64782
Practical services to disabled gardeners

Mouth and Footpainting Artists
9 Inverness Place
London W2 3JF   01–229 4491
Will provide training for prospective
talent and possible employment

RESEARCH AND DEVELOPMENT

International Spinal Research Trust
Nicholas House, River Front
Enfield, Middlesex EN1 3TR   01–367 3555
Sponsors research into spinal cord injury

National Fund for Research into Crippling Diseases
Vincent House, North Parade
Horsham, West Sussex RH12 2DA   0403 64101

Rehabilitation Engineering Movement Advisory
Panels (REMAP)
25 Mortimer Street, London W1N 8AB   01–637 5400
Makes aids not commercially available

SPORT

British Sports Association for the Disabled
Hayward House, Barnard Crescent
Aylesbury HP21 8PP   0296 27889

The British Paraplegic Sports Society Limited
Ludwig Guttmann Sports Centre for the Disabled
Harvey Road, Stoke Mandeville, Aylesbury
Bucks HP21 8PP   0296 84848

National Association of Swimming Clubs for the Handicapped
219 Preston Drive, Brighton, Sussex BN1 6FI   0273 559470

Scottish Council on Disability
5 Shandwick Place
Edinburgh EH2 4RG   031–225 8411

Scottish Spinal Cord Injury Association
3 Cargill Terrace
Edinburgh EH5 3ND   031–522 8459

Disabled Persons Information Centre
45 Park Place
Cardiff CS1 33B   0222 398058

Information Service for Disabled People
2 Annadale Avenue
Belfast BT7 3JR   Belfast 649555

Northern Ireland Paraplegic Association
26 Bridge Road
Helens Bay, County Down   0247 653310

UNITED STATES OF AMERICA

This is only a small selection of the many help agencies. The
Yellow Pages of the telephone directory will give the addresses of
the divisional offices in each state for the National Spinal Cord
Injury Association and the Veterans Association. Both these organisations will be able to supply a wide range of helpful literature
as well as indicating additional help and advice agencies.

National Spinal Cord Injury Association
369 Elliot Street
Newton Upper Falls, MA 02164

American Spinal Injury Association
250 E. Superior, Rm 619
Chicago, IL 60611

American Paralysis Association
4100 Spring Valley Road
Suite 104 L.B. 3
Dallas, TX 75234

Paralyzed Veterans of America
801 18th Street, N.W.
Washington, D.C. 20006

National Rehabilitation Association
633 S. Washington Street
Alexandria, VA 22314

Accent on Information (computer information retrieval)
PO Box 700
Bloomington, IL 61701

Access for the Handicapped
1012 14th Street N.W.
Suite 803
Washington, D.C. 20005

CANADA

Canadian Paraplegic Association
520 Sutherland Drive
Toronto, Ontario M4G 3V9

Spinal Injury Units

ENGLAND

The National Spinal Injuries Centre
Stoke Mandeville Hospital
Aylesbury, Buckinghamshire HP21 8AL   (Aylesbury) 0296 84111

Regional Spinal Injuries Unit
Hexham General Hospital
Hexham, Northumberland NE46 1QJ   (Hexham) 0434 606161

The Duke of Cornwall Spinal Treatment Centre
Odstock Hospital
Salisbury, Wiltshire SP2 8BJ   (Salisbury) 0722 336262

The Midland Spinal Injuries Centre
Robert Jones & Agnes Hunt Orthopaedic Hospital
Oswestry, Shropshire SY10 7AG   (Oswestry) 0691 655311

The Spinal Unit
Lodge Moor Hospital
Sheffield S10 4LH   (Sheffield) 0742 306555

The Spinal Unit
Promenade Hospital
Southport, Merseyside PR9 0HY   (Southport) 0704 34411

Royal National Orthopaedic Hospital
Stanmore, Middlesex HA7 4LP   01–954 2300

The Spinal Unit
Pinderfields General Hospital
Wakefield WF1 4DG   0924 375217

SCOTLAND

Philipshill Hospital
East Kilbride Road, Busby
Glasgow G76 9HW   041–644 1144

Edenhall Hospital
Musselburgh, Midlothian EH21 7TZ   031–665 2546

WALES

Spinal Injuries Unit
Rookwood Hospital
Cardiff CF5 2YN   0222 566281

NORTHERN IRELAND

The Withers Orthopaedic Centre
Musgrave Park Hospital
Belfast BT9 7JB   (Belfast) 0232 669501

EIRE

National Medical Rehabilitation Centre
Our Lady of Lourdes Hospital
Rochestown Avenue, Dunlaoghaire
Dublin, Eire   (Dunlaoghaire) 0001 854777

UNITED STATES OF AMERICA

California Regional Spinal Cord Injury Care System
Santa Clara Valley Medical Center
751 South Bascon Avenue
San Jose, California 95128

Department of Rehabilitation Medicine
University of Washington Medical Center
1959 N.E. Pacific Street
Seattle, Washington 98195

Department of Rehabilitation Medicine
University of Minnesota Medical Centre
412 Union Street, S.E.
Minneapolis, Minnesota 55455

Institute of Rehabilitation Medicine
New York University Medical Center
400 East 34th Street
New York City, New York 10016

Midwest Regional Spinal Cord Injury Care System
Rehabilitation Institute of Chicago
Northwestern Memorial Hospital
401 East Ohio Street
Chicago, Illinois 60608

Rocky Mountain Regional Spinal Injury Center Inc
Craig Hospital
3425 South Clarkson Street
Englewood, Colorado 80110

Southwest Regional System for Treatment of Spinal Injury
Institute of Rehabilitation Medicine
Good Samaritan Hospital
1033 East McDowell Road
Phoenix, Arizona 85006

Spinal Cord Injury System
Woodrow Wilson Rehabilitation Center
University of Virginia Medical Center
Fishersville, Virginia 22939

Spinal Cord Injury Unit
Boston University Medical Center
750 Harrison Avenue
Boston, Massachusetts 02118

Texas Institute of Rehabilitation and Research
1333 Moursund Avenue
Houston, Texas 77025

Index